DEATH BY ESPRESSO

I glanced back the way I'd come, but no one was sneaking up on me. I had an urge to call someone, just to let them know where I was. My phone, however, was back beside my purse, which in turn, was in my car. Someday, I'd learn to take it with me.

As I stepped into the kitchen, my foot bumped into something that clattered across the room. It bounced off the island counter and then rolled back to me.

"Huh." I bent over and picked it up. It was a silver candlestick, the candle broken off, top half missing. Vicki always kept a pair of them on the island counter. Trouble must have knocked one off.

Wasn't Trouble staying with Vicki and Mason?

A rumble outside scratched the surface of my attention, but was unable to fully break through. Clutching the candlestick, I walked slowly around the island counter.

First there was a stockinged foot. Then a leg, and finally, a severe, black pantsuit.

"Cathy?" I hurried over and dropped to my knees beside her. She was lying facedown, espresso beans scattered around her . . .

Books by Alex Erickson

DEATH BY COFFEE

DEATH BY TEA

DEATH BY PUMPKIN SPICE

DEATH BY VANILLA LATTE

DEATH BY EGGNOG

DEATH BY ESPRESSO

Published by Kensington Publishing Corporation

Death By Espresso

Alex Erickson

KENSINGTON BOOKS
KENSINGTON PUBLISHING CORP.
http://www.kensingtonbooks.com

KENSINGTON BOOKS are published by

Kensington Publishing Corp.
119 West 40th Street
New York, NY 10018

All Kensington titles, imprints, and distributed lines are avail-
able at special quantity discounts for bulk purchases for sales
promotion, premiums, fund-raising, educational, or institu-
tional use.

Special book excerpts or customized printings can also be
created to fit specific needs. For details, write or phone the
office of the Kensington Sales Manager: Attn.: Sales Department. Kensington Publishing Corp., 119 West 40th Street,
New York, NY 10018. Phone: 1-800-221-2647.

Kensington and the K logo Reg. U.S. Pat. & TM Off.

First Printing: July 2018
ISBN-13: 978-1-4967-0889-2
ISBN-10: 1-4967-0889-X

eISBN-13: 978-1-4967-0890-8
eISBN-10: 1-4967-0890-3

10 9 8 7 6 5 4 3 2 1

Printed in the United States of America

1

The Levington airport was a cacophony of sound, yet, despite the noise, there were people sleeping in chairs. Seemingly unattended children screamed and pointed as planes took off and as others landed. A few cranky adults stood at counters, yelling at anyone in a name tag, demanding flight changes or upgrades. It was utter chaos.

I stayed out of the way, impatiently glancing at the large clock on the wall every couple of minutes. I wasn't big on crowds in the best of times, and today, I was not at my best. The last week had been a flurry of activity as I helped prep for my best friend, Vicki Patterson's wedding to Mason Lawyer. The stress was really getting to me. I was the maid of honor, after all.

I should be home in Pine Hills. It wasn't necessary I meet anyone at the airport. The visiting guests all had rental cars waiting for them, so my drive back home would be a lonely one. Still, there was someone I wanted to meet and I'd much rather do it here, in neutral territory, rather than at home.

Vicki would have come with me, but with the wedding and work, she was already feeling overwhelmed.

And while I probably should have stayed with her to make sure she didn't pull her hair out, it was nice to get away from the madness for a little while.

Well, the wedding madness, anyway.

A kid shrieked by, arms flailing, as he ran toward an older couple waiting on him with dopey grins on their faces. A heavily burdened woman, carrying both her luggage and her son's, trailed after. She flashed me an apologetic smile before joining the happy reunion.

I watched them a moment longer before glancing at the clock yet again. I doubted my reunion would be full of shrieking and crying, but who knew?

Another minute ticked by. As long as the plane wasn't delayed, they should be entering at any minute.

A rush of nervousness nearly had me sinking down into the nearest chair. My mouth was dry and my hands were shaking so bad, I ended up clutching them behind my back so no one would see. I suddenly wished I would have taken more time to get ready. I'd settled on shorts and a nice blouse, going with my usual limited makeup. I was beginning to wonder if I should have gone with a skirt instead. Or maybe a dress. What if I gave everyone the wrong impression, that I didn't think them worthy of my time and effort?

A mental slap forced the thoughts from my head. I had a good reason to be nervous, but that was no excuse to start freaking out.

Tapping my foot, I waited. It seemed to take forever before a small group appeared, searching for their suitcases. And then it was another lifetime before the main reason for my presence appeared.

The man was bald, bearded, and looked much fitter than when I'd last seen him. His gut was gone, replaced by a flat stomach I hadn't seen in years. He was wearing glasses now, something I wasn't used to, and when he glanced my way, the eyes behind the lenses lit up.

"Krissy!" he called in his raspy voice, while waving.

I waved back, unable to stop the grin from spreading across my face. "Dad!"

He took the hand of the woman next to him and I did a quick appraisal of her as he led her my way. She had a full head of ultra-curly brown hair that looked entirely natural. She was dressed casually, which I appreciated. She was younger than I'd expected, but not so much that I thought it strange she was dating my dad.

"Hi, Buttercup." Dad gave me a quick hug. "I want you to meet Laura Dresden. Laura, this is my daughter, Kristina."

"You can call me Krissy."

"Krissy"—Laura beamed—"I've heard so much about you." She hesitated a moment before stepping forward for a quick, semi-uncomfortable hug.

We parted and I glanced at my dad, who had a goofy grin on his face. James Hancock had never been one to act the part of a lovesick teenager, at least not since I'd known him. By the time I came along, he and Mom had been well into the comfortable years, where that sort of thing was uncommon. It was odd to see him look so love-struck. Honestly, it was kind of cute.

"Was Vicki able to make it?" Dad asked, glancing around as if looking for her. More people piled into the small space, greeting friends or relatives, and gathering their luggage from baggage claim.

"She had some things to take care of at home." I looked past him. "Have you seen Gina and Frederick?"

Vicki's parents were due on the same flight as Dad, but I'd been so wrapped up in meeting him and Laura, I hadn't been watching for them.

A look passed over Dad's face, causing me to grow nervous.

"They're coming, right?" I asked. It would be just like them to cancel at the last minute.

"They are," Dad assured me. "They're around here somewhere, but . . ." He trailed off and frowned.

It took me a moment of scanning the crowd before I saw Gina's blond curls. Frederick stood next to her, his hair dyed a dark brown. They were talking to a rather large group of people in a way that seemed awfully familiar considering they were supposed to have come with only a couple of others.

Dad sighed when he followed my gaze and noticed them. "I told them they should have called first."

"Who are they talking to?" I asked. I was expecting to greet six, maybe seven people, not ten.

"Friends of theirs, apparently. I think one of them might be family, but they weren't keen on introducing me." Dad put an arm around Laura's shoulder, seemed to remember I was standing there, and dropped it. He was acting as nervous as I'd been the first time I'd brought a boy home as a teen.

"Why are they here?" I wondered out loud. Vicki had been pretty adamant about having a small wedding. She'd told her parents they could bring a couple of friends, since otherwise they'd be spending most of the week alone as they didn't know anyone and Vicki would be busy with the wedding. They'd agreed to keep it small.

And yet, here we were.

Gina happened to glance my way and her smile

faltered. She nudged Frederick, who followed her gaze before closing his eyes, as if counting to ten, before he nodded. They said something to the group they were standing with, and then headed over my way.

"Here we go," I muttered, steeling myself. If you knew anything about Gina and Frederick Patterson, you knew how difficult they could be.

I plastered on a smile, one I'd mastered while working in retail nearly all my life. I hoped it didn't look too fake, but I could already feel it start to falter.

"Kristina," Gina said, coming to a stop. She was dressed to kill, of course, head held high as if she expected everyone in the airport to worship her. She was still stunning, even at her age, and she knew it.

Unfortunately, her looks could only carry her so far. She was an actress who thought she deserved better roles than what she ever landed. If you'd seen her act, you'd understand why she never got anything more than a bit part.

Frederick was likewise handsome, though years of the good life had apparently started to play havoc with his figure. Like his wife, his acting skills weren't quite up to par, meaning he often played fourth or fifth fiddle to people who might not look as good as he did.

"Where's Vicki?" he asked. "I thought she'd be here."

"She's busy taking care of a few things for the wedding," I said. "She'll be waiting for us in Pine Hills."

"I see." The disapproval was heavy in Gina's voice. "Why are you here?"

My smile grew strained. "I thought I'd make sure everyone arrived okay."

"Did you now?" Gina looked back at the group, who were watching us.

"I think I'll check on our luggage," Laura said. "The last time I flew, they lost my bags and I had to wait nearly two weeks before it was shipped to me."

"Oh no! Did you get everything back?" I asked.

"Yeah. My suitcase looked as if someone had thrown it from the plane, but otherwise, everything was intact."

"Well, I hope nothing is lost this time," I said.

"Me too." She started away.

"I'll come with you," Dad said, hurriedly joining her.

I gave him a betrayed look. I couldn't believe he was going to leave me alone with these people. I often wondered if Gina and Frederick lived for insulting me. They rarely outright called me names, so that was a plus, I supposed.

"Who are all those people?" I asked, nodding toward the men and women the Pattersons had been talking to.

"They're here for the wedding," Frederick said as if it were obvious. "Why else would they come to a place like this?" His nose crinkled as if the mere thought of flying all this way offended him. Neither he nor his wife had bothered to come to Pine Hills before—not even in support of their daughter—let alone Levington.

"Vicki wanted to keep the wedding small," I said, knowing it was no use to point it out, but feeling the need to say it anyway.

Gina's brow furrowed. "She said we could bring some friends." For the first time, she actually looked concerned. "You don't think she'll turn them away, do you?"

"No," I said, resigned. "I'm sure we'll find space for all of them." Though I was pretty sure she wouldn't be happy about it.

A woman approached the group then, asked one of the men a question, and then followed his point to where Gina stood. She hurried over to where we stood with a decided bounce in her step.

"There you are," Gina said, giving the woman a brief hug. "I can't believe they put you in coach. We missed you in first class."

The woman reached into a bag she was holding and popped a chocolate ball into her mouth. She chewed a moment before answering. "It was uncomfortable, but I managed." She spoke in a hurried tone, as if she was afraid someone would cut her off before she finished. She was a small woman, makeup dark and severe, as was her short haircut.

"Still, you should complain," Gina said. "Just because they lost your information doesn't mean you should be punished."

"I'd sue," Frederick added.

"It's no bother." The woman waved her hand dismissively. "I'll be sure to file a complaint and make sure they understand I'll accept no further screw-ups lest I stop flying with them." She glanced around the airport. "Awfully small, isn't it?"

"It's no wonder," Gina said. "Can you imagine trying to live out here? I looked out the window on the way in and thought we'd somehow been transported to a third-world country!"

"Or somewhere in Idaho," Frederick added.

"And this town, Pine Hilltop, it's supposed to be smaller?"

"Pine Hills," I said, drawing all their eyes. I think they'd forgotten about me.

"And you are?" the woman asked.

"Krissy Hancock," I said. "Vicki's friend."

"Oh." She glanced at Gina as if for confirmation.

I could almost see the "unfortunately" in her nod.

I waited for someone to introduce the woman, but it didn't appear as if either of the Pattersons was willing, so I asked her myself. "You are . . . ?"

The woman popped a few more chocolates into her mouth. She shifted the bag, and I noted she was eating chocolate-covered espresso beans. My mouth watered.

"Cathy Carr." She said it like she couldn't believe I didn't know her by sight alone.

Having never heard her name before, I looked to Gina.

She heaved a put-upon sigh. "You don't know Cathy Carr, do you?"

I shrugged, feeling stupid. The Pattersons had a way of doing that to me.

"She's only the most important wedding planner in all of the United States," Gina said.

"The world, actually," Cathy said.

"Some call her the planner to the stars," Frederick added.

"Okay," I said, drawing out the word as I looked from one to the other. "So, why is she here?"

The Pattersons shared a look. It was Cathy who answered.

"I'm a wedding planner." She spoke like she was talking to someone who was hard of hearing—loud and slow. "I'm here to plan the wedding."

I looked to Gina. "But Vicki's wedding is already planned."

"She doesn't have a Cathy Carr–planned wedding, now does she?"

"Well, no." And as far as I knew, she didn't want one.

"I know that it's too late for her to plan the entire thing," Gina said. "But Cathy is a genius."

"Vicki deserves the best," Frederick added. "Cathy will look over what Vicki has planned already and improve upon it. It's our gift to her."

Another couple of chocolate-covered beans entered Cathy's mouth as she looked around the airport. "Is there a coffee shop around here somewhere?" she asked. "I desperately need a triple shot after that flight."

"I don't readily know," Gina said, before turning to me. "Kristina?"

"Over there." I pointed. "Take a left. You can't miss it."

Cathy nodded and hurried away, legs flashing as she just about ran for the coffee. I was someone who loved her coffee, yet it appeared Cathy Carr had my addiction beat.

"Okay, Buttercup," Dad said, rejoining us. "We have our bags and nothing is lost." He held up a pair of suitcases as if in victory. Laura had a bag of her own.

"Perfect," I said, turning to the Pattersons. "Does everyone have everything they need?"

"We do. I had Trey grab our bags for us." I assumed Trey was one of the people she'd been talking to.

"Then we should probably get going. The drive isn't too long, but it's quiet. It's mostly trees and farms."

"I could use some quiet," Gina said. The airport had gotten a lot louder with everyone crammed into baggage claim.

"Does everyone know how to get to Pine Hills?" I asked, not wanting to lose someone along the way.

"We have GPS," Gina said. "We should be fine."

"Vicki will be waiting for us at Death by Coffee. Once we're in Pine Hills, we'll meet there. Does everyone have a ride?"

Frederick said, "We all have rentals."

"Good. I'll see you all in Pine Hills."

For the first time since they'd arrived, Gina looked nervous. "Do you think she'll be happy to see us? I know we don't always see things the same way, and well . . ." She looked to Frederick, who put an arm around her shoulder.

"She's excited," I said. "She can't wait to see the both of you."

"We'd better gather everyone," Gina said, and then, as if it pained her, she added, "Thank you, Krissy."

"Sure thing."

Both Frederick and Gina turned and headed back to the others as Cathy Carr appeared, carrying a large coffee, likely her triple-shot espresso. She was still chewing away on the chocolate-covered espresso beans.

It'll be a wonder if she doesn't explode before we get there. I loved caffeine, but this was ridiculous.

"Are you going to be okay driving alone?" Dad asked as we started for the rental car park.

"I'll be fine," I said. "I can use the time to figure out how I'm going to tell Vicki about all of them." I nodded back toward the group, who were just now starting to head for their cars.

He laughed. "I'm sure you'll figure it out." He paused, glancing back at Laura, who was walking a few feet behind us as if not wanting to interrupt father and daughter time. "I hope you like her," he said, keeping his voice down.

"I'm sure I will," I said, and I meant it. We hadn't had a chance to talk all that much as of yet, but from what I'd seen of her so far, I had a feeling Laura and I were going to get along just fine.

Dad put an arm around me and squeezed. "This is going to be a great week." He released me and then held out a hand for Laura, who took it.

As I watched them walk together, I realized that despite Cathy's presence, and the extra couple of people the Pattersons had brought along, it would all work out in the end. Happiness was contagious, and Dad and Laura were the epitome of happiness. Nothing could ruin Vicki's wedding, not even a gaggle of strangers.

I would stop anyone who tried.

2

It was dark by the time I reached the bookstore and coffee shop Vicki and I co-owned, Death by Coffee. My back hurt from the journey, having sat bolt upright the entire way. I'd called Vicki on the way over, warning her of what was coming, and to say she wasn't happy about it was a major understatement. I was definitely not looking forward to the confrontation that was sure to come.

I got out of my car, wishing my boyfriend, Will Foster, had been able to make it. Unfortunately, he was in Levington, working at the hospital there. I'd considered stopping by before heading to the airport, but I hadn't made it to the larger city in time. He'd been so busy as of late, I'd barely gotten much of a chance to see him over the last few months. I would have liked to have spent a few minutes in his presence, even if it was only a glimpse. He *was* something special to look at.

Dad and the others found nearby parking spaces along the street and made their way to the front of the store, where I was waiting. The downstairs lights were still on, though Death by Coffee had been closed for the last hour. The lights by the books were dark, so all that could be seen of the shelves were shadowy outlines. I could see Vicki pacing inside. She still looked stunning with her long legs, blond hair, and movie-star looks, even in her agitation. Mason looked helpless from where he watched her beside the counter. He kept running his fingers through his dark hair, good-looking face contorted in worry.

This is going to go great. Even my inner voice had turned sarcastic. I forced a smile in the hopes that it would magically make everything better as I turned to the group.

"Everyone here?" I asked, doing a quick head count.

"I think so," Dad said. He rested a hand on my arm, and lowered his voice. "It'll be fine."

"I hope so," I told him, before taking a deep, calming breath. There was nothing I could do about it now but press forward. I led the way inside.

Vicki immediately stopped pacing as we entered. Mason put an arm around her, which seemed to calm her some.

"Mother," she said.

"Victoria."

Vicki's eye twitched. No one called her Victoria. Ever. It wasn't even her given name. Years ago, Gina had decided that Vicki wasn't a good enough name for an actress, and had started calling her Victoria in the hopes it would catch on. Vicki hated it. Gina didn't care.

"Why are all these people here?"

Gina glanced to Frederick, as if for support, before saying, "They're here for your wedding. I know I should have told you how many I was bringing ahead of time, but well, it slipped my mind in all the excitement."

"Yes, you should have."

"It's too late now," Gina said. "I promise they won't be too much bother." She glanced around the coffee shop. "Small, isn't it? And simple. I thought it would have a little more . . . flair."

I had to give Vicki credit. She merely stood there as her mother insulted our life's work. I would have said something if it was my place to do so. Still, it took all my self-control not to speak up. What did Gina Patterson know about running a coffee shop? I clenched my teeth and continued to smile, even though my face was starting to hurt.

"Maybe we should do introductions?" Mason suggested, stepping forward and extending his hand. "Mason Lawyer. Vicki's fiancé. You must be Gina."

Gina put her hand in his own, but not to shake. He hesitated a moment before raising her fingers to his lips.

"Frederick." Vicki's dad actually took his hand and shook, much to my relief. I wouldn't have put it past him to make Mason kiss his ring, just to see if he'd do it.

A tense silence followed. Mason stared at the Pattersons, who stared right back. I shifted from foot to foot, glanced at Dad, who shrugged. It wasn't our place to speak up, but if no one said anything soon, I very well might.

Finally, Mason turned his attention away from Gina and Frederick, and to the couple behind them. "And you are?"

"Sage and Trey Herron," the man said. He looked to be in his fifties, was well groomed, and had a soul patch dyed black. The woman next to him, Sage, looked twenty going on fifty. She'd apparently spent quite a lot of money to preserve her youth. Her skin appeared stretched, almost plastic, though she couldn't hide the age in her eyes.

"Pleasure," Sage said, flashing a smile.

"We apologize for coming on such short notice," Trey added. "I hope we didn't offend."

"No, you're fine," Mason said. His shoulders seemed to ease at Trey's friendly tone and kind words. "We're just surprised. We were expecting only a couple of people. We'll make room."

"I'm Jacques Kenway." A man in his mid-thirties, maybe early forties, stepped forward, hand extended. He was good-looking, and had a wide, toothy smile. Despite his name, there was no indication he had any French in him. "Friend of the family."

Mason shook. "Vicki hasn't mentioned you."

Jacques glanced past him, to where Vicki looked on. "We haven't had the pleasure before today," he said. "Though, I would like to get to know her. Gina has spoken highly of her."

"She is something special," Mason said, which caused Vicki's frustration to crack as she smiled.

He then turned his attention to the two people behind Jacques.

They hovered near the large, plate-glass window, apart from everyone else. The woman was inspecting her nails, as if the introductions were boring her. She was tiny, almost elfin, and gorgeous. I couldn't place her age. She could have been anywhere from twenty to her late thirties, early forties.

The man next to her was tall, kind of gangly, and was watching her every move. Like everyone there, he was good-looking, but in a goofy sort of way. His hair was shoulder-length, and hung loose around his face and ears. He kind of reminded me of Shaggy from *Scooby Do,* just better groomed.

Neither looked up nor spoke, as if they didn't realize everyone was looking at them. Jacques chuckled, and jerked a thumb at the tall man with a roll of his eyes, in a "Get a load of this guy" sort of way.

"That's Vince Conner," Gina said, breaking the brief, uncomfortable silence. "And Lyric Granderson."

"It's good to meet you both," Mason said, stepping forward to shake.

Vince jerked at his name, eyes briefly going wide, before he took Mason's hand. "The pleasure's mine," he said. Jacques laughed again, drawing a glare from Vince.

Lyric's lips twitched into something that wasn't quite a smile when Mason looked her way. She didn't offer her hand and, apparently, had nothing to say.

Dad stepped forward and introduced Laura next. I think he was trying to keep anyone from getting offended, but I could tell it wasn't going to work. Mason's eyes lingered on Lyric, whose own gaze had returned to her nails, before he turned to greet Laura.

"I'm glad you could make it," he said.

"I've heard so much about you," Vicki added, crossing the room to give Laura a quick hug before stepping back.

"I'm happy you invited me," Laura said. "I would have understood if you hadn't—I don't know many of James's friends yet."

"I couldn't imagine doing this without you," Vicki said. "If you're with James, then you're just as much a part of the family as the rest of us."

Someone cleared their throat. Loudly, and with obvious intent.

All eyes turned toward the short woman who'd gotten lost in the taller crowd around her. She popped a pair of espresso beans in her mouth and stepped forward. "Cathy Carr," she said, eyeing the empty coffeepots behind the counter. "I'm going to be making adjustments to your wedding."

Vicki stared at her for a long couple of seconds before her gaze drifted to Gina. "Mother?"

"She's the best, dear. Trust me."

"I wanted a small, uncomplicated wedding. You know, with *my* friends and *my* family."

Gina sighed dramatically. "I know that's what you said, but honestly, Victoria, you'll regret it if you don't think bigger. You only get married once."

Someone snorted a laugh, though I couldn't tell who. My guess, it was Jacques, who looked amused by the whole thing.

"Our wedding is already planned," Mason said, trying his hardest to be diplomatic. "And we're so close to the wedding date, I don't think it's feasible to make changes at this point."

"I was given an update by Mr. and Mrs. Patterson," Cathy said. "I can make subtle changes that will drastically improve the quality of your wedding. The flower arrangement seems so . . . simple." She fluttered a hand, and then tossed back another pair of beans. She chewed a moment before continuing. "I can have a more suitable arrangement here within two days if need be."

"I like my flower arrangements," Vicki said, and I had to agree. We'd both gone to Flower Power, a local business, and picked them out together. "I don't want them to be changed."

"Don't be obstinate, Victoria," Gina said, both

hands finding her hips. "Trust me, I know what's best for you."

Vicki made a sound that was akin to a growl low in her throat. I don't think she would have actually leapt at her mother like a rabid animal, but I could tell it was a near thing. I didn't know of anyone else who could elicit such a reaction from the normally even-keeled Vicki.

"Excuse us a moment," Mason said, taking Vicki by the arm and leading her upstairs, toward the books, and away from her mother, before one of them could say something they'd regret.

"I don't know why she's so upset," Gina said, turning to her husband. "We're just trying to help."

"She'll understand eventually," Frederick said. "Give her time. We're throwing a lot at her."

I met Dad's eye. He gave me a look that said, "Hang in there," and put an arm around Laura's shoulders. She looked a little overwhelmed, and quite honestly, I didn't blame her. Gina and Frederick were overwhelming people at the best of times. With a contingent of their Hollywood friends behind them, they were even more frustrating to deal with. In their world, image was what mattered.

"You tell her we were coming?" Sage asked in a stage whisper.

"She doesn't seem very happy to see us," Trey added.

"It slipped my mind," Gina said. "Victoria can be overly dramatic, especially when she doesn't get her way."

The pot calling the kettle black? I wondered. Dramatic stubbornness was practically a way of life for Gina.

"I just hope she realizes we aren't trying to make

things harder on her," Vince said. "We might not know her all that well, but we did come for the wedding." He glanced around the room, and then quickly lowered his eyes, as if he was afraid to meet anyone's gaze for long.

"That we did," Jacques said. His gaze lingered on Lyric longer than it should have before he looked away.

"What do you think, Buttercup?" Dad asked, keeping his voice low so the others wouldn't hear.

"She'll get through it," I said. "She's just surprised by everyone. It's sudden."

"I know I wouldn't be happy," Laura said. "Weddings are pretty personal." The way she looked at Dad then made my heart flutter just a little.

She really does love him, I realized. We'd barely spoken, but I could see it in the way she would reach out and touch his hand briefly, the way she spoke to him. It could have upset me since I'd never forget Mom, but I found I was okay with it. Dad deserved to be happy.

Vicki and Mason returned then, looking much calmer than they had before they'd left. I hoped that meant they'd worked everything out and we'd be able to proceed with the wedding without further trouble.

"It would probably be a good idea if everyone got a good night's sleep before we discuss this any further," Mason said. Apparently, he was going to get to play peacekeeper, which was fine by me. I definitely didn't want the job.

"At least let me give you this," Gina said, producing a long black box from her purse. She weighed it in her hand for a few seconds before she handed it to Vicki.

"What's this?" she asked, looking down at the box like it might be full of spiders.

"Open it and find out."

Vicki's brow was pinched, eyes worried, as she opened the box.

I couldn't help but gasp when I saw what it contained. It was a necklace, studded with diamonds the size of Skittles, and had a large red gem in the center that I took for a ruby. If it was, it was the largest one I'd ever seen, though, granted, I hadn't seen many. The piece was absolutely gorgeous.

"I'd like you to wear it in the wedding," Gina said. "It's quite valuable."

Vicki looked at it for a long, pregnant moment, face unreadable, before she snapped the box closed. "It's lovely," she said. "But I've already chosen my accessories." She handed the box back.

Gina looked stunned. "Victoria . . ."

"No, Mom. I don't want it. I don't want any of this." She gestured vaguely toward the group of actors.

"Vicki, please," Frederick said. "Your mother is trying her best to make you happy. Consider the necklace."

"It was a gift to me," Gina said. "It was worn in *The Nest of the Viper* by an actress I greatly admire. The director gave it to her as a gift after we wrapped, and then she passed it on to me afterward. I've waited all this time so I could give it to you."

Behind her, Lyric's eyes narrowed, her lips thinned. Her gaze never left the box, even as Gina clutched it to her chest.

Vicki looked like she was going to continue to argue, but at a look from Mason, she sighed. "I'll think about it," she said. "Keep it for now."

Gina held on to the box a moment longer before slipping it into her purse.

"Does everyone have a place to stay?" Mason asked, looking relieved that another crisis had been averted before it had truly begun.

There were nods around the room. Dad and Laura were staying with me, and the Pattersons were going to be staying at Vicki's place. They'd asked about hotels, but Pine Hills doesn't really have any, and definitely didn't have ones they would find suitable.

Gina glanced back, "Lyric? Did you find somewhere? I know you were having a beast of a time finding a place to stay."

"I did," she said. "It's a place called Ted and Bettfast, if you can imagine."

"Have you seen the names of most of the places here?" Jacques asked. "Coming in, I thought it was some kind of joke."

Admittedly, Pine Hills did have some strange names when it came to businesses. When I'd first moved here, I'd found it odd, but now, I thought the goofy names were charming.

"Will you be showing us to your house, Vicki?" Frederick asked. "I'm not familiar with the area and wouldn't mind a tour of the place. We don't want to intrude where we don't belong."

"Of course," Vicki said, softening. For all their disagreements, she still loved her parents. "I'll be staying with Mason, so you'll have the house to yourselves."

"I'll be staying with them as well," Cathy said, stepping forward, mouth full of espresso beans.

Vicki gave her a tight smile and a nod. "That's fine. There are two bedrooms."

"What about that terrible cat of yours?" Gina asked. "Please tell me you've found him a new home."

Vicki took a sharp breath, but when she spoke, she remained calm. "He's staying with me."

"Good." Gina glanced back at her friends. "Everyone else know where they're going?" There was a murmur of assent. "Good. Shall we?" Without waiting for an answer, she started for the door. The others piled out after her.

"I'll get the car," Mason said, hurrying out with the others.

"Meet you at your place?" Dad asked me.

"You have the key?" I'd given him one when he'd last stayed with me. He lived so far away, and his visits were rare, but it made me feel better knowing he had one. I missed having him around.

He nodded and patted his pocket. "Never leave home without it. Besides"—he grinned—"If I didn't, I'd just pick the lock."

"Of course you would." I couldn't help but smile. Over the last couple of years, I'd learned a lot about my dad.

He stepped forward and wrapped me in a warm hug. "It's good to see you, Buttercup."

"You too, Dad."

He stepped back, took Laura's hand, and together, they left Death by Coffee.

"I can't believe Mom and Dad would do that," Vicki said. "Why do they always feel like they have to have the last say? A wedding planner? Now?" She shook her head in wonderment.

"I'm sure they mean well," I said. In their own way, they truly did, even if they didn't know how best to show it.

Vicki sighed and rubbed at her temples. "This is going to be a long week."

"You'll get through it." I gently took her hands in my own. "Remember. You're getting married!"

That brought a smile to her face. "I am."

"And I'll make sure nothing goes wrong," I said. "This is going to be the best wedding ever."

"Thanks." A horn honked outside. "I'd better go. Mom will want more than just a tour of the house." She stepped back and looked around. "I'd better lock up first."

"I can do that," I said. "Go ahead and go."

"You sure?"

"Positive."

Vicki gave me a quick hug. "Thank you." She started for the door.

"Good luck," I told her as she left.

I took a deep breath and let it out in a huff. While things weren't exactly going to plan, I thought the brief meeting *had* gone better than expected. No one had started yelling, so that was a win. I just hoped that by the time the wedding rolled around, Vicki and her mother wouldn't be at each other's throats.

Mason honked once more as the car pulled away. Even though they couldn't see me, I waved anyway. And then, finally alone, I went about locking up Death by Coffee for the night.

3

"Good morning, Buttercup."

I yawned and trudged my way into the kitchen, guided by the smell of coffee and eggs. Dad was at the stove, apron tied around his waist, spatula in hand. Laura was sitting at the counter, watching him with a smile full of pure adoration.

"Thanks for letting us use your room last night," she said. "You didn't have to put yourself out for our sake."

"I'd be perfectly fine on the couch if you'd prefer it," Dad said, stirring the scrambled eggs.

I'm not normally used to talking before my morning coffee, so I poured and took a sip before responding. "It's no bother," I said. Besides, I was the one who'd forced them to take the master bedroom while I slept in the spare room. Dad had tried to convince me to let him take the couch, acting as if he and Laura had never shared a bed. From the looks they'd given one another, I knew that not to be the case, and quite frankly, we were all adults here. It might be a bit strange to think of Dad sleeping next to someone other than Mom, but it wasn't offensive.

"We can always find a hotel," Dad said. He opened a cupboard, found the plates, and began shoveling eggs onto them. "You've got a lot on your mind with the wedding, and don't need us getting in the way."

"Dad, I'm good." I leaned against the counter and closed my eyes. "I've got to work today anyway, so it's not like I'll be needing the space." Though, I was worried about what awaited me at Death by Coffee. If Vicki and her mom got into another fight, it could make for another challenging day.

"Do you have time to eat?" Dad asked. "I made you a plate."

I glanced at the clock. "Let me hop into the shower real quick. I should have a few minutes before I've got to go."

I set my coffee down, the cookie already breaking apart into soft little chunks, and hurried to the shower. Most mornings, I tended to stand under the spray for an extended period to let the water wake me, but today, I rushed it. I not only wanted some of Dad's cooking, but I also thought it might be good to sit down with Laura for a few minutes. I really wanted to get to know her better, especially since it was clear she really did care for my dad.

After toweling off and getting dressed, I returned to the kitchen. My long-haired, orange cat, Misfit, was sitting at Laura's feet, paw in the air, begging for scraps. He knew better, but with someone new to beg from, he must have figured out he'd get pampered if he looked cute.

"You didn't have to wait for me," I said, noting their plates were still full. I snatched up my coffee, topped it off, and joined them at the table.

Dad merely smiled. "I added a little homemade

seasoning to the eggs," he said. "Laura showed it to me, and I think it improves the taste dramatically."

"I hope you like them," she said. "Some people believe it makes the eggs too spicy, especially for breakfast, but I like it."

I took a bite, eyes widening as the heat hit my tongue.

"It's too much?" Laura asked, half rising out of her seat, as if she might run to grab me some water.

I swallowed. "No. They're really good. Just caught me off guard."

"Are you sure? I could get you something else." She eased slowly back down.

"Positive." I glanced at the clock and took another couple of quick bites before pushing the plate away. "I'd eat more, but I really do have to go. I slept in later than I should have."

"We might stop in to visit you later, if that's okay," Dad said.

"I'd like to try some of your coffee and browse the books," Laura added.

"That'd be great." And if Vicki was still down about her parents, she could use the positive vibes coming off the two of them.

I chugged the rest of my coffee, which had cooled during my shower. I would have liked to spoon up the remains of the cookie, but I hadn't been kidding when I said I had to go. I was already going to be late.

With a quick good-bye to Dad and Laura, and a loving scratch behind Misfit's ears, I headed in for work.

It was a bright and sunny summer day, and I found myself whistling by the time I walked through the door of Death by Coffee. Lena Allison was behind the counter, ringing up a sale. Her hair, which had been purple a week ago, was now neon pink, and cut short. She grinned and waved when she saw me. I returned the favor.

Upstairs, our other employee, Jeff Braun, was shelving books. We'd gotten a new shipment yesterday while I'd been picking up the wedding guests, or else I would have done it. He glanced down, saw me, and then redoubled his efforts. The guy was trying so hard, harder than he really needed to, truth be told. He was coming out of his shell more and more, and with it, his desire to impress increased.

I appreciated the both of them to no end, but was starting to wonder if we'd need to hire someone else to help fill in when one of them couldn't make it in to work.

I'd just gone to the back, grabbed an apron, and returned to check the cookie and coffee levels when the door opened and the resident gossip, Rita Jablonski, walked in. Her eyes immediately suctioned to me and she started my way, already talking.

"Can you believe it?" she said. "Our little town is rife with celebrities! I was on my way here when I thought I saw a woman I remember seeing in *The Robber Train*."

I had no idea who exactly she was talking about, nor had I ever seen *The Robber Train*, let alone heard of it, but I figured she'd come across one of the Pattersons or their friends since there were no other actresses hanging around Pine Hills as far as I knew.

"They're here for Vicki's wedding," I said, checking the cookie case to find it fully stocked and fresh. The coffee was likewise full.

"That explains it then." Rita leaned her bulky frame against the counter. "I considered stopping her and asking for an autograph, but she looked upset. She practically bristled when someone walked too closely to her." She huffed. "I'll never understand these Hollywood types. They never know how to relax! I mean, really! How hard would it be to treat other people with respect? All actors are the same, let me tell you. They only care about themselves."

I doubted she knew anyone who'd ever been in a movie or television show before, but held my tongue. Instead, in an attempt to change the subject, I said something even dumber.

"Dad's here too."

Rita's eyes lit up and she practically floated from the floor. "James Hancock is here?" Her head jerked around as she scanned the store. "Where?"

Not only was Rita the town gossip and busybody, she was also my dad's biggest fan, a fact she made sure to remind me of every chance she got.

"Not *here*, here. But in town. He said he might stop by later." And then I added what was probably the second-dumbest thing I could have said right then. "He'll be bringing his girlfriend."

It was like watching a building implode. Rita's eyes, which had been wide and excited, dulled, her mouth opening in a pained, shocked "O." Her forehead crumpled, and I swear I saw a tear glimmer in her eye. Her entire demeanor seemed to crumble, as if I'd just destroyed every hope and dream she'd ever had with those five simple words.

"His girlfriend, dear?"

There was nothing to do but plow forward. "Her name's Laura," I said. Beside me, Lena slunk away, as if afraid to get caught in Rita's inevitable breakdown. "She's nice."

Rita blinked at me before her hand fluttered to her chest. "I . . . I think I need to sit down."

A little worried, I hurried around the counter and took her elbow. I guided her to a chair and helped her down before saying, "Let me get you something to drink." She looked pale, and maybe a little shell-shocked. The last time my dad was in town, she'd practically thrown herself at him, so I guess I shouldn't have been surprised by how hard she was taking the news that he now had a girlfriend.

I filled a cup with water, and another with coffee, just in case. I carried them both to where Rita sat. She took them wordlessly and turned to stare blankly ahead.

Huh. Who would have thought anyone could say anything that would knock her speechless?

Damage done, I slunk back behind the counter, feeling like an insensitive jerk. I hadn't meant to hurt her feelings. I hadn't meant anything at all by it, really. It had just slipped out.

"She'll be okay," Lena said.

"I hope so." With as bad as she looked, I was afraid Rita might wither away to nothing in her misery. Her infatuation with my dad was the closest thing to a relationship she had.

I didn't have time to come up with some way to cheer her up, however. The door opened and Vicki entered, looking irritated. Mason was right behind her, as was his dad, Raymond Lawyer; Regina Harper; and both the Pattersons. I was surprised to see Regina, but I guess I shouldn't have been. Before she started dating Raymond, her daughter, Heidi, had been married to his other son, Brendon. After Brendon's untimely death, Regina and Raymond had been drawn together, and were now dating.

The door swung closed, and I thought that would be everyone until it opened again and Cathy Carr strode inside, mouth full of espresso beans. While everyone else found a table together, she made a beeline for the counter.

"Give me the strongest coffee you've got," she said, looking as if she was already hopped up on enough caffeine to fly to the moon.

"Coming right up," Lena said, hurrying back to fill the order.

"How's everyone doing?" I asked, nodding toward where the others had sat. Vicki already had her arms crossed and was glaring at her mother, who'd shoved the necklace box across the table toward her. It looked like last night's frustrations were boiling over again.

Cathy glanced at me, surprised, as if she hadn't even noticed I was there. "Oh, fine, I suppose." She gave a fluttery laugh. "I don't get why there's so much pushback. I'm going to make this wedding one to remember."

Not in a good way, I thought, but kept it to myself. "Vicki was hoping for something small and simple."

"Everyone says that," Cathy said, popping a bean into her mouth. She chewed a moment before going on. "Weddings are a one-time deal for the bride and groom. People who go for small weddings always regret it. They look back and wish they would have taken the time to do it right. If you go small and for-gettable, no one remembers it, and the memories are lessened by it." She nodded once. "Trust me, we'll make this the kind of wedding everyone will remember."

While I was sure that was true, I had my doubts about her assessment. Mom and Dad had a simple wedding; they couldn't afford much else. But I never once heard them complain. Dad always said it was the best moment of his life. They didn't need a DJ or a five-tier cake or a fancy flower arrangement, not when they had each other.

But I doubted Cathy Carr understood that.

Lena returned and handed over the coffee. Cathy eyed her in a way that was just this side of condescending before dropping change onto the counter. She took a sip from her cup, sighed as if it had hit the spot, and then she turned and strode quickly away.

"She seems high strung," Lena said, gathering the scattered coins. She counted it, frowned, telling me Cathy might have shorted us, and then put it into the register without another word.

"That she is," I said, watching as she joined the others. Cathy was wearing a dark pantsuit that was as severe as her makeup and short hair. Even her nail polish didn't do anything to soften her in any way. It made me wonder if she had any other clothes, or if this was how she looked all the time.

Almost as soon as she reached the table, Vicki stood, very nearly knocking over her chair as she did. She leveled a finger at her mother, then pointed to Cathy, who was so busy chugging her coffee she didn't seem to notice.

"Uh-oh," I muttered, watching. Voices had yet to be raised, but it was clear it was coming.

Gina Patterson motioned toward Regina Harper,

who nodded sagely at whatever was said. It was followed up by Raymond saying something that had Mason scowling and Cathy Carr nodding right along. Frederick looked content to let everyone else argue it out.

"Should I go over there, you think?" I asked, kind of hoping I'd be told no.

"If you don't mind getting your face melted," Lena said. When I glanced at her, she shrugged. "The atmosphere over there is toxic. I can feel it from here."

Voices started rising then, though I still couldn't make out what they were saying. Vicki looked as if she wanted to tear her hair out, as did Mason, while the four older people—Cathy excluded—looked calm and, quite frankly, acted as if they were in the right.

"I'd better go help," I said, taking off my apron and tossing it on a shelf beneath the counter. I couldn't let Vicki and Mason face off against all of them alone.

"Good luck."

I walked across the store much like I would if I was heading for the gallows. Lena was right; you could *feel* the toxicity in the air. *And I'm willingly walking toward it.* Somehow, I knew I was going to regret it.

"I was thinking we could order from Elsie's," Cathy was saying through a mouthful of beans. She took a sip from her coffee to wash it down. "Their cakes are phenomenal."

"I already *have* a cake ordered!" Vicki said. "Someone is putting a lot of time and care into it."

"But, Victoria, it won't be from Elsie's," Gina said.

"I don't care!" Vicki was near shouting now. "And don't call me that."

"Vicki, please," Frederick said. "You're making a scene."

Mason tried to put his arm around her shoulder,

but Vicki shrugged him off. She looked hot, and rightfully so. "I don't want your stupid cake. I don't want new flowers." She snatched up the box with the necklace inside. "And I don't want this!" She threw it at her mother, who, though surprised by the outburst, caught it before it fell to the floor.

Before anyone could say anything, Vicki stormed past me, and up the stairs, into the bookstore, right past a startled Jeff. He looked at me, eyes wide and uncertain. All I could do was shrug.

"What was that all about?" Regina asked.

"Women," grunted Raymond, as if that explained it all.

Mason started for the stairs, but I stopped him. "Let me see if I can calm her down," I said. "You can deal with this."

He grimaced, but nodded. "Thanks."

I left him to it and went upstairs to find Vicki.

She was standing in the back corner, where no one could see her. There were tears in her eyes, and her fists were clenched so tightly her knuckles were popping white.

"Can you believe them?" she asked, gesturing toward where everyone was sitting.

"They're trying to help in their own way," I said, and before she could get angry, I added, "It doesn't mean they're right."

"I just want a small wedding," she said. "I don't want some big production with fireworks and people I've never met watching on. Is that too much to ask?"

"No," I said, wondering if someone had actually brought up fireworks. "We'll make them understand."

"I don't know if we can." She sighed and leaned against the wall. "What am I going to do?"

"Focus on your wedding, what *you* want. Just because they suggest something doesn't mean they can change anything. It's your decision."

"Don't sell my mother short." A bitter smile played over her lips. "If she can find a way, she'll do it. I wouldn't put it past her to call the local businesses to cancel all my orders."

"Well then, we'll call them first to tell them not to listen to her." I put an arm around Vicki's shoulders and pulled her in close. "It'll be okay," I said. "You know they only want what's best for you."

"I know." She sagged into me. "It's just hard sometimes. I'm so stressed about everything, I feel like every time someone sneezes, it's going to blow this whole thing over."

"We just have to get through the next few days," I said, "and then you'll be married!"

Vicki smiled at that. "I will, won't I?"

I squeezed. "Don't let them ruin this for you. This is your time."

She nodded. "Thank you, Krissy. I don't know what I'd do without you."

"Your life would probably be a lot less hectic." I smiled and released her. "Go back there and put your foot down, okay?"

"Okay."

Vicki took a moment to catch her breath and then led the way back downstairs. She headed straight for her parents, who were shaking their heads at Mason, while I started for the counter. Before I made it all the way back, however, another disaster walked through the door.

Well, the couple coming through the door wasn't *the* disaster. It was what followed that qualified.

"James Hancock, how could you?"

Both Dad and Laura came up short at Rita's wail. She was up and out of her seat almost immediately, and crossed the short distance between them in seconds. She latched on to Dad's arm, nearly dragging him over as she dropped to her knees.

"I trusted you! And look what you've done to me."

"I . . . I . . ." Dad looked my way, silently pleading for help.

I considered letting him deal with it on his own. I'd just dealt with one tense situation, and really didn't feel like dealing with another. Besides, in a way, he'd brought it on himself by not warning Rita about Laura ahead of time. He knew just as well as I did how she could get.

"You can't do this to me!" Rita said, tugging on his arm so hard he actually did stagger this time. Laura was forced to grab his wrist to keep him from toppling over.

"Rita," I said, hurrying over. She looked at me as if I, too, had betrayed her. "Let him go."

She dropped his arm and took a step back. "I'm sorry, I . . ." Her hand went to her chest before she straightened. "I'm okay."

Worry had me putting a gentle hand on her arm. "Are you sure?" I asked. "If something's going on . . . ?"

She forced a smile. "It's okay, dear. I'm fine." She glanced at Dad and Laura. "I'll be on my way."

"Rita," Dad said, but she didn't give him a chance to speak. She walked out the door and down the street without looking back.

"What was that all about?" Laura asked.

"She gets emotional," I said, though it felt like there

was more to it than that. I knew Rita was infatuated
with Dad, but this went beyond that.

"I hope I can make it up to her," Dad said. "I don't
want her to be upset."

"I'll talk to her," I said. The only challenge would
be finding time to do so. Looking back, it appeared
Vicki and Mason were handling their parents, and
now that Dad and Laura were here . . .

I turned to them, putting Rita out of mind. "So,
you two, what can I get you?"

4

The house smelled of buttery popcorn, yet I hardly noticed it. A near full bowl sat in my lap, untouched. The television was on; a movie I wasn't even watching flickered across the screen. Normally, I would have chowed down on the popcorn and gone back for seconds within fifteen minutes, yet my mind was about as far from what was happening around me as it could get.

I might have helped Vicki feel a little better about her parents' involvement in the upcoming wedding, but I wasn't feeling the same way. I knew her mom, knew how she could get. It's one thing to say you're going to stand up to her. It's another thing entirely to actually do it.

Well, you can stand up all you want; it's whether she even deigns to see you that's the problem.

I'd already made a few calls around town to make sure nothing had been canceled. The cake was still on, as were the flowers. If Gina planned on replacing them with something Cathy Carr decided on, she had yet to inform anyone else of that fact.

Maybe she's all talk this time.

And maybe I'll live an uneventful life.

The TV snapped off mid-explosion, drawing me out of my ruminations. Dad and Laura were sitting on the couch, close to one another but not touching. It was as if Dad was afraid I'd freak out about displays of affection. I had half a mind to tell him to keep the bedroom door open when they retired for the night, just to see him blush.

"You okay, Buttercup?" he asked. He started to stretch his arm across the back of the couch, but that would have put it behind Laura's head. He quickly pulled it back down and let his hands fall into his lap. "You seem distracted."

I looked down at my now-cold popcorn and set the bowl aside. "I'm just worried about the wedding."

"Totally understandable."

"It's just, Gina and Frederick are making it harder on Vicki than what she deserves. Can't they just be happy for her for once?"

"They are," Dad said. "They see the world differently than we do. Gina thinks she's helping. And I see nothing wrong with wanting your daughter to have the best of everything." He gave me a meaningful look.

"I guess." My eyes drifted to where Misfit was curled up in Laura's lap. He'd really taken to her. Ever since she'd arrived, he'd followed her everywhere. I could hear his contented purr even from across the room. "I just wish they'd help a little more . . . helpfully."

Dad chuckled. "It'll work out, Buttercup. These things always do."

I wished I could believe him, but I was truly worried. Not only were Gina and Frederick on board with Cathy taking over the wedding, but so were Raymond Lawyer and Regina Harper. Both, like the Pattersons, tended to control their children's lives. I wasn't sure I'd ever heard Raymond say a kind word to or about Mason. And Regina's daughter, Heidi, was struggling to get out from beneath her mother's thumb; had been since I'd met her years ago when her husband was murdered.

With all those strong personalities pushing, it was only a matter of time before Vicki caved.

I rose from my seat, brushing stray popcorn pieces from my shirt as I did. "I think I need to get some fresh air," I said.

Dad rose with me. "Do you need company?" he asked.

"I can always clean up a bit while you're gone, so don't worry about me," Laura said. She shifted slightly, causing Misfit to bring out the claws to hold on. I couldn't help but smile. She wasn't going anywhere until his nap was over, not unless she wanted ten little puncture marks on her leg.

"No, you two stay here and watch another movie. There's more popcorn and I can put on some coffee if you want." I picked up my purse and fished out my keys.

"We're okay." Dad stepped forward and gave me a reassuring hug. "Stay safe." He kissed my temple.

"I will."

I left them to the movie, and headed outside to my car. Even before I was buckled in, I had my phone out and was dialing.

"Krissy?"

"Hi, Will." I sagged in relief when he answered. Will Foster and I had been dating for a while now, yet it felt like I never saw him anymore. Since he was a doctor, his hours were often unpredictable and long. And now, with me being busy with the wedding, we'd barely spoken, let alone seen each other. It was well past time we got together, lest I explode.

"Is everything okay?" he asked. "You sound stressed."

"I guess." I quickly related everything that had happened as I got the car started and backed out onto the road. "Vicki is beside herself, and I'm not much better."

"They sound like a couple of characters." He was referring to the Pattersons, obviously.

"You don't know the half of it."

A moment of silence before: "Jade and Gemma say hi." Jade was Will's sister, and Gemma her unfathomably cute daughter.

"Tell them hi right back."

"Will do."

More silence.

I was hoping he'd offer to come over to my place, or better yet, invite me over to his house, where we could be alone. I desperately needed contact, even if all we did was sit on his patio with my head on his shoulder as we stared at the stars.

But no offers were forthcoming. Instead, he yawned.

"I should probably go," I said. "You sound tired."

"I am. It's been a really long day. I'll have to tell you about it sometime."

"Soon?"

"Very."

"Good."

Another brief silence, before, "I'll talk to you tomorrow, Krissy. Good night."

"Good night, Will."

He disconnected.

I sighed and tossed my phone onto the seat next to

me. I'd called Will to make me feel better, yet now I felt worse. I don't think he was intentionally avoiding me, but darn it, it was sure feeling like it.

Putting Will out of my mind, I realized I hadn't been driving mindlessly this entire time like I'd thought. Instead, I found myself on a familiar road, heading to a familiar destination. If there was one thing that could make me feel better after my brief chat with my boyfriend, it would be to set Vicki's wedding to rights.

I pulled into the driveway and parked, determined that, tonight, I'd be the hero. No more hoping things worked out. No more waiting for something good to happen. I was the one who was going to make the difference.

Vicki's house was an old Victorian, which suited her name, I supposed. It was large and clean, and put my little place to shame. While her parents might not have approved of her running off to live her life in Pine Hills, they weren't going to let her leave California without providing for her in some way, hence the house. It might seem like they argued with their daughter all the time, but they truly did love her. They just needed to show it better sometimes.

Lights were on inside, both upstairs and downstairs, but only one car, a silver Prius, sat in the driveway. I shut off the engine and got out of the car. The house sat on a semi-private acre of land, surrounded by pine trees, planted in a way that formed a natural fence against prying eyes. I could see the lights of neighboring houses through the branches of the trees, but heard or saw no one else.

Maybe if Vicki moved in with Mason once they were married, she'd be willing to sell me her house at a discount. I couldn't even hear any cars on the nearby road. It was quiet, peaceful, and quite pretty.

I shook off the thought and steeled myself for what was to come. Gina and Frederick needed to lay off Vicki, let her decide what she wanted for her wedding. I'd put it nicely, of course, in the hopes they would hear me out, but I wasn't confident it was going to work. I simply had to try to stand strong and refuse to take no for an answer.

I made my way to the front of the house, mentally prepping myself for what I was going to say. If I could get them to concede, just a little, it would be a win. I took a deep breath, let it out in a huff, and then knocked on the door.

The light upstairs immediately went out.

A cold chill swept through me then. Were Gina and Frederick avoiding me? Or were they simply turning in for the night and hadn't heard my knock?

I hammered harder, just in case.

The door popped open.

This time the cold chill was a full-scale blizzard. I nudged the door with my foot, pushing it open farther. It didn't creak ominously, though my brain did provide the horror soundtrack mentally.

"Hello?" I called. "Gina? Frederick? It's Krissy." No lights came on upstairs, though the downstairs one was still blazing. All was quiet inside. "Cathy? You there?"

No answer.

Thoroughly creeped out, I stepped into the house. The floors were hardwood, causing my footfalls to sound loud as I moved toward the light. The foyer was empty, as was the living room to my left. The light was coming from the kitchen. It spilled out into the dining room, casting shadows over the table and chairs.

I scanned the dining room and just about screamed when I saw a dozen shining eyes staring back at me. I sucked in a breath and let it out through my teeth, remembering Vicki's porcelain doll collection. I shuddered and looked away from their terrifying faces. How could anyone ever stand those dead, shining eyes staring at them all the time?

"Hello?" I called again, though I knew I wasn't going to get an answer. *Maybe Gina, Frederick, and Cathy went out.* They were used to Californian time, so it was likely dinnertime for them. It made sense they would find something to eat, leaving the house empty.

Then why did the light upstairs go out?

I glanced back the way I'd come, but no one was sneaking up on me. I had an urge to call someone, just to let them know where I was. My phone, however, was back beside my purse, which in turn, was in my car. Someday, I'd learn to take it with me.

As I stepped into the kitchen, my foot bumped into something that clattered across the room. It bounced off the island counter and then rolled back to me.

"Huh." I bent over and picked it up. It was a silver candlestick, the candle broken off, top half missing. Vicki always kept a pair of them on the island counter. Trouble must have knocked one off.

Isn't Trouble staying with Vicki and Mason?

The blizzard was now an icy dread. A rumble outside scratched the surface of my attention, but was unable to fully break through. Clutching the candlestick, I walked slowly around the island counter.

First, there was a stockinged foot. Then a leg, and finally, a severe, black pantsuit.

"Cathy?" I hurried over and dropped to my knees beside her. She was lying facedown, espresso beans scattered around her. A few feet away lay an empty coffee mug, the handle broken from where it had fallen.

My immediate thought was that she'd had a heart attack or maybe a stroke from all the caffeine, and had fallen, knocking over the candlestick, and dropping the mug in the process. There was a mostly full, steaming pot of coffee on the counter, telling me she must have just fallen.

I felt for a pulse, and found none, though she was still somewhat warm, further confirming that her demise was recent.

I started to rise so I could rush out to my car and grab my phone—Vicki had long ago cut the cord, so there was no landline—when heavy footfalls sounded from the front room.

I froze, still at a crouch. My legs started burning almost immediately, but I was too afraid to move. What if this *wasn't* an accident. Lights didn't turn off by themselves. The killer could still be here!

I clutched at the candlestick and waited. The footfalls stopped in the dining room. There was a shuffling sound, like cloth on cloth, and then the steps continued on, toward where I was hiding.

It was now or never.

With a scream that startled even me, I rose from my crouch, candlestick poised above my head, ready to strike.

"Dear me!" Frederick cried, falling back a step, hand going to his chest. Behind him, in the dining room, Gina held a bag of takeout, just above the table, frozen in the act of putting it down.

I brought myself up short, thankfully not clunking Vicki's dad on the head and knocking him out.

"Kristina?" Gina said. "What on Earth are you doing here?"

I lowered my trembling arm. Slowly, I set the candlestick aside. I was so upset, I very nearly missed the counter, before I found the hard surface. It hit with a loud clunk.

"Krissy?" Frederick asked, eyes growing concerned. For the first time, I think he saw me as a real person, not just the person who'd led Vicki astray. "Are you all right?"

I shook my head, took a deep breath.

"Gina. Frederick. You might want to sit down. I have some bad news." When neither of them moved, I swallowed, and stepped aside so they could see past me. When I spoke next, it came out mechanical, almost rehearsed. "I hate to be the one to tell you this," I said, "but Cathy Carr is dead."

5

The dark looks the Pattersons were shooting my way had me shrinking in on myself as I sat at the dining room table, waiting for the police to arrive. Gina had called them while Frederick, against my advice, rolled Cathy over onto her back to check her over. I caught a glimpse of a bluish face and immediately turned away. I couldn't bear to look.

It was starting to become a habit, finding bodies. I'd been repeatedly told that, before my arrival in Pine Hills, there had been little to no crime. Since then, murders had sprung up like holes in an old inner tube. Somehow, I always found myself in the middle of them.

Sirens blared in the distance, growing closer. After I'd told the Pattersons about Cathy, we'd barely spoken more than a dozen words to one another. They didn't want to hear my defense. They had shut me down almost the moment I'd tried to speak. As the police neared, however, I felt the need to defend myself, especially against those stony, accusatory stares.

"I found her like that," I said.

"Did you now." Gina didn't sound convinced.

"I swear! I came over to talk to you about Vicki's wedding and found the door open. I walked in and found her on the floor. I thought she might have had a heart attack."

"You just walked in, uninvited?" Frederick asked, cold as ice.

Realizing I wasn't going to convince them of anything, I merely nodded and looked away. The sirens became near deafening, and then abruptly shut off as a pair of cruisers pulled to a stop behind my car in the driveway.

Frederick rose and pointed at me. "Stay here." Then, to his wife, "Keep an eye on her."

Gina clutched at a baseball bat she'd found by the front door and did as she was told. Vicki had placed the bat there the day she'd moved in and had never once felt the need to use it, let alone move it. I think she'd actually forgotten it, to be honest, but Gina sure hadn't. She glared at me, hands flexing on the grip of the bat, daring me to try something.

Frederick went outside to meet with the cops, leaving me alone with Gina. I considered pleading my innocence some more, but figured it would be pointless. The Pattersons had never liked me, and finding me kneeling over their favorite wedding planner, meager weapon in hand, had likely made their evening in some sick, depraved way. Now, they had a solid reason to tell Vicki to stay away from me.

Voices neared, and then Frederick entered, Officers Paul Dalton and John Buchannan right behind him. The moment I saw Paul, I rose from my seat, a sigh of relief on my lips.

"She did it," Frederick said as they stepped into the dining room.

"I did no such thing!"

Gina's hands tightened on the bat at my raised voice, and I took a ginger step away from her, just in case.

"Let us sort it out, Mr. Patterson," Paul said. He walked over to me. "All right, what happened?"

I watched Buchannan, who was moving toward the kitchen. He glanced back at me, as if feeling my gaze. His mouth pressed into a grimace and he shook his head sadly, as if he'd already condemned me.

Knowing him, he probably already had. Buchannan and I never quite got along. I thought things were getting better between us lately, but this would only sour our already tense relationship. Nothing I ever did seemed to make him happy. And even when I had nothing to do with whatever crime was committed, he always acted like I was guilty of some part of it.

Paul, on the other hand, was the proverbial one that got away. We'd had a single date, one that had been set up by his mom, the police chief, Patricia Dalton, of all people. Then, thanks to my penchant for getting into trouble, we'd drifted apart. I'd moved on to Will, he started dating a waitress named Shannon, yet we still found ourselves drawn to one another.

Unfortunately, it was usually murder that brought us together.

"I found her like that," I said, motioning toward where Cathy lay. "Well, not like that exactly. She was facedown, but Frederick moved her." I glared at him, taking a bit of glee in tattling on him. Petty? Sure. But he'd accused me of *killing* her first, so I felt justified.

Paul removed his hat and ran his fingers through his sandy-brown hair, which was growing longer. I actually thought he looked better with longer hair. It made him seem a little wilder, not so—I don't know—good-old boy. "Why were you here?" he asked me.

"I wanted to talk to them about Vicki's wedding. She was upset because they were messing with her plans. I thought I could make it better."

"By killing Cathy Carr?" Gina asked, incredulous.

"*No*," I said. "By talking to you. I didn't think I'd walk in and find a dead body." I shuddered and hugged myself. "I think she might have had a heart attack. She was always eating those chocolate-covered espresso beans and drinking coffee. That can't have been good for her."

"She was holding a weapon when we came in," Frederick said.

"I always told Vicki she was a bad influence," Gina added.

"It was a candlestick," I said, motioning to the item in question. "I found it on the floor." And then I realized how it must have sounded. *Krissy, in the kitchen, with the candlestick.* Just like a game of Clue. "I swear I didn't kill her."

"Did you see anything or anyone else?" Paul asked. He looked frazzled, and a little annoyed. I wasn't sure if it was because of me, or because of the Pattersons' accusations. I had a feeling it was a little of both.

"No, I . . ." I frowned. "Wait. The light upstairs. When I got here, it was on. It went out when I knocked on the door. Someone was here!"

"We were getting takeout," Gina said, touching the bag of cold food, when Paul looked to her.

"Is there anyone else staying with you?"

"No, there shouldn't be anyone here." This from Frederick.

"Wait here." Paul removed his gun, and then

carefully made his way over to the stairs. Buchannan was done looking at Cathy and moved to stand by the front door, presumably in case someone else *was* in the house and decided to make a run for it.

I had a near overwhelming urge to follow him as Paul made his way up the stairs, but at a harsh look from Buchannan, I decided to remain behind. Gina had yet to put down the bat, and was holding it with a death grip as she watched the stairs, while Frederick had taken up position between me and the kitchen, like he thought I might go in to destroy evidence while the police were distracted.

A tense couple of minutes followed where no one spoke. My hands were clutched to my chest as I waited, fearing the worst. *Has someone been here the entire time?* What if Gina and Frederick hadn't come home when they did? Could someone have startled Cathy, causing her to have a heart attack, and then gone upstairs afterward? I mean, Vicki had been staying with Mason more and more for months now. The house was usually empty. Could a thief have come, thinking no one would be home, and startled the life right out of Cathy?

It was possible. It was also possible the light had simply burned out the moment I'd knocked on the door, one of those cosmic coincidences that rarely happened, but did occur at times. This could be all one big misunderstanding, an accident no one could have prevented.

And if someone *had* been upstairs when I'd arrived, that meant they could have come down and attacked me at any moment. I very well might have been saved by the people who were now accusing me of murder.

Paul returned a minute later, gun holstered. "No one's here," he said. "John? What do you think?"

"Looks like she hit her head," he said. "There's blood in her hair."

"Or someone hit her," Gina said, shooting a meaningful look my way.

An ambulance pulled up out front then. Buchannan went outside to meet the EMTs, while Paul returned to question me and the Pattersons some more.

"Were you expecting company?" he asked Frederick.

"None. Gina and I went out to pick up something to eat. Cathy remained behind. We got her her favorite." He wiped a tear from his eye. I couldn't tell if it was genuine or not.

"Krissy could be right and she had a heart attack," Paul said, though he didn't sound entirely convinced. "Someone will check her out and we'll know for sure soon." He turned to me. "Until then, I think it's best you come down to the station and give a statement."

"What?" I gaped at him. "You think I had something to do with her death?"

Paul cringed at my tone, which was admittedly, earsplitting in my horror at the implication. "No, but I can't rule anything out just because we're friends."

"She's always been sketchy," Gina said, pointing the bat at me. "It was only a matter of time before she snapped!"

Buchannan returned then, a pair of EMTs in his wake. They pushed past us into the kitchen to deal with Cathy. Suddenly, the house felt overly full and I wanted out of there, though I wasn't so sure the police station would make me feel any better.

"You have to believe me," I said to Paul. "I found her like that."

"I do," he said, though he kept his voice low so no one else could hear. "But you do need to come with me. Please, Krissy, don't make this harder on us than it already is."

In the kitchen, Buchannan had removed a baggie and was using a gloved hand to slip the candlestick into it. His eyes flickered to me, and he shook his head again. Clearly, he already thought me guilty of what could very well have been an accident.

"Fine," I muttered. "If it'll make things *easier*." I might have been a tad sarcastic with the last.

"It will."

A car screeched to a halt out front. A moment later, Vicki and Mason rushed through the door, dressed in their PJs and looking as if they'd just woken. They very likely had, considering the hour.

"What's going on?" Vicki asked, voice high-pitched with near hysteria. Her gaze found both her parents alive and well, and she sagged. "You're okay. I was so worried." And then she turned to me, expression confused. "Krissy?"

"What are you doing here, Victoria?" Gina asked, cutting me off before I could respond.

"Neighbors called," Mason said. "Said there was something going on at the house. And then we heard the sirens and saw the cop cars and ambulance. We thought . . ." He trailed off as he took in the paramedics in the kitchen.

"It's Cathy," I said. "I think she had a heart attack."

"We found her hovering over her!" Gina said. "She killed her!"

"Mom." And then, Vicki looked to me. "Is she really . . . ?"

I nodded. Just like Vicki, I didn't want to utter it out loud.

"Oh no." Vicki's hand went to her mouth. She might not have known Cathy Carr at all, but to have a murder happen in your own home . . . it was a shock.

Mason put his arm around Vicki's shoulder and hugged her close, never once taking his eyes off of what was going on in the kitchen. The paramedics were doing their best to preserve the scene, while blocking off much of the view. Paul watched them a moment before looking to me.

"Wait here," he said before going over and taking both Mason and Vicki aside.

"You're not going to get away with this," Frederick said the moment Paul was out of earshot.

"We know you despised having her here," Gina added, head jerking toward where Cathy lay.

I couldn't deny not wanting Cathy, or the others the Pattersons had brought along, around, but I never would stoop to killing one of them. They had to know that, right?

I sank down into a chair and refused to speak. Everyone was in shock. Once they took Cathy away and the police figured things out, life could go back to normal. The Pattersons could continue to bicker at their daughter, I could spend time with Dad and Laura, and then, after the wedding, they could all go back home.

The wedding! I glanced up at Vicki and Mason, heart skipping a beat. This was supposed to be a happy time for them, yet it was one disaster after another. Would they be forced to postpone the wedding? Everything was already booked and paid for. Even if they wanted to put it off for a few months, I wasn't so sure they could.

Or should.

Cathy's death was an accident. It had to be.

Right?

Paul patted Vicki on the shoulder, shook Mason's hand, and then walked into the kitchen. He spoke briefly to Buchannan, who shot me another look, and then nodded. Paul then returned to the dining room, thumbs tucked into his belt. He looked us all over once, as if trying to decide how to attack the situation without causing too much commotion. There were some pretty volatile personalities in the room, and sadly, I think I was one of them.

"Officer Buchannan will handle things from here," he told Frederick. "Please remain here in case he needs anything from you." He paused, eyes drifting to Gina and her bat. "I'm sorry for your loss. We'll get to the bottom of this."

I expected the Pattersons to throw more accusations my way, but instead, they shook Paul's hand and then moved to comfort a clearly distraught Vicki. Paul helped me to my feet.

"Come on," he said. "Let's get this thing sorted out."

I nodded, numbly, not quite sure what else to do.

Paul took me by the arm, and while I wasn't handcuffed or anything, I felt like a criminal as he led me slowly from the house. All eyes were on me, but I refused to meet any of them, even Vicki's. I didn't want to see accusation there, though I knew she couldn't possibly think I had anything to do with Cathy's death.

Outside, Paul released my arm and turned to face me. "Are you okay to drive?" he asked, eyes growing concerned. "If not, I can take you."

"I'm okay," I said. I might be a little shaky, and a lot worried, but I didn't feel as if I was going to faint or anything.

"Are you sure?" He put a hand on my shoulder, forcing me to meet his eye. "Because if you think you need a few minutes, we can wait. Or I can take you there and bring you back after you give your statement."

"No," I said, forcing a weak smile. "I'll be okay. Just a little shocked. I can't believe she's dead."

"Did you know her well?"

"Not at all. She came with Gina and Frederick, and other than knowing she's a wedding planner who really liked coffee, I knew nothing else about her."

"I see." Was that incrimination in his voice? I didn't get the chance to ask because he then said, "Meet me at the station. I'll call ahead and let them know we're coming and that everything is under control here."

"Okay."

"Krissy." He waited until I looked up. "It'll be all right."

I nodded, couldn't bring myself to smile any longer. How could anything be all right when someone had lost her life? Accident or not, Vicki's wedding had just taken a serious turn for the worse.

Paul was parked directly behind me. I leaned briefly on a silver SUV, legs feeling a little wobbly, and then, once I felt strong enough to walk, I made my way to my car.

6

I sat alone in the interrogation room of the Pine Hills police station, foot tapping rhythmically beneath the table. Paul had promised he'd be right back, but that was over thirty minutes ago, and I was starting to get antsy.

The room was identical to when I had last been inside it. The table, the plastic chairs, the old couch, and the forgotten dartboard. I would have liked to have sat on the couch and treated this like a social visit, but Paul had led me straight to one of the hard plastic chairs. While he hadn't explicitly told me I *had* to sit in it, it was implied.

Thankfully, not many people had seen me on my way into the station. Pine Hills is a small town, and the police department is likewise small. Both Buchannan and Paul were on duty that night, and they'd been at Vicki's place. Only two other cops had been visible when I'd entered, and I didn't know either. I'd never seen more than four or five on duty at once, and doubted there were ever many more. As I've said, there's usually not that much crime in town, not until someone dies, which was happening far too often as of late.

I picked at a hangnail, and tried to think pleasant thoughts as the seconds ticked by. What could be taking him so long? Paul had to know I was innocent. Cathy was a high-strung caffeine addict. Even if someone else *was* in the house at the time of her death, there was still a chance she'd died of natural causes.

It was far too stressful to think someone could have gone as far as murder. I mean, it had happened in Vicki's house. She used to live there. Alone. With only a cat for protection. And while Trouble's claws should be registered deadly weapons, they would do little against a determined killer.

Vicki could have been home with her parents. She didn't own a gun. The only knives she owned were kitchen knives. And the bat had been a forgotten piece of the scenery, right up until Gina had picked it up to ward me off. If someone *had* broken in that night, it wasn't like they'd had much to be worried about.

After what felt like an eternity, the door opened, but it wasn't Paul who stepped through the doorway.

"Chief Dalton?" I asked, surprised. She looked bedraggled, as if someone had called her and woken her up just a few minutes ago. She was in uniform, but it looked decidedly unkempt. She was wearing her hat, despite the fact we were indoors, but from the hair poking out around it, I had a feeling she was trying to hide a serious case of bedhead.

"Ms. Hancock." She had a folder with her that she set down on the table before she took a seat across from me. She didn't riffle through papers and photos like you'd see on TV, but she did fix me with an unhappy stare.

"Where's Paul?" I asked. No one else had come through the door, making me more worried than ever. *I didn't do anything!*

"Filling out some paperwork, I imagine." Chief Dalton sighed. "How do you keep getting yourself mixed up in these situations?"

"I wish I could tell you," I said. "It's terrible what happened to Cathy."

"It is."

"But I had nothing to do with it."

"Why were you there?"

I took a deep breath and let it out slowly. This definitely didn't feel like a friendly chat. It was feeling more and more like a true interrogation.

"I wanted to talk to Gina and Frederick Patterson," I said, keeping my voice as calm and neutral as possible, though I was a tangle of hyped-up emotions inside. "They're staying at Vicki's house with Cathy until the wedding." I paused and frowned. "Well, were. All I wanted to do was ask them to stop messing with Vicki's wedding plans. When I got there, I found Cathy on the floor, unresponsive."

"And the candlestick?"

"It was on the floor too, on the other side of the counter. I picked it up before I realized she was there."

Chief Dalton stared at me a moment before nodding. "I figure you're telling the truth," she said. "I don't have all the details, let alone all the names, but we'll work that out soon enough." She flipped open the folder, read the page, and then closed it again. "EMTs are saying it is likely she was struck on the head by the candlestick you found. We can't be sure until tests are run and so forth."

I gaped at her for a long couple of seconds before

I could answer. "She was *murdered?*" The thought *had* crossed my mind of course, but hearing it confirmed was still a shock. *And the killer might have still been there.*

"Well, I'd say it's kind of hard to accidentally hit someone on the back of the head so hard, you cause them to choke to death."

"Wait. She choked?"

"On the candies found at the scene."

"Espresso beans."

"What?"

"They're espresso beans. She was popping them like candy, and I guess since they are chocolate covered, they could be confused for candy." My mouth snapped closed as I realized I was starting to babble. "So, you're saying someone came in, hit her on the head, and caused her to choke? Why?"

"I was hoping you could tell me."

"I don't know!" I sat back and looked to the ceiling. There were hundreds of little holes in it, as if someone had sat here and tossed pencils into the soft tiles. "No one knew her very well. She came with Vicki's parents and their friends."

"So, they knew her."

"Well, yeah, but they wouldn't hurt her. I mean, they brought her to plan Vicki's already planned wedding."

"She's a wedding planner?"

"Apparently the planner to the stars." It was hard not to make air quotes as I said the last. "She's why I went to see them. Cathy was talking about changing the flower arrangement, and the cake, and so on. Vicki didn't want them changed. I was hoping if I talked to them about it, they'd lay off." I paused, realizing how that made it sound. "You know I wouldn't kill anyone over something like that, right?"

Chief Dalton flashed me a noncommittal smile. "Did Vicki Patterson want the wedding planner involved?"

"No."

"She was upset?"

"Well, yeah."

"What about her fiancé?" Chief flipped open the folder again, scanned the sheet, and then closed it. "Mason Lawyer."

"He wasn't happy about it either." And then, just so she knew: "Neither of them would have hurt Cathy. They weren't happy about the situation, but would have found a way to manage without resorting to violence."

Chief considered it a moment before asking, "Do you have the names of anyone else who might know the deceased? You said the Pattersons brought friends?"

"They did." I rattled off the names, hoping I got them right. Could one of them have held a grudge against Cathy Carr and decided to come all the way to Pine Hills to off her? It sounded like a stretch, especially considering these people were here for a wedding, not to kill someone they could have just as easily killed in California. I mean, who kills someone right before a wedding? It's rude.

"Know where I can reach these people?"

I couldn't recall if anyone had said where they were staying, and I told Chief Dalton so. I was sure one or two of them had said something, but my brain was such a jumble, I was having a hard time remembering for sure.

"We'll find them," she said. "Trust me on that."

Oh, I did. Chief Patricia Dalton might look like a small, innocent woman, but she was determined and could be scary when she wanted to be. Out of everyone at the Pine Hills police department, she was the only one who I felt acted like a true, hard policewoman. Everyone else seemed a little Mayberry, if you asked me. I almost felt bad for the visiting actors and actresses.

Almost.

"Are you sure she couldn't have just fallen and hit her head? Buchannan said it was possible."

As an answer, Chief Dalton opened the folder again and pulled a photograph from it. She slid it across the table in front of me.

"Do you recognize this?"

I picked up the photo and frowned, not quite sure how it could have anything to do with Cathy's death.

"It's Gina's necklace."

"Do you know how it ended up in the deceased's possession?"

My frown deepened. "Last I knew, Vicki had given it back to her mom." I left out the fact she'd *thrown* it at her, since it wouldn't help anyone. "I assumed she still had it."

"The box was still in the room the Pattersons are using, but it was empty. Ms. Carr had the necklace tucked away in a pocket. One of the EMTs found it when she was searched."

About a zillion thoughts rushed through my head then. Had Cathy tried to steal the necklace? If that was the case, did that mean one of Vicki's parents had killed her? It seemed strange. I mean, why steal something like that now? Why not wait until they were about to board the plane for home. If she'd tried to take it tonight, and Gina found it missing, it would have been only a matter of time before someone would look to her as the likely thief since she was currently living there. But to kill Cathy over something like that?

I doubted it. There's no way either Gina or Frederick was capable of murder. They might not be the nicest of people, but that was partially because of their lifestyles. They might have killed people—and been killed—on screen, but never could I imagine them actually physically harming anyone.

"Maybe she was holding it for them," I said, not very convincingly.

One corner of Chief Dalton's mouth turned down, while her eyebrows rose in a "Do you really believe that?" look. I had to admit, it was pretty unlikely Gina would have given it to Cathy to hold, especially out of its box.

"Take another good look at the picture," she said. "Really look at it and tell me if you think that's truly Mrs. Patterson's necklace."

I looked again, studying it. I hadn't seen the thing for more than a few seconds when Vicki had first looked at it, but it shone just like the one I'd seen—diamonds and ruby and all. It truly was very pretty.

"I think so," I said. "Though I never actually held it or got an up-close look at it."

"I see." Chief Dalton took the photograph and slid it back into the folder. "Well, the necklace recovered at the scene is a fake."

"A what?"

"A fake. You know, a forgery. A replica, or whatever they call it when the gems aren't real."

"But . . . how?" I couldn't imagine Gina trying to

pass off a fake necklace as the real deal. She was too concerned about her image to do something like that.

"I don't know," she said. "We'll be sending it away in the morning for testing, but one of the EMTs on the scene has an interest in jewelry. She apparently collects the stuff." Chief Dalton shook her head as if she couldn't imagine anyone doing such a thing. "Said she could tell right away the thing wasn't the real deal."

All sorts of new thoughts zoomed through my head. Why would Cathy be carrying a replica of the necklace Gina had brought? Could she have wanted one of her own and had one made that looked just like it? If so, where was the original? And why would that culminate in her death? The only person who cared about the necklace was Gina, and as I said before, I didn't think there was any way she could have killed Cathy. It had to be one big coincidence.

"It's late," Chief Dalton said, punctuating the statement with a yawn. "We all need some rest."

I nodded, though, at this point, I wasn't feeling all that tired. Murder had a way of doing that to me.

"We're not going to hold you, but I don't want you leaving town. As much as it pains me to say it, you are a suspect in the possible homicide of Ms. Carr."

"But I didn't kill her!"

"I know that." And by the way she said it, she sounded genuine. "But still, I can't in good conscience let you off the hook just because of my gut feeling. There's procedure to follow, and I, for one, plan on following it."

This time, my nod was contrite.

"Go home. Get some sleep. And if you think of

anything else that might help, call me or Paul and let us know."

"Okay."

Chief Dalton rose. "Thank you, Krissy. Paul will be waiting for you outside." She left the room.

I remained seated for a good couple of minutes more. Talk about escalating quickly. We'd gone from a manageable wedding disaster to a dead wedding planner, right into a murder and counterfeit jewelry. Why couldn't anything be easy in this town?

With a surprising yawn, I rose and left the interrogation room. Buchannan wasn't around, and I wondered who'd filled Chief Dalton in so quickly. I suppose Paul could have brought her the photographs, or perhaps Buchannan had already been here and left again. It was all happening so fast. I didn't even know what time it was anymore.

And I'm a suspect.

Paul was standing by the doors, brow furrowed in concentration. He perked right up when he saw me and hurried over to take my elbow. I must have looked faint because his grip was firm and secure, and he asked, "You okay?"

"Not really," I said, and let him guide me out the door and to my car.

He didn't say anything more until I was safely seated and buckled in. He watched me a moment, as if trying to determine if I was fit to drive, before speaking.

"If you need someone to talk to, I'm here," he said, leaning his arms on the top of my door so he could look in at me.

"I think I'll be okay," I said. "My dad's staying with me." I looked up, met his eye. "But thanks."

"Anytime." He smiled, and did I notice a hint of sadness in his gaze? Was it because I was smack-dab in the middle of yet another murder investigation? Or was it something else entirely? Just because we'd stopped seeing each other after one semi-disastrous date, that didn't mean we stopped caring for one another.

My stomach did one of those slow flips. "Perhaps we can get together some other time," I said.

The sad smile remained. "Of course."

We remained like that a moment longer, each of us unsure what to say. Here I was, a possible murder suspect, and he, a cop, and we were acting like two love-struck kids, too afraid to let our real feelings be known. Yep, we definitely had a complicated relationship.

"Seems familiar, doesn't it?" I asked, hoping to lighten the mood, yet it came out sounding sad.

"Just as long as it ends the same as the last couple of times," Paul said.

I smiled at that. It seemed like every time something good happened to me, someone ended up dying. Some sort of cosmic justice? Or was it fate's way of keeping Paul and I in the same orbit? These murders *had* put us closer in some ways.

They were also the reason Paul and I had stopped hanging out.

My smile faded and I fished out my keys. "I'd better go."

Paul stepped back. "Drive safely, Krissy."

"I will."

I closed the car door, started the car, and then, with one last hopeful glance Paul's way, I put the car into drive and headed for home.

7

Lights were on in my house when I pulled to a stop. It was late, and I'd expected Dad and Laura to be in bed. Not even my neighbors were up. It was strange not having Eleanor Winthrow looking at me from the chair by her window all of the time. In some ways, I kind of missed her nosiness. It was like having my own personal watchdog. Sure, her prying had often ended with a cop showing up with the wrong impression of what was going on, but at least if something *did* happen, I used to be able to count on her to call someone.

Now, I only ever saw her when she stepped outside for the mail or the morning paper. I hoped she was doing okay all alone.

I removed the key and sat in the car, listening to the ticking sound of the cooling engine. I might have wanted Cathy Carr gone, but not in this way. And the suspect list hit awfully close to home. I mean, I had been found with the murder weapon in hand, while standing over the body. Vicki and Mason had been angry with her for thinking she could come in and change everything about their wedding, which gave them motive.

And then who? No one else in town knew her. She'd come all the way from California with Gina and Frederick and the rest of their friends. Could one of them be the culprit? It had happened where Gina and Frederick were staying, but once again, they were practically family. Despite how they treated me—and Vicki, to be honest—I wouldn't want to see anything happen to them.

"Maybe it was an accident," I said, speaking out loud to calm my nerves. I wasn't sure how she would have managed to fall and hit her head on the candlestick, but it *was* possible. She could very well have swallowed an espresso bean wrong, which in turn, caused her to stagger and fall, hit her head, and then, unconscious, she'd choked to death.

But that doesn't explain the fake necklace. Or the light snapping off.

I got out of my car. I was afraid that no one would ever know what had happened for sure, not unless she truly *had* been murdered and the killer was caught. I was still hoping for an accident.

Dad was sitting at the island counter, a mug of coffee between his hands, when I entered the house. He looked up as I stepped into the kitchen, brow furrowed with concern.

"It's late," he said.

"I know. Sorry about that." I crossed the room and poured myself a cup of coffee so I could join him. I so didn't need the caffeine at this hour, but I doubted I'd be able to sleep anyway. I grabbed a cookie, plopped it in, and watched the bubbles form as it sank to the bottom.

"Do you want to talk about it?"

I shrugged, considered what to say, and came up blank.

"If you're mad at me . . ." He cleared his throat and frowned.

"Why would I be mad at you?" I asked, pushing the coffee away. For the first time in my life, I didn't actually want it.

"For bringing Laura. For not, I don't know, telling you more. I know it has to be weird for you; it's weird for me. Your mother still means the world to me, even though she's gone. That will never change."

I blinked at him. "I'm not upset with you," I said. "Actually, I like Laura. I'm glad you brought her."

"Then why do you look like you have the weight of the world on your shoulders?" He snapped his fingers. "It's the wedding, isn't it? It'll be all right, Buttercup."

"It is. Kinda." I sighed, frustrated. I didn't want to dump Cathy's death on his shoulders, but he'd hear about it soon enough anyway. The rumor mill was likely already working overtime, spreading the news. I was half afraid to hear what they'd come up with, considering how I had been discovered.

I told him all about my night, about going to see Gina and Frederick, but finding Cathy instead. I told him how they'd accused me of the murder, though I made it sound like they had done so because I was holding the murder weapon, not because they're mean people. I told him of my visit to the police station and how, because of how it had all gone down, I'd ended up as a suspect, despite the fact Chief Dalton didn't think I had done it.

Dad listened, elbow on the counter, chin in his hand. He didn't interrupt, didn't try to force me to say anything more than I wanted to. He simply watched me, brow pinched, waiting for me to get it all out.

It felt good to be telling someone who wouldn't immediately judge me for what had happened. By the time I was done, I thought I could drink my coffee without bursting into tears. I reached for my mug and took a large, satisfying gulp.

"It appears I'm bad luck," Dad said, sitting back in his chair.

"What do you mean?"

"I've been to Pine Hills to visit you twice now. Someone has died both times." He grimaced. The last death had been someone he knew.

"Trust me, it's not you," I said. "This is like the sixth murder since I moved to Pine Hills. Maybe I'm the one who's bad luck. Apparently, this sort of thing never happened around here before I got here. Now, I can't go two steps without tripping over a dead body." It might have been an exaggeration, but lately, it sure felt like every time I turned around, someone was dying.

Dad smiled. "Maybe fate brought you here to help."

I grunted and took a drink of my coffee.

There was a long moment of silence. It was then I noticed Misfit wasn't prowling around, looking for his dinner like he normally would be at this hour. Dad smiled as I checked his dish to see the remains of his dinner, telling me someone had already fed him.

"He's in bed with Laura," he said. "They've really taken to one another."

"She can't have him," I said, only half joking.

Dad laughed. "I'll be sure to tell her." He sobered quickly. "Are you going to . . . you know?" He cleared his throat. "I mean, if you're going to look into it, I can help." His eyes seemed to sparkle as he said the last. Dad had always had a thing for mysteries—he *was* a mystery writer, after all—and to be smack-dab in the middle of another one would turn this little trip to town into an adventure.

I swirled my coffee a moment. Cookie chunks were floating in it now. I watched them circle, and thought about it.

The last time Dad had been here, we'd worked together to help put a killer behind bars. He'd kept his head when I'd lost mine. Let's just say, I tended to be a little more high-strung and didn't think about what I was about to do or say until I did or said it. He tended to think things through and roll with the punches. I simply took them.

I rubbed my wrist in memory. I'd sustained bruises, broken bones, and more than enough wounded pride for a lifetime. Was there any reason to get involved again, especially since bringing him along would put both Dad *and* Laura in danger if there was indeed a murderer running around? I mean, I wanted to help Vicki and Mason. But to risk Dad? Never.

"Let me think about it," I said, not wanting to commit to anything quite yet. As far as we knew, it was an accident, and there was nothing to investigate. "I'm pretty sure the wedding is still on, so I'll need to focus on that for now. If the police need something from me, I'll gladly help, but otherwise, it'd probably be best if I spent my time making sure nothing else happens to ruin Vicki's wedding."

Dad nodded, though I noted the slump of his shoulders. "Of course, Buttercup." He rose, leaned forward, and kissed me on the forehead. "I'm going to get some sleep. If you do look into her death, please be careful. I don't want anything to happen to you, especially if I could have prevented it."

I smiled. Dad knew me so well. I might think I've convinced myself I'll avoid the entire mess, but inevitably, I always found myself involved, even when I didn't want to be. "I will."

He gave my shoulder a squeeze, and then headed for the bedroom.

Despite what I'd said, there really was no way I could let this go. Cathy might have been annoying and on the verge of ruining my best friend's wedding, but she hadn't deserved to die. And it had happened in Vicki's house, a place where no one but Vicki, Cathy, and her parents were supposed to be. And if solving the murder would somehow help keep Vicki from postponing—or worse, cancelling— her wedding, I couldn't simply sit back and hope the police figured it out when I knew there had to be *something* I could do.

I mean, how many cases have the local cops solved on their own anyway? Not a lot when you really thought about it.

But first things first. I picked up my phone, considered calling, and then, instead, shot Vicki a text, letting her know I was out of jail and safe, and that if she needed me, to call. I wasn't sure if she was still up, or if she was busy dealing with her parents and the aftermath of Cathy's death. No sense interrupting with a call when a simple text would do.

It took only a few seconds before I got a quick, Thanks. Will do reply. I sent a silent prayer her way, and then, this time, made a call.

A muffled response that went something like, "Mrello," made me realize how late it really was.

"I'm so sorry, Will," I said, regretting making the call, despite the fact I desperately wanted to hear his voice. "I should have waited until morning."

There was a shuffle, and then, more clearly: "Hey, Krissy. I was asleep."

"I noticed." I took a deep breath and then launched into my tale without preamble. Getting it out for Dad had helped. Telling Will about it finally lifted the dark cloud that had been hovering over me from the moment I'd found Cathy Carr's body.

When I was done, Will sounded fully awake when he asked, "Are you okay?" I knew he meant more than just mentally. I rubbed at my wrist, which was now aching in remembered pain. It seemed like something was always hurting these days—a product of all the times I'd run into a killer determined to escape. Most of the time, the pain was in my head, like now, but sometimes—like when I'd hurt my wrist originally—it was all too real.

"I'm fine," I said. "Well, as fine as I can be."

"I can come over if you want." He punctuated that with a yawn.

"No, not tonight," I said, smiling. I'd woken him up, told him a horrible story about people he didn't even know, and he was still willing to come all the way out here to make sure I was okay. How had I gotten so lucky? "But I'd like to see you soon, if that's okay."

There was a long stretch of silence that made my smile slip away and some of the dark cloud return. "I think that would be a good idea," he said, making it sound as if it was just about the worst thing he could think of doing.

I swallowed back a lump that had grown in my throat. "Is everything okay?"

"Yeah, sure. I'm fine." He sounded anything but. "I'll let you know as soon as I'm free. It's been crazy busy lately. I feel like I'm being pulled in a million directions half the time, and dead on my feet the rest."

Tell me about it. "Okay," I said, sounding a little too wounded for my taste. The man *was* busy. I just had to look at his work schedule to know that.

If Will noticed my gloominess, he didn't say anything. "I'll talk to you soon."

"Okay. Good night." *Again.* That first call had felt like a lifetime ago.

"Night."

He disconnected.

I sat there, staring at my phone a long time. Something was up with Will, and I had no idea what it could be, other than thinking he might be done with me. We'd barely seen each other over the last six months or so, though when we did get together, it was always nice.

But I couldn't rid myself of the nagging doubts that he was too good for me and had finally realized it.

I pushed away from the island counter, dumped the remains of my cookie and coffee, and dispelled any and all thoughts of Will and what could be bothering him from my mind. There was something far more important I needed to focus on.

Cathy's death.

And Vicki's wedding.

If I was going to look into it, then I had to find a place to start. There was only one thing that stood out in the whole mess, and that was the fake necklace found on Cathy's body. It was my only lead, and I was going to use it.

But not tonight. I had to go in to work tomorrow

and would need a decent night's sleep to function anyway. I would let nothing stop me from making sure that if someone *had* killed Cathy Carr, they wouldn't go unpunished. And I was going to make doubly sure that when it was all said and done, Vicki's wedding would go on as planned.

8

"Have you registered these as deadly weapons?" I asked, gently tapping one pointy tip of Lena's pink hair.

She grinned. "I should. There's this guy down at the park who keeps catcalling me and has been a nuisance to all the other girls. The guy's a jerk, and a little bit of a pervert. I should run him through."

Her two-inch spikes wouldn't be running anyone through, but I was sure it wouldn't feel too good to be stabbed by them. I didn't even want to know how much gel and hair spray it took to get hair that hard and pointy. It was all I could do in the mornings to make sure my hair wasn't a tangled ball of fuzz.

"Well, if you do, try not to leave any evidence behind."

"Might be hard since I'll be stabbing him with my hair."

Jeff snorted a laugh, and then, looking as if he was appalled he'd made such a sound, he hurried to the back.

Death by Coffee was surprisingly slow this morning, though I couldn't say I was unhappy about it. I'd struggled to get to sleep last night, and waking up had been a chore. Every time I closed my eyes, I saw Cathy's lifeless body, felt the candlestick in my hand. When I had slept, I'd dreamed that the weapon was glued to my hand, and no matter what I did, I couldn't get rid of it. Everyone was pointing at me and was shouting "Guilty!" over and over again.

I shuddered and turned my mind back to more pleasant things.

"Have you given much thought to school?" I asked.

Lena shrugged and refused to meet my eye. "I don't know. I keep wondering if it's worth it."

I didn't like the sound of that. "What do you mean?"

"Well . . ." She glanced around, as if looking for a way out of the conversation, before sighing. "I like working here. I like my life. What point is there going to college when all it'll end up doing is putting me in debt for the rest of my life? I know a few people who went who are now working menial jobs that have nothing to do with their majors. They would have been better off not going at all, if you ask me."

"You wouldn't want to work here forever," I said. While I loved having her around, Lena deserved more. She was smart, had a good attitude. She really was the kind of person who could do anything she set her mind to.

"I know." She shrugged again. "I'm still saving and everything, but the longer it takes, the more I wonder if I'd be better off staying here, saving up, and figuring out what I really want to do with my life later. Nothing says I have to work for someone else. Maybe I could start my own business or something." Her face turned a light shade of red, and she refused to look up. "I don't know, it's something to think about anyway."

"Well, don't wait too long," I said. "Life is shorter than you think." I stopped short of saying she should definitely go to college, no matter how pointless it seemed, mainly since it wasn't my place. If she decided her life needed to go down another track, who was I to judge?

"I won't," she said.

The sound of running water came from the back, as did the clank of dishes, which reminded me of something.

"What do you think of us hiring someone else to help out around here?" I asked. While it wasn't busy now, if we had a rush, Jeff would need to abandon the dishes to work upstairs in the books while Lena and I handled the coffee, leaving no one to deal with the mess in the back. One more person could really ease the burden.

Lena looked surprised. "Is that your way of pushing me out the door?"

"No!" At her mischievous smile, I laughed. "No. But Vicki's getting married and you have your future ahead of you. It would make it easier on everyone if we had one more person who could help out or come in when someone couldn't make it."

"It would be nice for rush to have another body around," Lena said. "When someone is working upstairs, and there's just one or two of us down here, it can get hectic."

I nodded, liking the idea even more. Sometimes, Death by Coffee could be more than two or three people could handle. And then, when something happened, like when Lena broke her arm a few months ago, there was no one else to come in to take their place, leaving us shorthanded.

And then there was my penchant for chasing after murderers. It really did cut into my time around the shop. I also had no idea what Vicki would do once she was married. Would she stop coming in and working, choosing instead to focus on the business end of things? Would Mason pull her in another direction? Take her on constant vacations? Or would life go on like nothing had changed?

"I think we should do it," I said, feeling good about my decision. Now, I just had to get Vicki on board.

The door opened then, and Rita Jablonski walked in. She was dressed in all black, her makeup dark. Her dress went down to the floor, but I knew she was probably wearing black shoes as well. She kind of looked like a past-her-prime goth reject as she made her way to the counter. In all my life, I didn't think I'd ever seen anyone look more miserable.

"Hi, Rita," I said, leaning on the counter. I already knew what the problem was, but I wasn't going to bring it up myself.

Rita heaved an exaggerated sigh, and then, instead of talking in a slow, depressed drawl like I'd expected, she burst into her usual high-speed, overzealous way of speaking.

"Did you hear about what happened?" she asked, hand fluttering to her chest. "A murder! I swear, this place is coming apart at the seams." She tsked. "But we are lucky, aren't we? James Hancock is in town and can help solve the case like he did the last time he was here!" At mention of my dad's name, she closed her eyes and just about hugged herself. "It's just the thing to brighten my day."

I didn't see how a murder could brighten anything, but didn't say so. "He's here for Vicki's wedding," I said. "I don't think he's going to be getting involved this time. And no one has said it was actually a murder." Other than Chief Dalton, and I was still hoping she was wrong.

"Oh, pah." She waved a hand at me. "He just *has* to. I mean, he was on the same flight as that woman, wasn't he? He might have seen something on the plane, a clue." Her eyes widened. "Do you think he already knows who did it? He's probably already put it together! I should find him and ask." She started to turn as if she was going to do just that, but stopped. When she looked at me, her eyes were downcast.

Must have remembered Laura. Poor woman. I didn't much care for how she lusted after my dad, but darn it, I hated seeing her so down.

The only thing I could think of that would make her feel better was to gossip. I mean, she *did* have a good point. If something had happened on the plane, then Dad very well might have seen it.

I considered the possibilities.

If Cathy Carr had been killed by someone who'd come with the Pattersons, perhaps something *had* happened that would point to the killer. It could be something as simple as a spilled drink or a rude word. There might have been an all-out brawl, though I figured Dad would have said something if there had been. He'd flown coach with Cathy, while the others had flown first class, so it was unlikely she'd interacted with anyone during the flight.

Then again, how sure was I that everyone had flown first class? Just because Gina and Frederick had didn't mean everyone else had. I'd have to ask Dad about that when I got the chance.

"What have you heard about what happened?" I asked, knowing that word of the murder and its suspects had already made the rounds in Pine Hills. Rita, being the main culprit when it came to spreading gossip and rumor, would have the scoop.

"Just that *you* are the prime suspect." She sounded oddly smug about that, as if she blamed me for Dad dating someone else and having me accused of murder made up for it. "I don't believe for one second you had anything to do with it, of course, dear. I mean, you'd have to have guts to murder someone! It takes a certain type to pull off something like that."

I wanted to protest, but if she thought I was too much of a coward to kill anyone, then it was probably best not to give her another impression. "It might have been an accident," I said.

"An accident?" She laughed as if that were the most ridiculous thing she'd ever heard. "How do you kill someone by accident, dear?"

I felt myself flush, but pressed on. "It could happen," I said. "She could have fallen awkwardly. She could have been surprised by something and tripped. No one knows what happened that night." My mind went back to the light turning off as I knocked. I had a feeling that someone *did* know; they just weren't talking.

Rita gave me a flat look. "Well, how I hear it, that woman wasn't anyone's friend. Georgina heard that this Cathy lady came in and started demanding everyone do things her way! Upset Judith, if you can believe it." She said it like she couldn't imagine anyone getting on Judith Banyon's bad side. All it had taken for me was to open Death by Coffee. Judith hated me for it, claiming I was trying to steal customers from the Banyon Tree.

"And then she involved herself in the upcoming wedding, as if she had a right to do so," Rita went on. "It's no wonder someone decided to put an end to her meddling."

"Has Andi heard anything?" I asked. Georgina McCully, Andi Caldwell, and Rita were the three biggest gossips in all of Pine Hills. If anyone knew who had motive to kill Cathy Carr, they would.

Upstairs, a customer headed for the counter with a stack of books in hand. Lena, who'd been listening to the conversation while trying to look as if she were simply wiping down the counters, headed up to take care of her without a word.

"Funny you should ask," Rita said, leaning over the counter so far she was practically face-to-face with me. "Andi heard it from her sister that one of the actors in town was up for a big role recently, but lost it to someone else. He wasn't too happy about it, and made sure people knew."

I frowned, unsure how that could lead to Cathy's death. "Did she say which actor?"

"No," Rita admitted. "But I'll ask her. We're due to meet and have a little talk in a few minutes."

The door opened and both Georgina and Andi walked in, as if summoned. Georgina looked the same as always, white fluffy hair, glasses perched at the end of her nose. She looked like someone's grandma. Andi's hair was steely gray, and the fine lines around her eyes had deepened, making her look even older than the last time I'd seen her. They both looked upbeat and anxious, as if they couldn't wait to start gossiping.

They paused just inside, saw Rita, and made for the counter. I was abruptly forgotten as the women began talking about local, non-murder-related things in between orders. I filled Rita's black coffee order first, then grabbed Andi and Georgina's iced lattes. They barely stopped talking even as they paid and headed for an empty table.

I watched them for a few minutes, wondering if they would talk about Cathy Carr and her murder, or if they'd continue to discuss whether someone named Ruby would end up breaking it off with Stan and go after a man they called Tiger.

Since no one else was looking to put in an order, and Jeff had returned to the front, I decided to get some other things done. I made my way to the office and picked up the phone. All this talk about Cathy and the actors made me want to check in with Vicki to make sure she was okay. I dialed, and she answered on the second ring.

"How are you holding up?" I asked her.

"As well as I can be," Vicki replied. "Mom's freaking out, and Dad's trying to use it as an excuse to get me to go back home. I'm ignoring them both."

"As you should." I hated asking what came next, but was hoping she would know. "Have you heard anything about one of the actors in town having lost out on some movie role lately?"

Vicki sounded confused when she answered. "No, why?"

"I don't know. Rita said something about it. You know how she gets."

She laughed, though it sounded strained. "I do. Do you think it could have anything to do with Cathy's death?"

"I hope not," I said. "I'm still hoping it was an accident of some kind."

Vicki was silent for a long moment before, "They're saying that necklace Mom tried to give me was fake."

"I know." I still couldn't believe it. Or figure out how it fit in to all of this. If Cathy had been killed because of it, then the killer would have taken it, right?

"Mom insists someone has stolen the real necklace. She was demanding the police search your place, saying they'd find it there. I told them they'd be wasting their time, but don't be surprised if someone comes knocking before long. Mom can be insistent, and while I don't think anyone believes her, I bet they do what she wants just to get her to shut up."

I groaned. Just what I needed; the police snooping around while Dad's new girlfriend was in town. I was sure I was already making quite the impression on her, and having cops show up on my doorstep would only make things worse. It wasn't like it'd be too hard for them to get a warrant, considering I was a suspect.

"Could Gina be wrong about the necklace?" I asked. "Don't movies often use costume jewelry in place of the real thing?" I didn't mention that most of the movies and shows Vicki's parents had been in were low budget—or that, when they were in something big, they were merely nameless extras no one would recognize if they happened across them in the street.

"Maybe," Vicki said. "But it sure looked real."

It had. And all I'd seen of the fake was the photograph Chief Dalton had shown me. Were the two necklaces one and the same? Or had someone replaced the real one with a fake, be it Cathy or someone else?

And had it somehow led to Cathy's death?

There was no way for me to know for sure, not with me working. And that's not to mention how bad I felt for talking about it with Vicki. She sounded stressed and tired, and I was only making it worse.

"I'd better get back to work," I said. "Take it easy today. You still have a wedding coming and you don't want to have bags under your eyes for it!" I meant it as a joke, but it didn't come out quite right.

Still, Vicki laughed. "I'll try."

"Oh!" I'd almost forgotten. "I was thinking about looking into hiring someone else to work at Death by Coffee to help fill in. We should talk about it sometime soon."

"Actually, I was thinking the same thing," Vicki said, sounding better now that she wasn't talking about Cathy or the murder. "I even bought a sign to hang in the window, just in case you agreed with me."

"Great minds think alike, right?"

"Right." This time, her laugh sounded genuine and relaxed.

"We can hang it up after all of this blows over," I said.

"Why not hang it now?" she asked. "I left it at the store. It's in the filing cabinet, bottom drawer. We can get the applications in now. Then we can decide whether we want to wait until after the wedding to hire, or get someone in earlier so they can get to training right away. I *will* be gone for two weeks on my honeymoon, so adding another hand around the store would be a good thing."

I'd completely forgotten about that. "I'll put the sign up as soon as I hang up here. Hopefully, we'll get some good applicants quickly. I'd like to get someone in as soon as possible." Especially since Vicki's honeymoon was fast approaching.

"Good deal."

"I'll talk to you later, okay?"

"Sure thing."

We hung up and I found the sign in the filing cabinet where Vicki had told me it would be. I took it to the door and placed it right where anyone coming in would see it. Once that was done, I started back for the counter, but stopped to stare out on the street, mind elsewhere.

Cars drifted by, windows down as their occupants enjoyed the nice weather. Quite a lot of people were walking, talking amongst themselves as they went about their daily lives. Parents fed children. Children played with friends.

And somewhere out there: a killer.

9

It was still light out when I left Death by Coffee and headed for home. I loved the work I did there, but boy, during the summer months, it could get hot in the kitchen. I desperately wanted a shower, and I hoped afterward I'd have a nice sit-down with Laura so I could learn more about her.

When I pulled into my driveway, I was disappointed to see Dad's rental was gone and the house empty. A note sat on the counter telling me he took Laura out to eat at J&E's Banyon Tree and I could join if I wanted. He tacked on a smiley face at the end, since he knew my thoughts about the place.

While meeting them was tempting, I wasn't on the best terms with the owners, so instead, I took my shower, got dressed into something that didn't have coffee stains splattered down the front of it, and headed out to do exactly what the police wouldn't want me to do.

Out of all the people the Pattersons had brought with them from California, I knew only where Lyric

Granderson was staying: Ted and Bettfast. It had come to me while at work, so I hadn't lied when I'd told Chief Dalton I didn't know where any of the Californian guests were staying. It had simply slipped my mind at the time, which, honestly, had to be expected considering where I had been and what had happened. And while it might be a good idea to call the police and tell them what I'd remembered, I decided against it. Buchannan would take it as me holding out on them, even if I did tell them. Best skip that unpleasantness altogether. I had confidence they would figure it out on their own.

I wasn't sure what Lyric might be able to tell me about Cathy or who might have wanted to kill her, but I did remember the look she'd given Gina when she'd tried to give Vicki the necklace. I hoped she might be able to tell me more about the piece of jewelry, because you didn't glare at someone over something you knew nothing about.

Ted and Bettfast was an old mansion turned bed-and-breakfast, nestled halfway up one of the hills that gave Pine Hills its name. The building was showing its age, and sadly, repairs had stopped long ago. Still, I liked the place and hoped to one day stay there, just to get away from the craziness that had become my life. Sure, it wasn't like I was leaving town, but something about the serene location, the hedge animals, and surrounding trees, made me feel as if the bed-and-breakfast was on an island all its own where nothing could get to me.

I knew it wasn't true, considering its history, but hey, I'm allowed to dream.

I pulled into the lot, just as a silver car sped around

the corner, nearly taking out my front end. I leaned on the horn, but the driver didn't slow.

"Jerk," I muttered, before I took note of the handful of cars already in the lot. The Bunfords, who own the place, would account for one or two of them. They also usually kept one or two staff on hand to help out since they weren't getting any younger. That meant, of the three remaining cars, one of them must be Lyric's. I was guessing it was the shiny silver Audi.

I parked a few spots down from the Audi, not wanting to accidentally ding the thing with my door, and then headed inside in the hopes of finding Lyric Granderson. As far as I knew, she was out, experiencing what little Pine Hills would have to offer someone like her, which meant my visit could very well be in vain.

A woman I knew, Jo, was standing by the counter, filling out a form of some kind. She'd worked at Ted and Bettfast ever since I'd discovered the place, and while she used to enjoy having me poke around, she seemed to have soured on me since. It was a shame, really. When we'd first met, she'd practically treated me like a celebrity. I kind of missed it.

I cleared my throat, causing her to glance up. As soon as she saw me, she stiffened, and her eyes darted around as if looking for an escape.

"You shouldn't be here," she said, setting the pen down and hurrying to where I stood.

"It's okay," I said. "I'm meeting someone." It might not be the full truth, but I didn't want to get thrown out. Let's just say, the owners, Ted and Bett Bunford, weren't exactly thrilled with me lately on account of that every time I showed up, someone ended up dead.

I didn't kill them, of course, but murder seemed to follow me around like mosquitoes during the summer.

"Bett told us to tell her if you showed up." Jo shot a glance toward a door I took to be the Bunfords' office. "I think she's going to ask you to leave."

Even though I solved all the murder cases involving the guests here, it did make for bad publicity. Who would want to stay somewhere where people kept dying?

And, in a way, I understood why they might not want me to come back. If I was poking around, it meant something bad had happened. Or was about to. If I was Ted or Bett Bunford, I probably wouldn't want to see me either.

"I'll just need a few minutes," I said. And before Jo could protest, I added, "Lyric Granderson. She said she was staying here. A friend of hers died and I was hoping I could talk to her about it, make sure she's okay." Once again, not quite the truth, but it was close enough that I didn't think I'd get into too much trouble if she found out the real reason I was there.

Jo went through a myriad of expressions, ranging from worried, to angry, to sympathetic, and finally to resigned, all in the span of a few seconds.

"You'll have five, maybe ten minutes." Her eyes darted around the room, as if afraid someone might overhear. "If Bett catches you, I'm going to tell her you snuck in."

"That's fine," I said. "I don't want you to get into trouble because of me."

She nodded, worried at her hands a moment, and then pointed toward the back. "She's out by the pool."

And then, before someone could see us together, she hurried away.

I shot Jo a silent thanks and then headed for the glass doors that led out onto the large patio and belowground pool. It looked much the same as when I was last here, including the volleyball net in the pool, the lounge chairs, and the empty bar that was likely only in use when there was a party. The water looked cool and refreshing. Despite my shower, I still felt a bit grungy from work and would have loved to dive in, but couldn't, not if I wanted to talk to Lyric. One of these days, I was going to bring a swimsuit and take a dip, regardless of why I was there. It'd been a long time since I'd been swimming, and I could use the exercise.

Lyric was seated in one of the lounge chairs by the pool, staring out over the water. She glanced up as I approached, face neutral, and then returned her gaze back to the water as if I hadn't even registered on her consciousness.

"Hi, Lyric. It's Krissy. I don't know if you remember me . . ."

"I do."

"Would you mind if I sat down?"

"Suit yourself."

I took a seat next to her and then stared out over the water to gather my thoughts. I didn't know how well Lyric knew Cathy, or even if she liked her, which made it hard to decide how to lead in. I didn't even know how well she knew the Pattersons, though I imagined they had to be friends or else they wouldn't have brought her along for their daughter's wedding.

"It's a shame about Cathy," I said, testing the waters as gently as I could. Hard to get offended about that.

Lyric grunted. "If you say so."

"You didn't like her?"

"Barely knew her, to be honest." She glanced at me out of the corner of her eye before returning her gaze to the water. "From what I gathered, she didn't try to endear herself to anyone. She liked to bully people into doing things her way, even if it meant no one liked her because of it."

That jibed with what I knew of Cathy Carr—abrasive and self-centered. "Do you think anyone had a reason to kill her?"

Lyric shrugged. "Look deep enough, you can find a reason for everyone."

I wondered if she was including herself in that. "So . . ." I stretched out the word while I figured out how to ask the next question. "The necklace—"

Lyric's head whipped around, eyes going hard. "It was supposed to be mine!"

I jerked back as if she'd come at me, but she remained seated. Her hands were clenched, as were her teeth. I had a feeling that if Gina were here with the necklace in hand, she would have tried to snatch it from her.

Lyric took a couple of deep breaths, which seemed to calm her, though her fists remained tightly balled. "My mother wore that necklace in *The Nest of the Viper.* It was supposed to be mine afterward, but that *woman* took it."

"Are you saying Gina *stole* your mother's necklace?"

"Well, no." Lyric turned back to the water to glare at it instead. "She weaseled her way into my mother's good graces and convinced her to give it to her instead of me. I've tried for years to get it back. Mother

died last year, which made me feel its loss even more.
I would like to have it to remember her by."

I hated to think it, but it sounded like something
Gina would do. She only cared about herself most of
the time, and something like a mother's death
wouldn't sway her, not if she would be forced to give
up something of her own. I was glad Vicki had turned
out differently.

"Did you get a good look at the necklace the night
she gave it to Vicki?" I asked.

Lyric shook her head. "I could barely look. I
couldn't believe she would do that in front of me.
That woman . . ." She made a "grrr" sound and then
leaned back in her chair. "I don't know why I bothered coming here at all if that's the way she was going
to treat me."

I wasn't sure how much I could tell her without getting on the bad side of the local police, but felt she
should know. "Lyric," I said, keeping my voice low,
soothing. "Your mother's necklace was found on
Cathy's body."

She looked over at me, eyes wide. "She was trying
to steal it?"

"I don't know," I admitted, watching her closely. If
anyone had a reason to sneak into Vicki's house after
the necklace, it was Lyric Granderson. "But when the
police found it, they were able to determine that it was
a fake."

"A fake?"

"The diamonds and the ruby aren't real."

Lyric sat up straight, shaking her head. "That
can't be."

"Do you think someone might have stolen the real
necklace and replaced it with a replica?"

"I . . . They . . ." She frowned. "It's possible, but who would do such a thing? I'm the only person here who cares about the damn thing." Her eyes widened again. "You don't think *I* could have had something to do with Cathy's murder, do you?"

"I'm sure you didn't." Though, honestly, I wasn't so sure. Lyric had made it abundantly clear she was interested in the necklace. And since it had been found on Cathy's body, or at least, a copy had been, there was a good chance it was the reason she was killed.

"If I would have stolen *my* necklace back and replaced it with a fake, do you really think I'd still be here in this pathetic little town? I'd be on the first flight back home, and away from these . . . people." She said the last as if referring to the lowest of the lowlifes.

"What about the wedding?" I asked.

"I don't care about the wedding. In fact, the only reason I'm here at all is because of some stupid movie."

"A movie's being shot in Pine Hills?" If so, it was the first I was hearing of it.

Lyric gave me a "how stupid are you?" look. "Of course not. Who would shoot a movie here?"

That stung a little. I mean, Pine Hills wasn't California, but it had its own charm. I'd take the rolling hills, the quiet vistas, over the bustle of the bigger cities I'd grown up in.

"Gina and Frederick have small, but significant, roles in a movie," Lyric explained. "They know the director pretty well, which is why they were given the parts." She made a face that told me she didn't think very highly of that. "I auditioned for one of the lead roles, but don't think I'm going to get it. I was hoping to get in close with Gina or Frederick and see if they could put in a good word for me. It's like that in Hollywood, you know? It's not always about who's prettiest or the best actress, but often about who you know."

"So, you came all the way out here to suck up to Gina and Frederick?"

She shrugged. "It sounded like a good idea at the time. I could get them to put in a good word for me, while spending some quality time away from the glamor and lights. Now, I'm thinking I would have been better served staying home and using my charms on the director himself." She shuddered, as if the thought was enough to make her sick.

"Your plan not working?"

"Gina will barely speak to me," she said. "I swear, that woman only cares about herself. Not only is my necklace missing, now it appears as if I wasted my time coming here. There's nothing to do, no one important to see." She rolled her eyes skyward, as if hoping for guidance from above.

And I didn't feel the least bit sorry for her. I don't know if it was the way she dismissed Cathy's death so easily, or how she acted like Vicki and Mason meant nothing to her, but she rubbed me the wrong way. Even if they didn't matter one iota, she could have at least pretended to care.

As casually as I could, I asked, "Where were you last night?" Then added, just so she wouldn't think I was implying anything, "Just curious. I saw a few of the others that night, but didn't see you."

"I was here," she said. If she was upset by my question, she didn't show it. "It was a long journey and I fell asleep by the poolside. The rest of the town might not be anything to look at, but at least it's quiet here."

I wanted to ask if anyone could confirm that, but figured that would be taking it too far. I was sure the police had already asked her that very same question, and if not, they would eventually get around to it. I could go in and ask Jo to confirm, but if she wasn't working, that meant I might have to go to the Bunfords. *That* was something I wasn't going to do.

I ran down my mental list, and decided there was little else I could ask her without raising her suspicions. I'd already pressed enough. "Thank you for your time," I said, rising. "I hope you find your necklace."

She nodded, leaned her head back, and closed her eyes. Apparently, I was dismissed.

Instead of going back through Ted and Bettfast, I decided to go around. No sense risking getting caught by Bett on my way through, though I hoped to make good with her sometime. I hated the fact she blamed me for the past disasters that had befallen her bed-and-breakfast guests.

As I got in my car, I considered what I'd learned. Lyric hadn't done a thing to make herself seem innocent of the murder. In fact, she'd given me more of a reason to suspect her than dismiss her, and I wondered if the police were doing the same. There were still too many unanswered questions for me to be sure one way or the other. And I was worried I was focusing on the wrong thing. Just because Cathy had had the fake necklace on her when she'd died, it didn't mean it had anything to do with her death.

And quite frankly, I still wasn't positive she'd been murdered. If she'd choked on those espresso beans she'd been popping like candy, it could very well have been an accident. A crazy, highly unlikely accident, but an accident all the same.

Yeah, I was probably fooling myself, but darn it, I so wasn't looking forward to yet another murder investigation in my quiet little town.

Either way, there was still more I could learn if I played my cards right. I just had to ask the right questions of the right people, without getting myself injured, or worse, killed.

I might not have all the answers now, but I suspected there were some people who very well might, and I knew exactly where to find them.

10

It was so eerily similar to before, I almost drove away.

Night had fallen, and after the murder, Vicki's house looked sinister in the dark. A light was on upstairs. Another downstairs. It was just like the night of Cathy's death. I was half afraid that if I were to get out and go to the door, everything would unfold exactly the same way, just with someone else lying facedown in the kitchen.

I sat in my car with the engine running, trying to decide if I wanted to take that chance. It didn't appear as if anyone was home, because my car was the only one in the driveway. But with the lights on, it did make me wonder. I watched for a shadow to pass over one of the windows, but nothing so much as twitched inside.

That doesn't mean anything. If someone *had* killed Cathy, and done it by accident while searching for something—let's say, the necklace—then they could very well have come back, looking for it. As far as I knew, only a handful of people knew Cathy had the necklace—or at least a replica—on her when she was killed. The killer might not even have realized there was nothing to find.

But if Cathy's killer was here, then where was his or her car?

I shut off the engine and listened. There were no screams coming from inside, no sounds of struggle, or someone rifling through drawers—not that I could hear that from inside my car. There wasn't even the telltale flicker of a television telling me that someone was indeed home.

"Calm down, Krissy," I said as my heart started hammering. "You're just paranoid." I pushed open my car door, but kept my keys in hand. If someone who wasn't supposed to be there was indeed inside, I wasn't going to go down easily.

Sticking my car keys between my fingers so I could use them as a weapon if the need arose, I started toward the door, listening for the slightest sound. Once there, I knocked with my free hand, albeit quietly.

A loud crack sounded somewhere far behind me, causing me to jump. A dog started to bark, a deep, vicious sound that had me more anxious than ever.

"Nope," I said as I started backing slowly toward my car. I wasn't going to do this, especially not at night. I stepped gently off the front porch, and prepared to make a run for my car, when the front door opened and a weary-looking Gina Patterson peered out at me, glass tumbler in hand.

"It's you," she said matter-of-factly. She didn't seem all that surprised to see me.

It took me a moment to calm my nerves enough to speak. I slipped my keys into my pocket, hoping she hadn't noticed me holding them like a weapon. Gina already didn't like me; I didn't need to give her more reason to think of me as a killer.

"I'm sorry to disturb you so late," I said. My voice only shook a little, which I counted as a win. Inside, I was still trembling like a leaf. "I was hoping we could talk."

"About?" She swirled her drink, causing the ice to clink against her glass. She watched it while I spoke, but didn't take a sip.

"Cathy. The wedding." And then, in the hopes of easing her mind about me: "How are you holding up?"

Gina sighed and looked up toward the half moon. "What did I ever do to deserve this?" This time, she did take a drink—a large one—before, "You'd better come inside, I guess." She turned and walked into the house.

The bang from somewhere past the trees came again, putting a little more haste in my step as I followed Gina inside Vicki's house.

I found her sitting in the living room, sipping from her glass, leaning forward over the coffee table. Old photographs were spread out in front of her. At a glance, I could tell they were all of Vicki, throughout her life, from baby to toddler and on to young adult and adult. Some were headshots. Others candid. She spoke as soon as I entered, as if reflecting.

"I was going to put together a montage for her, you know?" she said, taking another sip from the amber liquid in her glass. "A 'this is your life' sort of thing. It seemed like such a good idea when I'd had it, I'd started working on it immediately."

"You still can," I said. "Vicki is still getting married to Mason."

Gina nodded slowly, took another sip. By the looks

of her, I was guessing she was on her third or fourth glass. "I suppose. But it won't be the same. Cathy was going to build a portion of the ceremony around the montage. I have the frame already. It's in the bedroom, tucked away in the closet where it'll probably remain. All I'd needed to do was settle on the right photographs to put in it. But now . . ." She shrugged. "It doesn't feel important."

I sat down across from her, worried. This didn't sound like the Gina I knew. "Where's Frederick?" I asked.

"He left some time ago. I think he might be talking to the police. He didn't really say before he left." She glanced at me and frowned, before she returned her gaze to the photographs. "I suppose I should apologize for my accusations the other day. I was truly upset by Cathy's death and looked for the most obvious answer as to who could have done it. It was wrong of me."

I wasn't quite sure how I was the obvious answer, but didn't press. "Thank you," I said. It might not be the most genuine apology I'd ever received, but coming from Gina, it was the best I was going to get.

"This is going to put a stain on my reputation," she said. "Everything I've worked for might be gone for good."

There's the Gina I know. "You didn't have anything to do with Cathy's death," I reminded her, not that I thought she'd forgotten. I figured it was what she *wanted* me to say, and since I was hoping to learn something from her, it was best to give her what she wanted.

Gina flashed me a smile before downing the rest of her drink. "I know that, but other people won't be so understanding. I brought Cathy here in an ill-advised attempt to give something special to my daughter. So, in a way, her death is my fault. Without me, she wouldn't have been here. If I only would have . . ." She trailed off and glowered at her empty glass as if it were somehow responsible for her misery.

I fidgeted, unsure what to do or say. I wanted to ask Gina about Cathy, about the necklace, but wasn't sure how to go about it without sending her into another downward spiral of self-pity. Gina didn't like me; never had. If I said the wrong thing, she would have no qualms about kicking me out of the house, and then would do her best to remove me from Vicki's life for good.

But sitting there, watching her lament over old photographs and drink herself into a stupor would accomplish nothing. If the police were right, there was a killer on the loose. The answer could be right here, locked in Gina's brain.

"Do you know why anyone would want to hurt Cathy?" I asked as gently as I could. "I know the police have asked you the same thing, but maybe now, after some time has passed, you've thought of something?" The lilt of my voice made it a question.

She gave me a long, hard stare, before, "You're right; the police *have* already asked me these questions, as they should." She paused, and then looked away. "*You* aren't the police."

"I know," I said. "But this affects Vicki's wedding. I know members of the police department pretty well." In some ways, more than I'd like. "If there's something new you've thought of, I could pass it along to them. It'll keep you out of the news, and put the focus on me."

"You'd like that, wouldn't you?" I wasn't sure what

she meant by that, and she didn't give me time to consider it before she went on. "I don't know what I can tell you," she said. "Cathy was a great person, a real go-getter. She was the best wedding planner in the country, if not the world. She commanded a high price, and the quality was beyond compare. There are people who are bound to be jealous of that."

Perhaps, but not in Pine Hills. "Did she have any enemies?" I asked. "Did she fight with anyone recently, something that might push someone over the edge?"

Gina started to shake her head, but stopped mid-shake, brow furrowing.

"What is it?" I asked, sitting forward. She had the classic "Something just came to me" look on her face I'd seen hundreds of times before.

"It's probably nothing." She didn't sound convinced.

"Or it might be the reason why she was killed," I pressed.

"Well . . ." Gina rose, walked into the kitchen to pour herself another drink. She took a long sip before returning to her seat. "Just before the flight here, there was something of an altercation in the airport. It was nothing, really, I assure you—just a minor spat."

"What kind of altercation?" I asked. I still wasn't totally sold on Cathy's death being a murder—which was probably more wishful thinking than anything— but if someone *had* killed her, I needed to know who might have had a problem with her. Even a minor spat could turn into motive if things got out of hand.

"Yelling, mostly," Gina said. "It was old news, rehashing things better left forgotten. I mean, why fight over something that happened years ago when there was so much more to look forward to now?"

It was a long way from yelling about past grievances to murder, but it wasn't a stretch to think it could happen. I mean, some people held grudges for years, if not lifetimes. "Who did she fight with?" I asked.

"Are you sure it's relevant?" Gina looked as if she wanted to do anything but tell on one of her friends. "I'm positive they couldn't have had anything to do with Cathy's death." She rubbed at her wrist and refused to meet my eye. She looked worried, like she thought there was a chance someone she knew had killed her favorite wedding planner.

"It might not be," I said. "But it's better to know everything, even the little things, than leave something out that could be important. We can let the police decide its relevance." Not that I would simply drop it, mind you, but she didn't need to know that.

"If you say so." She took a long drink from her glass, as if to gather her thoughts. "Sage and Trey Herron used Cathy for their wedding some odd years ago. I don't know the details, but something went wrong with the whole thing. They still blame her for it, though I'm sure they're just blowing it out of proportion. Sage tends to think the worst of everyone, and will make things up just to get them into trouble." She leaned forward. "I imagine she just wanted to get out of paying for Cathy's services."

"So, you don't know what happened?"

She shook her head. "We haven't been friends that long. They were married before we met, so I wasn't there to see it firsthand. All I know is that it was early in Cathy's career, before she became who she is today. You'd have to ask them about what transpired, but as I said, I'm sure it was nothing."

And I would do just that. "Do you know why Cathy would have your necklace on her when she . . . you know?"

Gina paled slightly, took a large gulp of whatever it was she was drinking. "I have no clue," she said. "I can't imagine why she would have it, and to learn it was a fake?" She shook her head. "No, I can't believe it was *my* necklace. Mine was the real deal. Someone must have stolen the real thing and made a replica of it for some nefarious reason."

"Do you think Cathy might have found the replica, realized it was fake, and taken it to show you?" I wasn't sure how that would have led to her death exactly, not unless she'd found it while the thief was still in the house. She could have made a mistake and confronted him or her about it, not realizing the culprit was capable of murder.

"I suppose she might have," Gina said. "But that would mean she had gone into my room. Cathy would never do such a thing. She was a respectful person who would never stoop to snooping, even if she thought something was out of place. She would have come to me first."

"Was the door locked?"

"Why bother?" Gina asked with a dismissive shrug. "No one would invade our privacy like that." And then, almost under her breath: "It's Vicki's room anyway." As if that mattered.

"Did you ever have the original necklace appraised?" If someone *had* come after the necklace and killed Cathy for it, knowing the value of the item might help prove motive.

"Of course not." Gina sounded oddly offended. "I wouldn't want someone to get their grubby hands on it. Do you know that I heard it from a friend that these appraisers will often steal the real item and replace it with one of lesser value? I wouldn't risk such an important piece that way."

There was some pretty unscrupulous people out there, but I doubted there were appraisers running rampant, stealing all the nicest pieces of jewelry to sell on the side. If that was the case, no one would ever use them.

I was out of questions for Gina, but I wasn't done. If someone really was in the house that night, they might not have been there for the necklace or Cathy. This *was* Vicki's house, and if someone had been scoping it out, they would have known she'd barely spent any time here lately. This could all be one of those "wrong place at the wrong time" sort of things. If that was the case, then perhaps there was a clue tucked away somewhere.

"Do you think I could take a look around?" I asked. "I'd like to see where the necklace was kept. I've been here before, and could probably tell you if something is missing."

I figured Gina would balk at the idea, but instead, she waved a hand toward the stairs. "You know the way, I suppose." She took another long drink and slumped on the couch, eyes going distant.

I thanked her, though I'm not so sure she heard me, and hurried to the stairs before she could change her mind. Gina must've been really into her drink because normally, she would have thrown me out at the merest suggestion I poke around where she was staying. It might be Vicki's house, but right then, it was Gina's territory.

I made straight for Vicki's room, figuring it would

be the best place to start since that was apparently where they'd kept the necklace. Sure enough, sitting on the vanity was the empty black box. It was closed, but as soon as I touched it to open it, I could tell nothing was inside. Whether a thief had stolen it, or Gina had misplaced it, the necklace was indeed gone.

I glanced around the room, but nothing else appeared out of place. The bed was a large four-poster. Next to it sat a cat bed I knew Trouble rarely used. He didn't like the feel of the fabric on his fur and would fight against it if you tried to put him in it. Most of Vicki's private items were missing, but that was to be expected since her parents were staying in the room and she'd been spending most of her evenings with Mason. Resting against the wall near the closet were a stack of suitcases that had clearly come from California, thanks to the tags on them.

This isn't going to be as easy as I thought. With Vicki moving out, it was hard to tell what might have been moved.

I wasn't about to go through drawers or anything, so I returned to the vanity and the black box. I was surprised it hadn't been taken in for evidence. The police might have already checked it for prints, but if not, they'd likely be obscured by now. Between Gina and Frederick, and now me, it was unlikely it would be of much use in their investigation.

A pair of expensive-looking earrings lay next to the box. A jewelry box I didn't recognize sat pressed against the mirror. I opened it up to find the kind of jewelry Gina wore inside, all loops and dangles and shiny baubles.

Had this been here when Cathy was killed? If so, it made it seem pretty unlikely a thief was the culprit.

Even without the necklace, they could have earned a pretty tidy sum from the gold and diamonds inside Gina's jewelry box. I couldn't imagine someone breaking in, replacing the real necklace with a fake, and ignoring such a trove of treasures.

Then again, if the thief knew about Gina's necklace and had taken the time to have a forgery made, then it was likely they'd planned on making it appear as if nothing was taken at all. Stealing the rest of her jewelry would be counterproductive if they were trying to mask the real theft.

It did make me wonder, could Lyric truly be the culprit? She was the only one, outside of Gina, who seemed to care about the necklace.

Or was I following the wrong clue, one planted by the killer to throw off the cops, perhaps?

I closed the box and left the bedroom, not quite sure I knew what to think. I made a cursory check through the other rooms, but if something was missing, I had no idea what it could be. I hadn't realized how much of Vicki's stuff had already been moved out.

The front door opened as I came back downstairs, and Frederick entered. He paused when he saw me, looking startled, and then he turned to his wife, who was tottering to her feet.

"What are you doing here?" Frederick asked, eyes going to the stairs behind me. His mouth pulled into a tight frown.

"Gina said it was okay to take a quick look around," I said, glancing at her. She was nodding, but I don't think it was because she was confirming my statement. "I heard you and Gina recently landed roles in a movie?" I asked, remembering what Lyric had said.

Frederick's face cleared up as he smiled. "We did. The parts are small, but it very well might be the one to propel us forward, into the limelight."

"Lyric said she was hoping to land one of the lead roles. Do you think you'll be able to help her out with that?"

"She should learn to do things for herself once in a while," Gina said.

"Now, dear . . ."

"No, she's always wanting someone else to do everything for her. Just because she's built like a supermodel doesn't mean everyone should treat her any better than the rest of us."

They stared at each other, Frederick looking like he wanted her to stop talking, Gina looking ready for a fight. I decided not to press any further, lest I become the focus of her wrath.

"I'll get out of your hair," I said before anyone could say anything more. "Thank you for talking with me," I told Gina. "Frederick." I nodded to him.

He stepped aside when I made for the door. As it closed behind me, I heard him say, "You really shouldn't be talking about our friends that way." If he said anything more, or if Gina responded, it was lost behind the wood.

With my head practically spinning from the little I'd learned from Gina, and the implications of what I'd learned about Lyric, I got into my car and pointed myself for home.

11

I woke up to the smell of pancakes.

Living on my own, I'd forgotten how nice it was to have someone around to cook for me every morning. Dad didn't believe in cereal or bagels for breakfast, but preferred to go all out, every day. Back when he was writing full time, he'd sometimes forget about lunch or dinner, but breakfast was the one meal he never missed.

I stepped out into the hall, waved to Laura, who was sitting on the couch petting Misfit, and then headed to my room to grab a change of clothes. Next came my shower. Even with Dad making a heavenly breakfast, I couldn't cancel my plans so I could sit and eat with him.

Once I was ready for the day, I joined Dad in the kitchen. He was just finishing up some freshly squeezed orange juice. He must have picked oranges up from the store at some point, because I didn't have any on hand.

"Hey, Buttercup." He gave me a once-over. "Do you have time for breakfast before you go?"

"I wish I did, but I have to run." Still, I swiped a

pancake. It was dotted with chocolate chips, which was all the sweetening I needed. "I'm meeting Vicki and Mason for a wedding powwow and breakfast. We're so close to the actual date or else I'd ask them to reschedule."

"I understand." He washed his hands and kissed me on the forehead. "Will you be around this evening? Laura and I were hoping to go out to eat and would love for you to join us."

"I wouldn't want to intrude."

"You wouldn't be intruding," Laura said, coming into the kitchen. Misfit trailed behind her, until she stopped. Then he proceeded to weave in and out of her legs, demanding attention. "Actually, I'd like for you to be there. We haven't had much of a chance to talk."

It *was* a good idea. They might be staying at my place, but I'd barely been home. And if Dad and Laura were planning on staying together for more than just a few months, it would be a good idea to get to know the woman he was spending his time with. Who knew, maybe one day I'd be calling her "Mom."

Okay, it's unlikely I'd ever do that, but the idea was good.

"When we were out yesterday, I overheard some people discussing a new place in town," Dad said. "The way they were talking, it's supposed to be really good. I thought we might give it a try."

"Okay." How could I resist? "I'll come."

"Great!" Dad kissed my cheek, and then, surprisingly, Laura stepped forward and gave me a brief hug. Behind her, Misfit glared at me like I was intentionally hogging all the attention. As soon as Laura stepped back, he reached up and batted at her hand, claws nowhere in sight. She scooped him up and hugged him close, causing him to purr loud enough that everyone could hear it.

"I really should get going," I said, scratching my cat behind the ears. He accepted it, but instead of leaning into my hand like usual, he pressed himself closer to Laura, like he was afraid I might try to take him away. I took a large bite out of the pancake, considered leaving it behind, but decided to take it with me for a snack instead. "I should be home this afternoon."

"Perfect."

I eyed the orange juice with longing, but didn't have a cup with a lid. If I tried to take it with me, I'd inevitably dump it into my lap. I gave Misfit one last ear rub, grabbed my keys and purse, and then headed out the door.

Vicki and I had agreed on meeting at Death by Coffee, both because it was convenient and because it allowed us to keep an eye on the place since Jeff and Lena would be working alone during the morning rush. They'd managed it before, but it was a lot for two people to handle on their own. It only reinforced my idea that we needed to hire someone else.

Mason and Vicki were already there, seated so they could watch the counter. Mason's best man, Charlie Yow, was heading for the door as I entered. He was tall and good-looking, and was going to be on my arm for the wedding. Despite my dating Will, I felt kind of special such a good-looking man would be walking with me down the aisle. Heck, it felt like I was surrounded by good-looking men lately.

"Am I late?" I asked, checking the clock to be sure.

"No," he said. "Something came up at home. Mason said I could take off and he'd fill me in later."

"Oh. Well, good luck."

Charlie touched an imaginary hat brim, and then hurried out the door. I hadn't gotten much of a chance to get to know him as of yet, but he seemed nice enough. I wondered if his wife minded me walking with him at the wedding. Since Vicki didn't want a full bridal party, just the maid of honor and best man, she'd asked if we'd walk with one another down the aisle. We'd both readily agreed, but now, I was wondering how Will would feel seeing me walk with another man.

Death by Coffee was busy, but not so much Jeff and Lena couldn't handle the crowd. I waved to them, and then joined the line to put in my breakfast order. We'd started selling pastries a month ago, so I ordered a cheese Danish to go along with my coffee and cookie. Lena took my order, and Jeff filled it. They worked well together, barely needing to communicate much more than to pass on any special requests.

I carried my food to the table and sat down across from Vicki. "Looks like they have it under control," I said.

"I'm not surprised," Vicki said. "It's why we hired them." It was supposed to come out light and jovial, I think, but she sounded depressed.

It wasn't hard to figure out why.

"How are you two doing?" I asked, taking a bite of my Danish. It wasn't Dad's pancakes, but it was still really good.

"As best as we can," Mason said. "It's been a rough couple of days."

"I'm not sure it's such a good idea to go through with this," Vicki said.

"With what?" I set my Danish aside and swallowed.

"You can't be thinking of canceling the wedding, are you?"

"It might be best," Mason said. He looked as if saying it pained him. He reached out and took Vicki's hand and squeezed. She gave him a thankful smile, before the melancholy was back.

"Someone died," she said. "And it was so close to the wedding. It feels rude to go on like nothing happened."

My heart did a little pitter-patter. They couldn't really be thinking of canceling, could they? I scrambled to come up with something to say to ease their minds, but what? Cathy *had* died. And she'd done so in Vicki's own house, mere days away from the wedding. You couldn't simply scrub that away and pretend it never happened.

"We wouldn't simply cancel it," Mason said after a moment. "We'd reschedule. Maybe give it a few months for everything to get back to normal. We could make adjustments for the extra people your parents want to bring if we did that."

I looked to Vicki. "But this is when you've always wanted to get married." She'd always loved the summer, and used to talk about how overrated fall and spring weddings were. Sure, the leaves during the fall were beautiful, but the weather was often touchier. The summer sun was hot, but that meant she could take her honeymoon and go to a beach like she'd always wanted.

"I know." She closed her eyes and looked as if she might cry. "But how can we do it now, after all this?"

"What happened is terrible," I said. "But you shouldn't let it affect your wedding." It felt callous of me, but I needed to be realistic. "You'll lose all your deposits and since everything has already been ordered, you'd be out the money for the cake, the flowers, and everything else."

"And that's not to mention our friends and family who've flown in," Mason said, frowning as if he'd just considered it. "They might not want to make the trip again."

"Give it a few days," I said. "You'll feel better once the police have it all figured out." Hopefully, by putting the killer behind bars. *If there truly was a killer.* Oh, how I wanted to believe it all was one big accident and that nothing would need to be changed. Because if someone the Pattersons knew *was* responsible for Cathy's death, it could very well make Vicki's mind up for her.

"We really don't want to postpone the wedding, but felt as if it might be best," Vicki said, looking at Mason. "It wasn't our idea, not really."

"Dad." Mason's frown deepened. Raymond Lawyer did that to a lot of people. "He and Regina sat us down and gave us this long lecture about responsibility, saying it would be best to hold off until everything blows over."

"I think he hopes we'll change our minds and break up."

"He wouldn't want that," I said, though I wasn't so sure. Raymond Lawyer was downright mean, as was Regina Harper. The two of them together was a nightmare pairing that had somehow survived far longer than it had any right to.

"I'm not so sure it's Dad," Mason said. "He likes Vicki in his own way." He met Vicki's eye. "He might not say it outright, but since he hasn't actually told you he disapproves of you, it means he kind of likes you."

Vicki smiled and patted Mason's hand. "I know. I kind of like him too. Sometimes."

"But Regina's another story," I guessed.

Mason nodded. "She thinks Vicki is a bad influence on me."

I very nearly laughed. "How could she even *think* that?"

"You," Vicki said, turning to me.

"Me?" Why was everything always my fault? "What do I have to do with it?"

"Nothing as far as we can tell," Mason said. "But Regina is good at holding grudges, and you've made such a bad impression on her, she's holding it against everyone you know."

"That's . . . That's . . ." Unfair? Unwarranted? I couldn't even sputter the words.

"We don't hold it against you," Mason said. "We like your quirks."

"Gee, thanks."

Vicki laughed. It was good to hear there was still some good humor there. I hated seeing her so down. "We usually don't pay them any mind, but with Cathy's death, I think we both let them get to us."

"We did," Mason said. "It's really such a shame."

And right back to the murder we went. It seemed that no matter what I did, it reared its ugly head.

But since we were already on the subject . . .

"What can you tell me about the people that came with your parents?" I asked. "I only met them briefly. Do you think one of them could have had a reason to kill Cathy?" Or steal the necklace, for that matter.

"I don't know any of them all that well," Vicki said. "I never was one to get involved with their friends, because, well, you know."

I did. Whenever the Pattersons had a big get-together, Vicki and I would often find somewhere else to be. When we did try to be sociable, it always ended badly, often with creepy older men hitting on us.

"Anything you know might help," I said, drawing a knowing look from Mason. He knew I was going to involve myself in the investigation, and by the slight nod I received, I could tell he approved.

Vicki sighed. "Well, you know my mom and dad, so no need to go over them. Though, sometimes, I wonder if *I* even know them all that well."

"What about Jacques Kenway?"

Vicki shrugged. "I think he's a cousin. As you know, my family isn't all that close."

Other than her mom and dad, Vicki never saw anyone else from her family. Part of it was because Gina and Frederick were so standoffish, none of their relatives bothered to keep in touch. I'd met Gina's sister once, and from that single conversation, I realized how little Vicki's parents were liked. They were probably the most famous of the Patterson clan, but when you treat your siblings like underlings, it's hard to stay close.

It was kind of sad, really. There's usually a point in most people's lives where all they'll have left is family. Because of the way they've treated everyone, Gina and Frederick might one day find themselves alone.

"Do you know anything at all about him?" I asked, returning my thoughts to Jacques.

"Nothing," Vicki said. "I'm pretty sure Jacques isn't his real name, but other than that, he's a stranger."

"What about Vince Conner?"

"Up until the day he showed up, I'd never heard of him before," Vicki said. "So, there's nothing I can tell you."

Disappointing, but I wasn't surprised. Besides, it was the other guests I was most interested in since they had reasons to go after either Cathy or the necklace.

"Lyric Granderson?"

A tight smile flashed across Vicki's face before she answered. "Lyric doesn't like our family all that much. I was surprised to see her here, to be honest."

"Because of the necklace."

Vicki shrugged. "I don't know. We met on set a long time ago, and I guess you could say we became friends. Our moms were both in the same movie together."

The Nest of the Viper," I provided.

"That's the one." Vicki sighed. "We got along well enough back then. She was a couple of years older than me, and she'd often get me to do things for her, like steal her mother's hairbrush, or hide a prop. Childish mischief." A look of fond remembrance passed over her face, and then was gone. "And then something happened and she stopped talking to me. I never did learn what it was."

"The necklace," I said. "The one your mom tried to give you. Apparently, Lyric's mom wore it in the movie and she thinks it should belong to her."

"And she blamed you for that?" Mason asked.

"I suppose." Vicki shrugged. "I don't know. We were young. I just figured she'd moved on and found new kids to play with. And since our parents were never in the same movie together again, it wasn't all that strange that we lost touch. I wish I could tell you more, but we were just kids doing kid things back then. We never saw each other outside the set. I didn't even recognize her at first. It wasn't until I was on my way home the night she'd arrived that the name registered. I suppose that tells you all you need to know about how close we were."

Which wasn't well at all. It was also probably why I'd never met her. If Lyric had hung around Vicki outside the movie set, I likely would have been involved in some of their mischief. It made me wonder if we would have been friends, or if she would have looked down upon me, much like she did today.

"Okay, what about the Herrons?" I asked.

Vicki looked pained when she answered, "I don't really know them either. I've seen them around before, but never actually talked to them. Sorry."

"I heard Cathy Carr planned their wedding," I said.

"If she did, it would be news to me. Like I said, I barely knew them. I'd seen them around parties and whatnot, but never interacted with them at all."

"Gina told me about it," I said. "She claims something went wrong with the wedding and they blamed Cathy for it."

"Do you think they came all this way for revenge?" Mason asked.

"I don't know. It *does* seem excessive," I admitted. "But if they killed her here, maybe they thought it would be easier to get away with it because of how small Pine Hills is and because no one here knows them well enough to accuse them of anything."

It didn't explain why Cathy had had the necklace in her possession when she'd died, or why it was a fake. It very well might have been a coincidence.

A new thought slowly trickled through my brain. What if Cathy *was* stealing from the people she was planning weddings for? Could that be what had gone wrong with the Herrons? Had they caught her in the act back then? It would explain why they were so angry with her, because if all the fuss was over a cake or the wrong flower arrangement, you'd think they would have gotten over it by now.

Maybe the Herrons hadn't come all the way to Pine Hills to kill Cathy, but instead, happened upon her while she was attempting to steal from the Pattersons. One thing leads to another, and the next thing you know, you have one dead wedding planner, and a necklace no one could explain.

In a way, it made sense. Cathy steals from the Herrons, gets caught, and learns from her mistakes, but not in the way you'd think. Instead of stopping, she decides to make replicas of the jewelry she plans to steal, replaces the real thing with the fake, and no one is the wiser.

Of course, all of this was pure speculation without a hint of proof one way or the other. I tucked it into the back of my mind to consider later.

Conversation moved on from there to the actual wedding, though my mind kept drifting back to my top suspects. While I might have talked Vicki and Mason out of postponing their wedding for now, it was obvious they were still considering it. Vicki kept second-guessing everything about the ceremony and reception, and Mason spent an inordinate amount of time frowning. It was sad to see, considering these were the two cheeriest people I knew—well, maybe outside of Jules Phan and Lance Darby, that was. My neighbors were about as happy as you could get.

And then, as if she could hear my thoughts . . .

"Do you think you could stop by Phantastic Candies

for us?" Vicki asked. "We have to meet with my parents after this, but I want to make sure our order is okay."

"Of course," I said. Jules was handling sweets for the wedding. Every table would have specially made chocolates that would very likely be to die for, knowing Jules.

"Thank you so much. With everything that's happened recently, I'm just so paranoid that something else is going to go wrong." Vicki stood, gave me a hug.

"I'm happy to check," I said. And if it led to me getting to taste the chocolates, all the better.

Mason rose and shook my hand. "You're a good friend," he said without a hint of irony in his voice.

"I try."

And then with nothing further to discuss, we parted ways. Mason and Vicki headed for their conversation with Vicki's parents, while I got to visit a candy store.

I think we all know who got the better end of that deal.

12

My weakness for sweets is practically legendary. So, it was no wonder that, when I pulled up in front of Phantastic Candies, my mouth immediately started watering and a hankering for salted caramel nearly overpowered me. I parked, and all but floated through the door and inside to the sound of a giant piece of candy being unwrapped.

Jules looked up as I entered, a large smile spreading across his face. "Krissy!" he said, coming around the counter and giving me a big hug. "What brings you in today?"

"What else?" I stepped back and breathed in the scent of sugar and chocolate. "Candy."

He laughed. "Of course."

Jules Phan wasn't just the owner of Phantastic Candies, but he was also my next-door neighbor. He had an upward slant to his eyes, and caramel-colored skin that made me want to sink my teeth in the sweet stuff even more. Today, he was wearing a bright yellow suit and tie, and a hat with a long ostrich feather in it. When he walked, his shoes clicked, telling me he was wearing his tap shoes. He didn't always dress like this, but when working, he made sure to stand out for the kids who frequented his shop.

Always extravagant, always fun, Jules had become one of my best friends in Pine Hills.

I drifted over to the caramels and bought a bag for myself, and then one for Dad and Laura to share. I carried them to the counter, fighting the urge to rip into my bag as I did. Jules rang me up, whistling a jovial tune under his breath.

"How's the candy for the wedding coming?" I asked, looking around the brightly colored store. Chutes of candy lined the walls where there weren't bins and shelves of candy. Bright colors seemed to leap out at me from every corner. My teeth ached just looking at all the sugar. I was lucky I hadn't grown up where there was a place like this in town or else I would have been toothless by the time I was ten. Phantastic Candies was any child's dream.

"Very well, I think." Jules took my money, made change, and handed over the candy. "I can take you to the back and show you, if you'd like."

I'd always been curious about the back room of Phantastic Candies, especially since I knew Jules made some specialty candy on site. Usually, there was a spot up front for the chocolates made in house, but since he was working on the candy for Vicki's wedding, it was looking unusually spare.

"Sure," I said, daydreaming of something that would look akin to Willy Wonka's factory. "I'd love that."

Jules led me through a bright green door, into the mysterious back room. An air-conditioning unit that was running overtime kept the room extremely cold. It almost felt like I'd stepped into a refrigerator, and I suppose it was necessary since Vicki's candies were laid out on sheets that sat atop a long metal table.

There were no crazy vats or anything, which was expected, but the small child in me was somewhat disappointed. Something so magically delicious should be made with much more flair.

"I didn't want them to melt," he explained, seeing me shiver from the cold. "It's been so hot lately, I was afraid the lettering wouldn't hold up. The electric bill is going to be outrageous, but I think it'll be worth it."

I leaned over the table. The chocolates were slightly smaller than the palm of my hand. Each had a stylized "V" and "M" in the middle. They kind of looked like large M&Ms.

"I used a homemade crème filling," Jules went on as he opened an actual refrigerator, adding to the chill. He removed a bowl and held it out to me. "Try it."

He needn't ask me twice. I snatched a spoon from a nearby counter and dipped it into the crème filling.

"She asked for raspberry, so I hope you like it."

I didn't answer. Instead, I stuck the spoon in my mouth and was overwhelmed with a burst of the mouthwatering flavor of raspberries. I very nearly sank to the floor in bliss.

"Do you like it?" Jules asked, a knowing smile on his face.

All I could do was nod, before I handed over the spoon. If I held on to it much longer, I'd probably end up eating the entire bowl of filling. I'd regret it later, but it would be so worth it.

"I still have a few more to make to be sure I have enough," he said, returning the bowl to the fridge. "Inevitably, a few will melt or break, so I always make a few extra."

"You might want to add to your totals," I said. Looking at the candies laid out on the table, I was pretty sure there would be enough, even with the Pattersons' friends. But it was always best to be safe, and if I could possibly sneak a few of the candies away for myself, all the better.

"Oh?" Jules asked. He sounded nervous, like he expected me to tell him he'd done something wrong and would have to start anew.

"We have some . . . unexpected guests," I said, putting it as nicely as I could. "About two or three too many."

"I heard!" Jules leaned against the wall, his worry turning to concern. "One of them died, didn't they?"

"She did."

"Terrible. Absolutely terrible." He shook his head sadly. "I don't understand why all these horrible things have been happening lately. It's as if the entire world has gone insane and upended itself for no good reason."

"Tell me about it," I muttered. Not only were bad things happening in Pine Hills all the time now, they seemed to consistently happen around me.

"I think I met the woman once," he said.

"Really? Did she come here?" It wouldn't surprise me. In my book, Phantastic Candies should be on everyone's list of places to visit before they die.

"No." Jules shuddered, and I don't think it was from the cold. "Let's go back out front. It's chilly in here and the topic of conversation only makes it worse."

I fully agreed.

We returned to the front of the store, just as a pair of teenagers who were entangled with one another in what was quite clearly young love, stepped up to the counter. Jules excused himself long enough to ring them up before joining me again.

"I guess I shouldn't say I met her, but I did see her. Lance and I were trying out the new restaurant in town, Geraldo's, just the other day." He paused, as if remembering. "Have you been there yet?"

"Not yet," I said. "I'll be going tonight, though."

"It's fantastic." Jules's eyes went distant briefly. "The food is great, and the atmosphere is just right. Though, I'll admit, the owner doesn't much look like the Geraldo from TV."

And that was a good thing in my book.

"Anyway, we were there, eating, when an argument broke out a few tables away. I didn't know who the two people were at first, but Lance recognized the man as an actor in a cheesy movie he liked."

"What was the actor's name?" I asked.

Jules tapped his chin and frowned. "I can't recall. I don't even remember the name of the movie. Lance was the fan, and honestly, we were both too busy looking at his physique to pay attention to much else. He might not be the world's best actor, but he sure does look the part." He laughed at my shocked expression. "What? It's okay to look, just as long as you don't touch."

I supposed that was true. I mean, even though I have a boyfriend of my own, I've been known to let my eye wander, as I'm sure Will has. It's human nature.

"Can you describe him?" I asked, though I thought I already knew who he was referring to. Only one of the actors who'd come with the Pattersons had the sort of physique he was describing.

"Good-looking. Penetrating eyes. When he smiles,

he dazzles." Jules sighed. "Lance took me home that night and showed me a clip from the movie. He spends a good portion of it shirtless. The actor—not Lance." He chuckled.

"Jacques Kenway?" I asked as a mental image of the man popped into my mind—shirtless, much to my chagrin.

Jules snapped his fingers. "That's it. I think the movie Lance knew him from was *The Pirate Heist*. It was rather silly, when you think about it, but we weren't watching it for the acting or the plot, which didn't make much sense, to be honest."

I bet. "And he was with Cathy Carr? At the restaurant, not in the movie."

"I do believe so." Jules thought about it some more, and then nodded. "It was definitely her. I saw her picture on the news, and I'd swear it was the same woman."

"Do you know what they were arguing about?" If Jacques had been arguing with Cathy before her death, it could very well be the reason she'd ended up dead.

"Sorry, I don't. It was pretty busy, and even when they were yelling, they kept their voices low enough I couldn't make anything out. The man, Jacques, slapped the table so hard, the dishes rattled. It's what drew our eye in the first place. All I know for sure is he was angry, as was the woman."

Interesting. Other than their friendship to the Pattersons, I didn't know of anything that connected the two. Had something new come up, a rift between them that caused the fight? Or, like the Herrons, had Jacques had a prior grievance with Cathy that could have spilled over to genuine anger?

"What happened then?" I asked, wondering if anyone actually liked Cathy, outside Gina and Frederick.

"Nothing much. They realized they were drawing attention to themselves, and calmed down. After only a few more minutes, Jacques stormed away, leaving Ms. Carr to dine alone. I'm not sure she ate much after he was gone, and since the eye candy had left, Lance and I turned our attention back to our own table, so she might have left soon after. I didn't actually see her go."

The door opened and a gaggle of kids swarmed inside, spilling throughout the store like a bunch of rambunctious ping-pong balls. That was my cue to go.

"Thanks, Jules. You've been a big help. I'll let Vicki know the candies are turning out great."

"I can't wait to see how everyone likes them."

I hurried out before I could get caught in the swarm, and carried my caramels to the car. As soon as I was seated, I tore into my own bag, popping one into my mouth and chewing while I mentally reviewed what I knew.

First, there was Lyric Granderson. She thought the necklace Gina had tried to give to Vicki should belong to her instead. She could have gone to Vicki's place to confront Gina and take back what she thought rightfully belonged to her. Instead of Gina, she'd gotten into a confrontation with the overly caffeinated Cathy, and killed her, likely in a fit of rage.

But if she had killed her, why not take the necklace? Or had she, leaving the fake behind? If that was the case, then this whole thing was premeditated, or at least the theft was.

And then there were the Herrons. They'd once used Cathy's services and were unsatisfied, though I wasn't

sure why. They fought with her before their flight to
Pine Hills, once more bringing up the old grievance.
Could the frustrations and anger have boiled over
until one or the both of them decided to get payback
for a ruined wedding?

Finally, we have Jacques Kenway, a good-looking
actor who had apparently fought with Cathy the day
of her death. But why? Could it have something to do
with Lyric and the necklace? The Herrons? Something else entirely? I wouldn't know until I talked to
him, and even then, nothing said he would actually
tell me what they'd fought about.

There was still the possibility Cathy's death was an
accident, or perhaps the other guest, Vince Conner,
could have had a reason to kill her, which would make
for pretty much the entire Californian crew having
some grievance against her.

A worrying thought crept through me then. What
if one of Vicki's parents had killed Cathy? They were
both pretty strict when it came to what they wanted. If
she'd screwed something up, or said the wrong thing,
or even tried to take the necklace for herself, one of
them might have hit her out of frustration, and then
panicked when she'd choked.

But they had been out getting dinner when it had
happened, right? Or had they left after killing her
to give themselves an alibi? It was awfully convenient of them to come home just when I'd discovered
the body.

I shook off the thought. I refused to believe either
of the Pattersons could be involved in a murder, just
as I refused to believe Vicki or Mason could have done
it. No, it had to be one of the others.

Still, I thought it might be a good idea to learn the

estimated time of death to clear them for good. I just wasn't sure how I'd get it without going to Paul, who would give me one of his patented sighs and lectures about not getting involved in his murder investigations.

I drove home, playing over all the scenarios, chewing away at my caramels. It wasn't until I pulled into my driveway that I realized all wasn't well at Casa Hancock.

Eleanor Winthrow was standing outside her house, staring toward mine. When I got out of my car, she shook her head, an amused smile on her face, before she shuffled slowly back inside her own house.

I groaned inwardly as I grabbed the caramels and closed the car door. Dad and Laura were home; their rental was sitting right where it had been when I'd left earlier that morning.

But behind them was another car.

A car I recognized.

I peered inside the backseat of the familiar car to find a clutter of romance novels and a little pink laptop tossed carelessly among them. I half-expected to find a cardboard cutout of my dad looking back at me, but it appeared that had been left at home.

"This can't be good," I muttered. Then, steeling myself for yet another disaster, I started for my front door.

13

"I can't believe you would do this to me!"

I tossed my caramels onto the table, and then hurried into the living room, where Rita was kneeling in front of the couch where Dad and Laura sat. She was clutching at Dad's hand, holding on so tightly, I wasn't sure he could easily remove it. He looked uncomfortable, as anyone would, while Laura looked mildly amused. Rita, on the other hand, was clearly beside herself.

"What did I do?" she asked, scooching forward on her knees so that she was practically leaning into Dad's lap. "If I did something, just tell me what it was and I'll fix it."

Dad looked up at me and I could see the relief wash over his face. "Krissy," he said, extracting himself from Rita and rising. "How was your day?"

Rita abruptly stood and wiped a hand over her eyes. Her makeup was smeared, dress rumpled. I actually felt bad for her. She couldn't help how she felt about my dad. She was his self-proclaimed number-one fan and had no problem telling everyone, Dad included, that fact. Ever since I'd come to Pine Hills,

Rita had attached herself to me, all because my father was James Hancock. She was smitten with him, more than an avid reader should be.

But this took her fascination with him to a whole new level. Something else *had* to be going on in her life for her to act out like this.

"It was fine," I said, and then, knowing I couldn't just ignore her, I stepped past Dad and put an arm around Rita's shoulders. She flinched, like she thought I might take a swing at her for simpering at Dad's feet, before she leaned into me, sagging as if her strings had been cut.

"I'm so sorry, dear," she said. "I don't know what came over me." She sniffed and produced a handkerchief from her dress pocket to wipe her nose.

"It's okay," I said. "I understand. These things can be hard."

Dad moved slowly to Laura's side and sank back down onto the couch. I led Rita across the room to the recliner and helped her into it. I didn't think she'd collapse if I stopped supporting her, but figured it would be better if we did this with her sitting down.

"I was sitting at home, all alone, and I got this urge to come over here and see James," Rita said. She dabbed at her eyes, removing some of the smeared makeup. "It's the anniversary, you know? I get all weepy and confused." She gently touched her hair to make sure it was still in place. "I got that bug in my rear and just had to come over and ask why he turned against me. I know it was wrong of me, but, well, I just couldn't sit by and let it happen without speaking my piece."

"He didn't turn against you," I said, wondering what she'd meant by "the anniversary." Could she have been married before and her husband passed? Left her? Some other anniversary? I would have asked, but was afraid it would open an already painful wound further. For now, I needed to diffuse the situation, not make things worse. "He lives far from here, has his own life."

"But . . ."

I cut her off before she could protest. "He didn't want to hurt you, right, Dad?"

"No. No, I didn't."

"See? And Laura is a very nice person. She didn't know how you felt, couldn't have. You might like her if you'd take the time to get to know her."

Rita glared at Laura and then shrugged. "I don't know about that." She straightened, wiped at her eyes one more time, and then put on a brave face. "But I suppose it can't hurt to try."

"Good." I left the room briefly to grab a dining room chair. I carried it into the living room and placed it so I could see everyone at once. This had gone far enough, and I wanted to make sure nothing like this ever happened again. "Now that we're all here and calm, let's talk."

They all looked at me like I was insane.

"It'll be good for us," I said.

"I'm not sure what we could possibly talk about, dear," Rita said. She looked far more like the Rita I knew, even if her eyes were rimmed red and her makeup was still a mess. That look of stubborn defiance was back.

"Anything. I've recently learned that sometimes, if you just sit down with someone and talk, you can hash out any problems you may have." I shot a glance toward the window that looked out onto Eleanor

Winthrow's own place. Things were much better between us ever since her daughter had come to town last Christmas and forced us to talk. I wouldn't say we were besties or anything, but she'd stopped spying on me constantly, and I had a better understanding of why she was the way she was.

"How did breakfast go?" Dad asked, wisely starting small and avoiding the proverbial elephant in the room. No sense in rubbing Rita's nose in his relationship.

"It was okay," I said, knowing it was anything but. "Vicki and Mason are struggling with deciding what to do. Raymond and Regina are pushing for them to postpone, if not cancel, the wedding. For a little while there, I thought they might do just that." My heart ached just thinking about it.

"I hear they're getting married themselves," Rita said, eyes lighting up at the chance to gossip.

"Regina and Raymond?"

She nodded vigorously. "They've been planning it in secret for months now. I believe they would have been married already if it wasn't for Vicki and Mason's wedding, or at least, that's what I've heard."

"You don't think they are pushing for Vicki and Mason to cancel so that they can step in and get married instead, do you?" As ludicrous as it might be, it *did* sound like something both Raymond and Regina might do. They were the kind of people who always put themselves first.

Come to think of it, they were a lot like Gina and Frederick Patterson in that regard.

"I can't swear to it, but I wouldn't put it past them," Rita said, echoing my own thoughts.

"Could one of them have killed that wedding planner?" Laura asked.

I shook my head. "Raymond is a jerk, and Regina isn't much better, but I don't think either of them would kill anyone. They'd happily call the police, or threaten someone to get their way, but I'm pretty sure murder is beyond them." Or at least, I hoped it was.

"I have it on good authority they were together at the time of the murder, anyway," Rita said, giving me a meaningful look. "And they were nowhere near that house."

I struck that from my memory and moved on. "I did hear something interesting today," I said. "Apparently, Jacques Kenway fought with Cathy Carr the day of her death."

Dad sat forward, a familiar gleam coming into his eye. Like me, he loved a good mystery. "Do you think it escalated to the point of murder?"

"I'm not sure. I want to talk to him and see what he knows."

"That might be dangerous," Dad said.

"If he killed her, wouldn't you be putting yourself at risk?" Laura added.

"I would talk to him in public," I said. I'd learned my lesson over the last few years. Talking to people where no one else could step in and help if things went sideways was on my strict "do not do this" list. "I'll ask him to share a meal with me, telling him it's about the wedding or something. If he tries to come at me, I'll make sure someone will be around to stop him."

"I can assist you in that," Dad said, sounding far too eager for my tastes. I appreciated that he wanted to help, but if Jacques *was* the killer, I didn't want Dad anywhere near him.

"Or I could do it," Rita put in, sounding just as eager. "I could even take the meeting for you. He might suspect something from you, but me?" She grinned. "He'd never see it coming."

I didn't doubt that, but the last time Rita tried to talk to a suspect in my stead, it had ended up with her sitting in a jail cell. I didn't want to have to go through *that* again.

"I'll do it on my own," I said, not wanting to put anyone else I cared about at risk. "Dad, you should stay here with Laura, just in case my talking to him triggers a reaction from him, or someone else. They may decide to stop by and pay me a visit." Of course, I didn't like the idea of Dad being anywhere near a killer, but there was only so much I could do to protect him, other than send him home. "Rita . . ." I frowned. What could I have her do to keep her out of trouble?

She leaned forward. "Yes, dear?"

"Check with the rumor mill, see what anyone might have heard about Cathy or one of the wedding guests. She could have had a run-in with someone from town. If she did, someone might have seen or heard something." Though I hated the thought that anyone from Pine Hills could have killed her.

Rita beamed. "I'm on it." She stood, phone already in hand.

"And see if you can find anything out about Sage and Trey Herron. They've also had a fight with Cathy recently." And then, to be safe: "But *don't* talk to any of them. Let the police"—or me—"handle it."

"Of course, dear," Rita said, dialing as she made for the door. "I know what I'm doing."

I wondered about that, but let it go.

I slumped back into my chair with a relieved sigh. This could have been a major disaster, yet it looked like we'd avoided any catastrophic meltdowns.

For now.

"Thanks, Buttercup," Dad said, briefly putting an arm around Laura before dropping it in his lap, a red ring creeping up his neck.

"Go ahead," I told him. "You don't need to be shy around me."

That only made Dad blush harder.

Laura, however, took it as an invitation. She snuggled in closer to him, all but forcing him to put an arm around her lest it get crushed between them.

"Do you think she'll find something?" Laura asked.

"I hope so." And I hoped she wouldn't go rushing off to take care of it herself if she did. Rita had always been a nosy busybody, but the longer she's known me, the braver she's become. Before long, I could see her opening up her own little detective agency. "I'd like for the police to solve this thing as soon as possible so it stops interfering with the wedding." I paused, realizing how callous that might have sounded, and added, "Cathy deserves justice."

"If you need anything from me, don't hesitate to ask," Dad said.

"Hopefully, it'll all be over soon and we can focus on nicer things." I grinned, taking the two of them in. They looked perfect together. "Are you thinking of going for the bouquet, Laura? It's going to be beautiful."

Dad's eyes widened as Laura's mischievous smile

joined mine. "I was thinking about it. I've always been one for following tradition, so if I catch it . . ."

Dad was up and off the couch in an instant. "That sounds like my cue to, um, make some calls." He cleared his throat, refused to meet anyone's eye. "Cameron has been working rather hard lately, and I should check in." Cameron Little was his literary agent, hired after his previous one met an untimely end.

Both Laura and I laughed as Dad scurried from the room.

"The poor man has gone through a lot today," she said. "I'm starting to worry his face is going to get stuck in that same shade of red permanently."

I rose and returned the dining room chair to the table. "I wasn't entirely joking," I said, returning to the living room.

"About the bouquet?"

"Yeah."

"Would you have a problem with it if those thoughts *are* going through my head?"

I took a moment to think about it. It was nice Dad had someone. He looked healthier, and was even sounding better. Ever since he'd had some problems with his throat, his voice had a raspy edge to it. I wasn't sure if Laura had given him some sort of remedy that was working, or if it was the mere fact of her existence, but he didn't sound nearly as bad as before. The rasp was still there, especially when he laughed, but it was definitely toned down.

When I came right down to it, Laura's presence was good for my dad, and really, that's all that mattered.

"No," I said. "In fact, I kind of hope you catch it."

Something passed between us then, a sort of unspoken understanding. She would never replace my mom; no one could. But she had my seal of approval to step in as Dad's lifelong companion and friend.

Laura rose from the couch and picked up a pair of empty bowls from the coffee table. "James has told me a lot about you and what happens here in Pine Hills. He's proud of you, of the work you do."

"I do what I can," I said, feeling a blush of my own rise up my neck. It was either genetic, or contagious.

"Sounds like you go above and beyond." She took the bowls to the kitchen, gave them each a quick wash, and then set them aside to dry. "I hope you're careful," she said, leaning against the counter. "I'd hate to think of anything bad happening to you. I really hope we get a chance to get to know one another better."

"I hope so too."

"Maybe we can work something out so you can come with us on a trip sometime," she said. "I have a few lined up over the next year or so. We'd both love to have you along."

"I wouldn't want to intrude."

Laura smiled. "You wouldn't be. And from the look of things, you could use a little time to get away yourself."

Thinking about the craziness surrounding the wedding, and yet another murder occurring in Pine Hills, I had to agree.

14

The afternoon passed with not much else happening, and before I knew it, it was time to head out for dinner. Unsure how to dress, I put on a nice pair of khaki shorts and a maroon blouse with gold thread-work. It wasn't super dressy, but neither was it my usual ultra-casual frumpfest. Dad and Laura likewise opted for casual, but not sloppy.

Dad drove us there.

Geraldo's was tucked smack-dab in the center of downtown. It had a small parking lot around back, but I noted a lot of parking spaces on the street were taken as Dad maneuvered us around to the lot. From the outside, the restaurant didn't look like much. A brick exterior, simple sign. It was probably why I hadn't noticed it before now.

The restaurant had only been open for a few weeks. The building was older, though I wasn't sure what it had been before it became Geraldo's. There'd been no grand opening or ad in the paper or on the news. The place had opened with a whisper, yet, from what I'd heard so far, it was always busy.

Dad pulled into a space and we piled out of the car.

The lot was pretty full, and a few people were standing outside, chatting amongst themselves by the front door. They stepped aside as we approached, looking full and content. It was a nice night to stand outside and relax.

Inside, Geraldo's was a different place. The brick exterior was nowhere in evidence. Fashionably painted walls were lit by dim, colored lights. The waitstaff was dressed in black and white. The men wore suit jackets, while all the women wore dresses, though I didn't get the impression the customers were expected to do the same. While a few people were dressed up, many looked like they'd just come from work, or had thrown on whatever was convenient. All good signs, in my book.

We were led to a table amid the clamor of forks on plates, and of loud voices. There were no TVs hanging from the walls. Light jazz came from the speakers interspersed among the lights and, not surprisingly, security cameras. I noted the napkins were cloth, which put it a huge step above anything else Pine Hills had to offer.

"Nice place," Dad said, taking his seat.

"Nicer than I expected," I admitted. I was surprised a place like this was so popular in a small town like Pine Hills. I was half afraid to look at the menu. The food smelled fantastic, and glancing at a nearby table, I saw they came on little rectangular plates.

"Seems pretty reasonable, too," Laura said, opening her menu. Apparently, she'd been thinking the same thing as me.

We took a few minutes to peruse the menu, and ordered when our waiter—a young man named Kyle who couldn't be any more than eighteen—appeared to take our orders. He even bowed when he left.

I glanced around at the other guests, hoping to catch sight of Jacques Kenway in the masses. Jules had said he'd come here to eat with Cathy, so I was hoping he would return. And since Geraldo's *was* nice, it might be more his speed than a place like the Banyon Tree.

But if Jacques was in attendance, he wasn't sitting where I could see him. Most of the tables were full of happy customers, busily chomping away at their meals, or gabbing the night away. I recognized quite a few faces, but none of them had anything to do with Cathy Carr, or the wedding.

"Looking for someone?" Dad asked.

"No." I returned my gaze to the table. "Just looking around."

I could tell by his crooked smile he didn't believe me. "You might want to take a look that way," he said, nodding toward the doors.

I turned to look. Trey and Sage Herron had just entered and were waiting to be seated. They were dressed nicely, Trey in a suit and tie, Sage in a sparkling mauve dress. Lyric Granderson entered behind them, dressed in a tight black number that put every woman in the room to shame.

I waited to see if Vince Conner, Jacques Kenway, or the Pattersons would join them, but they'd apparently come without the rest of the Hollywood crew.

They were led to a table off my left and in front of me, where I could watch them, but it was too loud for me to overhear anything they said. Almost before they'd hit their seats, Lyric began talking animatedly, hands flying through the air. If she wasn't careful, she was liable to smack someone.

"Can you hear what they're saying?" Dad asked.

"No." I forced my gaze away, though I could still see Lyric's frenetic gesturing in my peripheral vision. "And it isn't nice to eavesdrop."

"Where're your manners, James?" Laura asked, nudging him with her shoulder. "It's not polite."

He rolled his eyes and then shook his head. "Have it your way."

Our food arrived a few minutes later. It smelled as good as everything else, and when I took the first bite, I very nearly melted into my seat. I wasn't sure I'd ever eaten anything as heavenly that wasn't full of chocolate or sugar.

"This is good," Dad said. He'd gotten one of the fish plates, though I wasn't sure which. It smelled good, even though I'm not a big fish person.

"Mine's a little salty," Laura said, but spoke with good humor as she shoved a large bite into her mouth, which caused Dad to bark a throaty laugh.

Both Dad and Laura had ordered wine and, by the time we were halfway through the meal, had gone through two glasses each. I sipped my Coke, complete with grenadine to make it taste of cherry, and tried my darndest not to stare at Lyric and the Herrons.

Throughout the meal, Lyric looked agitated. Nothing the Herrons said seemed to calm her. Her gaze kept flickering toward the door, but no one came through—at least, no one she knew. By the time her food arrived, she looked practically beside herself.

The Herrons, on the other hand, appeared calm and collected. They sipped their own wine, nibbled at their appetizers, like nothing could bother them. I wondered if that was because they truly had nothing to worry about, or if they were content now that Cathy was dead.

Lyric jumped in her seat like she'd been shocked, and then reached into her purse for her phone. She put it to her ear and rose, nearly knocking over her glass of wine as she did. She glanced around quickly, spotted the restroom sign, and then started back that way.

"Excuse me a moment," I said, rising with her. Dad and Laura had been so focused on their food—and each other—they hadn't noticed Lyric's sudden exit or else I think one of them would have said something about my own abrupt departure.

I hurried toward the restrooms, hoping to catch a little of what was being said. Yeah, eavesdropping *was* impolite, but by the outraged look on Lyric's face when she'd started toward the restrooms, I knew the call had something to do with why she was in such a bad mood. It might not have anything to do with Cathy's death, but then again, there was always a chance it might.

I stopped just before turning down the hall toward the bathrooms. Pressing my back against the wall, I listened.

"What do you mean you aren't coming?" Lyric said, practically shouting. If it weren't for the clamor of diners, everyone would have heard her. "After everything I've done for you, you're going to leave me hanging like this?"

I eased closer as she stopped to listen.

"No, I don't think so. You do realize you've really

stepped in it, don't you?" Another pause. "I don't want to hear it. I said, I don't want to hear it!" She made a frustrated sound, and then loudly: "Jerk!"

The click-clack of heels followed, and I hurriedly tried to get out of the way, but apparently, Lyric hadn't gone far down the hall to talk because before I could escape, she strode angrily around the corner, phone clutched tightly in her hand.

She came to a dead stop the moment she saw me. The briefest flicker of guilt washed across her face, and then was gone in a flash. "What are you doing here?" she asked, the heat still high in her voice, though she tried to hide it.

"Eating." I flashed her a smile. "Needed to visit the ladies' room."

She grimaced and rolled her eyes skyward. "I really don't need to know that." She started to step past me, but I stopped her.

"Are you okay?" I asked. "I saw you head back here a minute ago. You looked upset."

"I'm fine," she said, and then, "No, I'm not, actually. But that's none of your business, now is it?"

"No," I admitted. "But with everything that's happened, I was concerned."

Lyric's eyes narrowed, as if she suspected I wasn't being totally honest with her, and then her shoulders sagged. "It's nothing," she said, sounding a little less annoyed than she had a moment ago. "I was expecting to meet someone here and I got stood up. Now I get to listen to those two blather on, by myself." She nodded toward the Herrons, who were both watching us with interest.

"Who were you going to meet?" I asked, genuinely curious.

Lyric's smile wasn't exactly kind. "My food is ready," she said. "I'd like to eat it before it gets cold."

I stepped aside and let her pass. She glanced back once, rolled her eyes, and then took her seat. This time, when she spoke, she wasn't nearly as animated, though I could tell she was still upset over the phone call.

The question was, who had stood her up? And did it even matter?

Not wanting to look like a liar, I went into the bathroom and washed my hands. I gave myself a once-over, nodded at my reflection, and then headed back to the table.

"Find anything out?" Dad asked the moment I was seated.

"I have no idea what you're talking about."

He smiled knowingly. "Uh-huh. You just happened to need the little ladies' room at the exact same instant as Ms. Granderson over there," he said, jerking a thumb toward where the actress was seated.

"Well, I did." I took a bite of food to hide my chagrin.

"Don't bother," Laura said. "His mind is already made up."

I swallowed my food, which was starting to get cold. "The answer is no," I said. I should have known I couldn't pass one over on my dad. "Lyric was supposed to meet someone here, but they stood her up. She didn't say who or why they were meeting, other than a date, I guess." Though, by her side of the conversation, it had sounded more than a simple date.

"Do you think it could be one of the men she traveled with?" Dad asked. "What were their names?"

"Vince and Jacques."

"That's it." He leaned forward and lowered his voice conspiratorially. "Could they all be in on the murder together, you think?" I could see the wheels spinning behind his eyes. If this was one of his books, it was very likely they'd all have had a hand in Cathy's death.

"It's possible, I suppose," I said. Yet I didn't believe it. Why come all the way to Pine Hills to do what they could have done in California?

A frown crossed my features. Why else? Pine Hills is a small town. No one knows these people, other than knowing that they are actors. I doubted many even recognized them from their movies, since they mostly were only extras or leads in low-budget movies no one watched. They could have used Vicki's wedding as a front, as a way to get everyone together. Could one of them have convinced Gina to bring Cathy along just so they could kill her?

I glanced across the room at the three people sitting there, and wondered if it was all one big conspiracy. It would explain why so many people who knew so little about Vicki would come to her wedding.

"You should talk to them," Dad said. "See what you can learn. We're right here and can back you up if need be."

"I don't think they'd appreciate me interrupting," I said. Especially not here, after I'd been caught eavesdropping on Lyric.

"Then talk to them wherever they're staying," he

said. "Get them alone, where they might let their guard down."

"Should you be encouraging her?" Laura asked.

Dad shrugged. He had that mischievous look in his eye that meant he was willing to do it if I didn't. "Why not? She's good at it."

"Didn't we agree it's dangerous to talk to these people alone?" Laura asked. "If one of them did kill Cathy, they might not stop there. Having Krissy interrogate them would be like poking a sleeping bear, don't you think?"

He glanced from Laura, to me, and then back toward the Herrons. "I suppose you might be right."

"I already spoke to Lyric a couple of times," I said. Now that Dad had suggested it, I was antsy to talk to them. Now wasn't the time or place, but if I could catch them somewhere else, like at their hotels, or in Lyric's case, the bed-and-breakfast, I might learn something. "I know where she's staying."

"But not the other two?" Dad asked.

"Nope."

He looked down into the remains of his fish, as if considering it, and then he abruptly stood. "Be right back."

I watched in horror as he strode across the restaurant, right up to Sage and Trey Herron. He spoke to each, and then shook everyone's hand, and then continued talking. Even from where I sat, I could hear their laughter when he said something they found funny.

"I can't believe he's doing this," I said, waiting for the moment when he'd accuse one of them of murder.

If someone went for a knife, there was no way I'd be able to stop them before they used it.

"He's bold, I'll give him that," Laura said. There was a healthy amount of affection in her voice.

Dad spoke to the group for a few minutes more, shook each of their hands once again, and then walked back over to the table, a mile-wide smile on his face. He sat down and crossed his arms over his chest.

"What was that all about?" I asked.

"You're to meet with Sage and Trey tomorrow morning."

"I have to work!"

"Which is why you're to meet with them at eight. I got their address for you. You don't have to be in too early, do you?"

"Well, no." Jeff and Lena had been taking care of opening more often lately. Soon, Vicki and I wouldn't have to help out at all, and we could focus our attention even more on the business side of things. And if we hired another person or two, all the better.

"Then you can stop by before you go in."

"How did you . . . why did you . . . ?"

He chuckled at my flustered state. I couldn't believe he'd done that, walked right up to them and set up a meeting. "I told them you were curious about who they were, what they were interested in. In an effort to make sure the wedding goes off without a hitch, you wanted to talk to them, get to know them. They were hesitant at first, but I assured them you were only doing it for the wedding."

I looked to Laura, who shrugged. "You did say you'd like to talk to them at some point."

I groaned and looked skyward. "Thanks a lot."

"My pleasure." Dad laughed and continued to eat as if nothing had happened.

The Herrons were looking at me, as was Lyric. I could feel their eyes on me, which was making me nervous. I gave them a halfhearted wave and smile, but no one returned the gesture. When they turned away, I slumped in my seat.

"This is going to be a disaster." I took a bite of my food, but it no longer tasted as good as it had before.

15

If I was going to visit the Herrons, I needed to know more about them. When I woke the next morning, I immediately went for my phone and brought up Facebook. Since they were both minor celebrities, they'd have social media profiles of some sort. I typed in their names as I headed for the bathroom to brush my teeth.

Both Sage and Trey had profiles, which were dedicated to their work. I scrolled through the list of movies they'd appeared in, and was impressed by the sheer number of them. Sure, their credits were often listed as "waitress" or "busboy," but at least they were working. They also seemed to work together more often than not. At least two-thirds of their roles were in the same movies and television shows.

Out of curiosity, I looked for *The Nest of the Viper,* and was surprised to see they'd both had tiny roles in the movie. Their parts were so small—listed only as "villager"—I doubted anyone would recognize them as Lance and Jacques had.

It did make me wonder how close they were with Jacques Kenway, or if it was just a coincidence that they'd appeared in the same film. They might not have shared a scene, or interacted in any meaningful way. They might not even realize they shared an acting credit. I'd heard, in some films, even lead actors rarely interacted if they didn't have scenes together. Maybe that was the case here, and it would come as a surprise to all of them if I told them they'd been in it together.

I finished brushing my teeth and took a quick shower before going back to their pages. There was little in the way of personal information, which I guess shouldn't have been much of a surprise. They wouldn't want an obsessive fan showing up on their doorstep, begging for autographs, or worse, accusing them of ruining a character or something like that. You had to be careful about that sort of thing these days. Even Dad, as a writer, didn't want people knowing where he lived.

"Morning, Buttercup," Dad said from the stove as I entered the kitchen. He was cooking again, and Laura was once more watching him with her chin in her hands, smiling. I got the feeling she did that quite a lot. Quite frankly, I didn't blame her. What woman wouldn't want a man to cook for her every day?

"Morning," I said. And before he could ask about breakfast, I added, "I'm going to grab some toast and coffee to go."

He nodded in understanding. "Sage and Trey said they'd be up by five, so you should be fine anytime."

I poured myself a travel mug of coffee, added a cookie, and then leaned against the counter while I waited for my toast to pop.

"What was your impression of them?" I asked Dad. "I know you didn't get to talk to them for long, but any insight might help."

He stirred some sort of egg-and-meat concoction that smelled absolutely blissful. "They were friendly enough," he said. "They come off as a little standoffish, I guess, but compared to some of the other jokers I've met recently, they aren't too bad. If I had to choose out of the people who'd come with Gina and Frederick to hang out with, I think they'd be the least offensive."

I got that impression too. "Do you think they could have killed Cathy?"

He stopped stirring to look to the ceiling, as if he might find the answer there. "Honestly, I really don't know. Seems anyone is capable of anything these days. If I were to take a guess based on what I know of them—which, granted, is very little—I'd say that no, they didn't. But, as you know, you can't always trust your gut. Sometimes, people do bad things without thinking about the consequences."

"Especially if they're caught in a corner," Laura put in.

I wasn't sure what kind of corner the Herrons might have been stuck in, but hey, that's why I was paying them a visit.

My toast popped. My mouth was watering from the smell of Dad's cooking. I seriously considered putting off the Herrons so I could stay and eat, but decided that this might very well be my only chance to talk to them. I quickly buttered my toast, said my good-byes, and got into my car.

I was surprised when I pulled up to the address Dad had given me to find a house, rather than a motel. It was nestled at the edge of town, surrounded on three sides by a man-made pond. Pine trees had been planted around the property, giving the place a sense of privacy, despite nearby houses. It was quiet, serene, and honestly not the kind of place you'd expect to find someone who was staying for only a couple of days.

I checked the address to be sure, and found I was indeed in the right spot. I got out of my car, went to the door, and knocked, fully expecting the Herrons to have given Dad a bogus address.

The door opened almost immediately, revealing Trey Herron, dressed as if he might be going golfing in a powder-blue polo, white khaki shorts, and a visor. He had a pink drink of some kind in one hand and was fiddling with his phone with the other.

"Ah, Ms. Hancock," he said, stepping aside. He tucked his phone into his pocket. "Sage is out back, if you'd care to join us."

"Thank you," I said, stepping past Trey and into the residence.

The inside of the house was much like the outside: serene and peaceful. No loud colors, no crazy themes. It was fully furnished, and as I passed the living room, I noted a photograph on the wall depicting a young couple holding a baby. They looked nothing like the Herrons, not unless Trey or Sage had some distant Asian relatives.

"Nice place," I said as we approached a sliding back door.

"Found it online," Trey said, not bothering to glance back at me. "Owners were looking for someone to rent it while they were overseas. We decided to pay for the full three months so we wouldn't have to stay in a flea-ridden motel."

I wondered how such low-end actors could afford

such a place, but then decided it was none of my business. "You're staying for three months?" I asked instead.

He chuckled. "Of course not. They might *think* we are, but I couldn't imagine staying here for that long." He opened the door and stepped outside onto a concrete, covered patio. "Sage. Our guest is here."

Sage was dressed much like her husband, although her polo was pink, as was her visor. She was sitting in a chair, past the patio and in the yard, an umbrella keeping the sun off her. She was looking out over the clear, blue water, which rippled in the breeze. It made me wonder why they simply hadn't registered at Ted and Bettfast since they could have had the same sort of thing there. It would have been a whole lot cheaper, and they wouldn't have had to clean up after themselves.

Then again, Sage and Trey could very well value their privacy enough they wouldn't want the hassle of dealing with the staff at the bed-and-breakfast. Not everyone wants to be waited on hand and foot either.

"Ms. Hancock," Sage said, paying me only the briefest of glances.

"You can call me Krissy."

She smiled, but said nothing.

"We were leaving for brunch soon," Trey said, hinting that he wanted me to hurry this along.

I had no problem with that, other than the fact that most people would still consider it breakfast at this hour. Looking around, we were pretty isolated. If they were indeed Cathy's killers, they could kill me and dump me in the pond without anyone knowing.

Well, anyone but Dad and Laura, who knew I was here, but weren't in a position to help if the Herrons turned suddenly violent. Already, I was doing a pretty poor job of doing all my investigations in public.

"How do you like Pine Hills?" I asked, deciding to start small. Get them talking, see if anything slipped.

Sage made a face. "It's rather simple and boring."

Trey took a sip from his drink. "There's nothing to do," he said. "We like a little excitement now and again. Here . . ." He shrugged. "We just sit around. It's nice to get away sometimes, but after a while, it gets tedious."

I supposed murder wasn't exactly the kind of excitement they were looking for. It definitely wasn't for everybody. "I like it," I said. "It's relaxing most of the time. I used to live in a pretty big city and got tired of all the bustle. Pine Hills is definitely more my speed."

"If you say so," Sage said.

I moved on, remembering that I was supposed to be asking about them so I could get to know them better for the wedding. "I checked you two out online and saw you had quite a lot of movie credits under your belts. You were in one with Jacques Kenway as well, weren't you?"

"*The Nest of the Viper,*" Trey said. "Dreadful movie."

So, they *did* know they'd been in the film together. "Did you know him back then?"

"Not really," he said. "Other than our friendship with Gina and Frederick, we don't run in the same circles. We like our excitement, but he's a little too wild for our tastes."

"He thinks he's better than us," Sage added. "He's younger, sure, but that means little in the long run. We have experience."

"You don't really like him, then?"

Sage and Trey glanced at one another. He was the

one to reply. "We don't know him well enough to say."
The diplomatic answer.

"What about Cathy Carr?" I asked as casually as
could be. I watched them both carefully, and wasn't
disappointed with their reactions.

Sage visibly flinched, while Trey immediately took
a long drink from his glass. I waited them both out. It
was clear they were both stalling, but was that because
they had something to hide, or because they didn't
want to speak ill of the dead?

Finally, Trey spoke. "She wasn't one of our favorite
people."

Sage shook her head, and then hugged herself. "I
have a chill."

Trey went to his wife and put an arm around her.
"We really should leave for brunch."

I refused to let them off that easily. I was here to
learn what I could about their relationship with Cathy,
and so far, I hadn't been told anything I didn't already
know. "I heard she planned your wedding and did a
poor job of it."

"It wasn't the planning that was the problem," Trey
said.

"Well, not the entire problem," Sage amended.
"The cake was the wrong color by a half a shade."

"Which wasn't entirely her fault," Trey said. It
sounded like they'd had this argument before.

"It didn't match the scheme. I was very specific on
what I wanted, and yet she let them serve us a cake
that stood out like a sore thumb!"

"What was your issue with her?" I asked quickly,
before they could get completely off topic and de-
volve into an argument.

Sage and Trey shared yet another look before he

started speaking. "We really don't want to talk about her now that she's dead. You understand, right? There's no sense bringing up something no one can do anything about now."

"And it happened so recently," Sage added, though there was some heat in her voice, like she wasn't too terribly upset Cathy had been killed.

"We wouldn't want you to think we could have had anything to do with her death."

I stared at them in silence. They were already doing a good job of babbling, telling me they had something to say. If I waited long enough, I was sure one of them would tell me what it was. It was one of the things I'd picked up from watching crime shows on TV.

Sage withered under my stare, and was the first to break. "It was my jewelry," she said.

Trey grimaced, closed his eyes for a moment, shoulders slumping, and then added, "It came up missing."

Bingo. I couldn't believe I'd guessed right. "And you think Cathy Carr took it?"

"Oh, I know she did," Sage said. "She was the only one in that wing of the house when I realized it was missing. It was small pieces, things you'd think I wouldn't easily miss. But I noticed, all right. They were my mother's earrings!"

"Could someone else have snuck in and taken them?" I asked, excited now. If Cathy *was* stealing from her clients, it would make her a target. "Did you have cleaners or other guests who might have come in and taken them when no one was looking?"

"We did, but it's unlikely any of them had an opportunity," Trey said. "The room was on the third floor and no one else was permitted up there, and that included our cleaners."

"She took them, even though she never admitted it." Sage clenched a fist, and took a deep, calming breath.

"Is that what you fought about at the airport?"

"How did you know about that?" Trey asked.

I merely smiled and touched my nose, as if I'd somehow uncovered it on my own, not that I'd had someone simply tell me.

"It was," he admitted after a moment. "She steadfastly denied it, but I'm positive she took them. I've talked to others about her and they've said the same thing: she's guilty. We aren't the only ones who suspects Cathy has taken things. I wouldn't be surprised if her thefts were the reason she's dead now."

Nor would I.

"I really wish we could put it all behind us," Sage said. "Though I do hope that when someone goes through her things, they find those earrings and return them to where they belong. I truly would like them back."

I had a feeling the earrings were long gone, whether Cathy had taken them or not, but didn't say so. You didn't steal jewelry to wear it.

"Thank you for letting me know," I said. "Cathy's murder is terrible, and I hope the police figure out who did it soon." I felt as if I was getting closer to the truth, though I still wasn't sure who had the most to gain by Cathy's death.

When neither Trey or Sage showed much reaction to my last comment, I added, "Do you have any idea who might have wanted to hurt her?"

"She probably did it to herself," Sage said, though she didn't clarify whether she meant Cathy's actions had caused her death, or that she thought it had been an accident.

"No one we know could do something like that," Trey said. "We're actors. We're not violent people. None of us are."

I wondered if they included everyone in that statement, or just the two of them.

"I'm getting hungry," Sage said, stepping out from beneath her umbrella. "We really should go."

Trey walked over and offered a hand. "It was nice talking to you, Krissy, but we really should get going. You could come with us for brunch if you'd like. We've always preferred dining with others, and since you live here, perhaps you could tell us about some places we might want to visit."

"There's this place we were told to try," Sage added. "The Banyon Tree. Do you know it?"

I nodded with an inward grimace. Any thoughts I might have had of joining them flew out the window the moment I knew where they were headed. Why did everyone always want to go there? It was like they *knew* I wouldn't follow.

"I have to get to work, or else I would," I said. "Maybe another time?"

"Perhaps." By the way Sage said it, I doubted I'd be receiving another invitation any time soon.

We left the house together, the Herrons getting into a Mercedes, and me getting into my Ford. I waved to them as they pulled onto the road and turned toward J&E's. Neither returned my wave.

I aimed myself toward work, mind working overtime. I wasn't sure I suspected the Herrons of killing Cathy anymore, but it was possible they'd tried to confront her about her presumed theft at Vicki's house and lost their tempers. Or Lyric could have done it if she'd gone to ask Gina about the necklace and found Cathy with the fake in her possession.

Of course, that made me wonder where the real necklace was. It couldn't have just up and walked away on its own.

And then there was Jacques and his argument with Cathy the night of her death. Could the theft have nothing to do with it? And what about Vince Conner? So far, nothing pointed to him, but that didn't mean he didn't have a reason to go after Cathy. He *had* been making himself pretty scarce lately.

And finally, there was Gina and Frederick. The necklace on Cathy had belonged to Gina. They both were staying in the house and had conveniently been grabbing dinner when the killer struck. I still didn't know if anyone could place them anywhere outside the house at the time of the murder or not. I was counting on Paul to know and, hopefully, to let it slip while I was within hearing distance.

It worried me that the Pattersons were rising up my list of suspects. If there was one thing that would put an abrupt end to the wedding, it would be Vicki's parents getting put away for murder.

16

I scanned the dining area of Death by Coffee, a frown creasing my features. When Vicki had originally started planning her wedding, she'd immediately said she wanted it to be small and personal. That meant fewer guests, which meant we didn't need a giant building for the reception, or a ton of catered food.

So, she'd settled on Death by Coffee.

We'd mapped it all out: decorations, seating arrangements, everything. Mason and Vicki were to sit at the top of the stairs so they could look out over their guests like royalty at court. The rest of the wedding party would be on the ground floor, paired off to either side of the staircase—this included parents, Regina, Charlie, and me. Everyone else would be seated in the dining area.

It should have worked. It might not have been ultra-classy like Gina and Frederick would want, but it had saved Vicki and Mason a lot of money and allowed us to be in control of everything from lighting to air-conditioning, since it was our store. We could change and move whatever we wanted, when we wanted, and no one would care.

"I think we can all fit," I muttered. Now that we had a few more guests to worry about, there just wasn't enough seating, not if we wanted to have some semblance of a dance floor. The DJ would be set up upstairs, so that wouldn't be an issue. Drinks would be served at the counter, as would snacks.

But where to put the new guests?

I considered putting them outside and leaving the door open. It was supposed to be a nice, warm evening that night, so it wouldn't be uncomfortable. The only issue would be the fact they wouldn't be able to hear or see what was going on inside. And honestly, it would be rude to separate them, even if they weren't invited in the first place.

Maybe they can stay that way. Just because they'd showed up, that didn't mean Vicki had to invite them to her wedding or reception. She could politely tell her mother no, and force Gina to tell her friends that they had come all this way for nothing.

Of course, Vicki wouldn't do that. She might be unhappy about the extra guests appearing out of nowhere, but she wouldn't turn them away. She was too nice for that.

With a sigh, I tore my gaze away from the space, which kept looking smaller and smaller the longer I looked at it. The wedding was only a few days away and I had no idea what we were going to do. When I'd arrived for work, Vicki had just been leaving. She'd been nearly beside herself with worry, and quite frankly, I didn't blame her. Things were quickly spiraling out of control. If it kept up, I was afraid she'd eventually throw in the towel and give up on getting married.

I glanced at the clock and removed my apron. Lena

was behind the counter, wiping down all the machines, while Jeff was upstairs, reorganizing the books. We'd moved a few of the shelves so there would be room for the DJ. It made space tight between the shelves, but there was little we could do about it. Not that it really mattered much. Today was the last day we'd be open until after the wedding. We'd decided it would be best to close for a few days, just to be safe. Vicki didn't need the stress of managing the shop, and there *was* quite a lot of organizing to be done.

But I could worry about that later.

Vicki had set up a few interviews for me today in the hopes we could hire someone and have them help with setting up for the reception. It would also make training them easier since we'd be closed for a few days and we could take our time with them, not throw them into the proverbial fire. I was surprised when she'd told me there were people coming in since I hadn't realized we'd gotten any applications. I'd hoped for good results, but after my first two interviews of the day, I wasn't so sure we were going to find anyone who could handle the job.

"I'm going to head into the office to prep," I told Lena. "Send the next applicant to the back when she arrives."

"Sure thing."

I'd just opened the door to the office when the bell jingled. I glanced back, expecting my third interview to be early, but instead was faced with my ex, Robert Dunhill, and his latest girlfriend, Trisha, coming through the door.

"Hey, Krissy, hold up a sec."

I took a deep breath, and then plastered on a smile as I walked around the counter to join him by the door. Robert and I had broken up years ago, when he'd cheated on me. I'd come to Pine Hills thinking I'd never see him again, yet here he was. Our relationship had gotten better recently, thanks to me helping him out of a sticky situation, but it still wasn't the best. His abrasive personality had a lot to do with that.

"Robert," I said. "Trisha. What brings you here?"

Robert put his arm around his girlfriend, and I was once more surprised that she put up with him. She was gorgeous and blond, and from what I knew of her, she was smart. Robert was drawn to the looks, but usually, anyone with half a brain knew not to get involved with him. I wasn't sure what that said about me—or her, for that matter—but there it was. Some guys got all the luck, I supposed.

"I heard about the wedding," he said. "That murder thing was on the news and they mentioned she was in town to plan it."

"That *murder thing* was a terrible tragedy," I said, not impressed by his choice of words. He was as insensitive as ever, I saw.

"Yeah, sure." He cleared his throat and shifted from foot to foot.

I waited him out and, after only a few seconds, realized I'd be standing there forever if I didn't prod him along. "What do you want, Robert?"

He cleared his throat and rubbed at the back of his neck, all while looking everywhere but at me. "So, like, Trisha and I were wondering why we weren't invited."

I blinked at him. "Invited? To what?"

"It's not a big deal," Trisha said, looking mildly uncomfortable. I imagined when Robert had included her in the inquiry, he'd really meant just himself.

He had a way of dragging other people down in his bad decisions.

"Vicki's wedding," he said. "I know she and I aren't exactly friends and stuff, but, you know, we came from the same place. I just figured she'd like, want me there. Old times' sake, you know?"

"You do realize she doesn't like you," I said, putting it as nicely as I could. When Robert had cheated on me, he'd permanently been placed on Vicki's "do not trust" list. I was afraid that the next time they were in the same room together, she would punch him in the face for how he'd treated me. That wasn't the sort of thing you wanted to happen at a wedding.

"Yeah, I know." Robert's face reddened. "But I thought after, you know, you helped me, she might reconsider?" He made it a question.

The smart thing to do would be to shut him down right then and there and send him on his way. I so didn't need Robert mucking around during the wedding and reception. Things were already tense enough with Cathy's death and the uninvited guests. I wouldn't put it past Robert to hit on all the women, Lyric and Sage included, even with Trisha right there.

No, Krissy, he's changed. I wasn't sure how much he'd changed, but Robert was definitely trying. Ever since he'd started seeing Trisha, he'd stopped begging me to give him another chance. I didn't know if that was truly because of her, or if he'd simply grown tired of failure, but it was a step in the right direction.

"I'll talk to her about it," I said. And then, when Robert grinned, I added, "I can't promise anything. We're already short of space. Everything has been ordered and adding two more people might not be feasible." Of course, we were already adding others; how much worse would squeezing in two more be?

"Thanks. I knew I could count on you." He turned to Trisha and pulled her in close. "See, babe, I told you she'd be willing."

Trisha put her head on his shoulder as he squeezed. It was an amazing sight, really. How could she care that much about a man like *that*? I liked her well enough, but I will say, she needed to work on her taste in men.

The door opened again, and this time, Beth Milner walked in. She came to an abrupt stop when she saw me standing by the door. "Krissy, right? I'm here for the interview."

Robert led Trisha toward the counter as I turned to Beth. She looked much the same as when I'd last seen her, which had been a rather long time ago. She was a bottle blonde, hair pulled into a bun, with painted nails. She looked like a model pretending to be a business professional, and I sometimes wondered if that was why she'd been hired at Lawyer's Insurance across the street. Last I knew, she was Raymond Lawyer's secretary there.

"Hi, Beth." When I'd skimmed the application earlier, it hadn't occurred to me who exactly I'd be interviewing until this very moment. "Let's head on to the back."

I led her to the office and sat her down. The space was tight, but she didn't seem to mind. She had her practiced, fake smile plastered on her face, and looked so uncomfortable, I actually felt bad for her. Years of working for Raymond Lawyer could do that to a person.

"Are you still working at Lawyer's Insurance?" I

asked, genuinely curious. If she was, I'd have to play this carefully. Raymond was likely to accuse me of poaching her from him if he caught wind that she was here interviewing for a job.

"No," she said. "I quit a few weeks ago. Couldn't take it anymore." Her smile cracked, showing a nervous woman beneath.

"I totally understand." And I did. As I'd said before, Raymond wasn't exactly a nice man. I wasn't sure he'd ever asked for anything—just demanded. That had to be hard on a secretary.

We got down to business and I went through the general questions any employer would ask of a prospective employee. While she didn't have much experience working with food or books, she *was* a dedicated worker. She'd stuck it out with Lawyer's Insurance through a murder, and through all sorts of verbal abuse, for years. That said a lot about her character, if you asked me.

"But I can help out other ways," she said, after she'd told me about her lack of experience.

"Such as?"

"Well, I can tell you that Raymond Lawyer is looking to match Regina Harper's daughter up with his son Mason if things don't work out with Vicki Patterson."

My eyes widened at that. "What? They're getting married!"

Beth nodded. "He's trying to take full advantage of that woman's death. He thinks that if he plays his cards right, he can sway Mason and get everything he wants."

"Did he tell you this?"

Beth leaned forward and lowered her voice. "I hear things when I work," she said. "He has a loud voice and often doesn't close his door when taking calls and it's just the two of us. I'm awfully good at listening." She gave me a knowing smile.

I knew her ability to eavesdrop on other people's conversations shouldn't impact whether or not I hired her, but I had to admit, it did. It would be nice to have someone around who could pick up a thing or two, even if it didn't have anything to do with a murder investigation. If the customers started talking about something they'd like to see sold in the store, or a drink they didn't much care for, it would be helpful to know.

And if she did happen to overhear a little bit of gossip, then all the better.

I finished up the interview a few minutes later, telling Beth I'd let her know later that day whether or not she got the job. So far, she was top on the list, and it wasn't even close. I wanted to run it past Vicki first, however, just to be sure.

As soon as she was gone, I took a few minutes to jot some notes down, but I kept having to stop when my mind wandered. Raymond wanted to use Cathy's murder to break Mason and Vicki apart. I already knew that, thanks to earlier conversations about a possible cancellation or postponement, but I hadn't realized how serious he was about it.

I finished up the notes, and made a plan to call Vicki before I left work to ask her about Beth. I was pretty sure she'd sign off on anything I decided, but I wanted to talk to her about it anyway. And I supposed I could pass along Robert's question. If she said no, I could at least tell him I'd tried, and wash my hands of it.

Robert and Trisha were gone when I returned to

the front, as was Beth. Only a handful of customers sat at the tables. Today was especially slow and I wondered if most of our regulars thought we'd closed today, instead of starting tomorrow.

I was about to check the cookie case to see if it needed to be restocked when I noted Vince Conner sitting alone in the corner, coffee held in both hands, but he wasn't drinking. He stared out the window, a contemplative expression on his face. He looked tired, and a little hungover.

Now's your chance, a little voice in the back of my mind whispered. I knew practically nothing about Vince, and that included how well he knew Cathy Carr. Now that he was here, in my store, it was the perfect opportunity to find out.

"Need me to do anything else?" Lena asked, before I could start that way. The counter was sparkling clean, and a quick glance into the display told me that the cookies were fresh and full. Even the dishes were done in the back.

"No," I said. "You can go ahead and head home if you want. I think Jeff and I can hold down the fort."

"You sure?"

"Yup. Enjoy your day."

Lena grinned and headed for the back, just as the phone rang. I answered, once more eyeing the dining area in an attempt to figure out the logistics for the reception, and to keep an eye on Vince, who had yet to so much as take a sip of his drink. The man was seriously lost in thought. Guilt? Or was it something else?

"Death by Coffee," I said, only half paying attention.

"Krissy! Thank goodness." Vicki sounded so frantic, I grabbed the phone with both hands, Vince forgotten.

"What's wrong?" I asked, heart leaping straight to

my throat. I was terrified she was going to tell me they'd found another body.

"I hate to call you like this, and I know you're at work, but I need you to do something for me."

I sucked in a relieved breath. *It's about the wedding.* "It's no bother. We're pretty slow. What do you need?"

"Could you run by the church for me? There's an issue that needs immediate attention. Mason is stuck at work and I have to meet with the cake decorator. Apparently, something has gone wrong there too." She sounded close to hysterics.

"Sure, no problem," I told her. "Do you need me to go now? Or can it wait until I'm done later?"

"If you could. I'm not sure it can wait."

I glanced back. Lena was standing in the office doorway, her backpack in hand. She smiled at me, nodded, and then returned it to the office.

"Yeah, I can do it."

"Thank you so much. I wish one thing would go right this week." She barked a half-crazed laugh. "I'd better go. Thanks again." She hung up.

"It's okay," Lena said, returning. "I could use the extra money anyway."

"Thank you," I told her, hurrying to the back to grab my own purse before returning to the front. "I'll be sure you get a bonus."

"Hey, I won't say no to that!"

I looked to where Vince was sitting, to find he'd gotten up and left. His coffee sat on the table, and even from here, I could tell he'd barely touched it.

"I'll check back in later," I promised Lena as I hurried outside, thinking I might catch Vince, at least to find out how I might contact him later, but he was already long gone.

With a sigh, I got into my car and started the engine, and with one last glance toward Death by Coffee to make sure Vince hadn't magically returned, I pulled out and headed for the church.

17

The good news was the church wasn't on fire. Since Vicki hadn't given me the details of what kind of disaster to expect, my mind had conjured up all sorts of horrible images and scenarios on the short drive over. I should have realized it wasn't something so drastic as a fire or anything that would require the police. The top of the church was visible from Death by Coffee, and if something like that had happened, I would have heard the sirens or seen the smoke.

I parked out front and headed for the doors, wondering what could possibly require my immediate attention. The air-conditioning unit might have gone out, or maybe a water line had burst, which would be an inconvenience, but that wouldn't put much of a damper on the actual wedding.

Inside, I looked around, trying to determine where to go. No one was immediately evident in the church. I'd only ever been upstairs, where the meeting rooms and the main worship room were located. Downstairs contained storage, and I thought they had some sort of dining area down there, though I'd never actually seen it. Normally, I was only ever here in the evening, for the writers' group meetings I'd stopped coming to.

"Offices then," I muttered, tromping up the stairs. I'd never seen anyone in the offices before, but I figured if something had indeed happened that required Vicki's attention, then it was the most likely place to find someone in the know.

Sure enough, as soon as I reached the top of the stairs, I heard voices coming from the office connected to the room where the writers' group meetings are held. I'd seen the door before, but it had always been closed, the room dark. Now, the lights were on, and two people stood just inside. I headed for the office, concern growing as I neared.

I recognized one of the voices.

Frederick was standing just inside the office door, arms crossed over his chest. He was shaking his head, frowning up a storm. He didn't see me approach since his back was to me.

"I don't think it will suffice," he said to a tall, thin woman who had sharp green eyes and a cute bob of a haircut and was wearing slacks with a button-up blouse. A silver cross hung from her neck on a delicate chain that was practically invisible against her skin.

"It's not up to you, sir," she said, and then, spotting me, she asked. "Are you Krissy?"

Frederick turned and his frown turned into a genuine scowl. "Great," he muttered under his breath.

"I am," I said, ignoring him. I stepped forward and took the woman's hand when she offered it. Her grip was dry and firm.

"Elsie Buchannan." She smiled when my eyes widened. "And yes, I know all about you. John is my husband."

I knew I was staring, but couldn't stop. *This* was

Buchannan's wife? I'd fully expected a scowling, stocky woman, not this lithe, friendly thing. And she was actually pretty. When she smiled, her entire face lit up with a glow that was just this side of heavenly. I didn't know why I'd expected Buchannan's wife to be on the unattractive side. Maybe it was because of his often ugly personality or because of some of the questionable rumors Rita had told me about the two of them.

"It's nice to meet you," I finally managed. And then, to the point: "Vicki called and asked me to check in for her. Is something wrong?" I glanced at Frederick.

"This venue will not suffice," he said. "The building is old, and not of sufficient quality to house my daughter's wedding."

"I assure you, sir, there is nothing wrong with the building," Elsie said. "It might be old, but it's still solid. The air works and the pipes are clean. We just had them replaced three years ago. Your daughter requested the site; we didn't force her into anything."

Frederick huffed. "I have the right to change the venue if I see fit."

"Can we have a moment?" I asked as I slid past him, into the office.

His jaw tightened briefly, but Frederick otherwise complied without complaint. He turned and marched out of the room to look at a painting on the wall that showed the Last Supper from a different angle than what was normally depicted—top down instead of from the front. I remembered reading the plaque beneath it claiming the artist had come from Pine Hills, though she had lived and died well before my time.

I eased the door most of the way closed, just in case Frederick tried to eavesdrop, but not so far I couldn't keep an eye on him. He glanced my way, scowled some more, and then returned his gaze to the painting.

"Vicki called me to take care of this," I said, keeping my voice low, though Frederick was far enough away, I doubted he would have understood me even if I'd spoken normally.

"She said she'd send you to speak for her. When he came in and started claiming he had authorization to change the venue, I thought it best to call Ms. Patterson and check instead of taking him at his word." She shook her head. "I don't get it. Why would he do something like this?"

"He's headstrong," I said, understating it quite a bit. "He wants what's best for his daughter, but he doesn't know how to go about it. If he tries to press the issue, don't let him. Vicki wants the church, and that's what she's going to get, no matter what Frederick says."

"That's what I thought." Elsie picked up a pen and wrote something down before facing me again. She tapped the pen on her chin. "I've been organizing events for the church for nearly fifteen years now, and I've never had anything like this happen before."

"Frederick is . . . different." Once more, an understatement, but I didn't want to talk too bad about him. For as difficult as he could be, he was still Vicki's dad and she loved him. And despite how poorly he treated me, I didn't hate the man. He lived a different sort of life from what I was used to, and I had to respect those differences, even if I didn't like, or agree, with them most of the time.

"That he is." She smiled. "John says the same thing about you, you know?"

"We've had our, uh, differences." To put it mildly.

She laughed. "So I've heard. Despite what you might think, he doesn't hate you. He's actually impressed with you, with how you handle yourself. I know he doesn't like showing it, but he thinks you've got a good head on your shoulders and appreciates your hard work."

"Really?" I was genuinely surprised. While his cold shoulder toward me had thawed considerably since we'd first met, he still acted as if he trusted me about as far as he could throw me. "I would never have guessed."

"He does wish you'd stay out of the way of his duties, but that's the cop in him talking. He's always been big on letting the police do their jobs, even in a small town like this, where that job includes saving kittens caught in drains more often than theft or murder."

"He's a good cop," I said, and I meant it. We might not always get along, but John Buchannan knew what he was doing. I just wished, sometimes, he wouldn't be so gung-ho about dropping blame at my feet.

"That he is." She glanced past me, toward Frederick. "I'm not sure how I'm going to convince him there's nothing I can do for him. The venue decision is Ms. Patterson's call. She's already signed the papers."

"I'll take care of it," I said.

"Are you sure? I'm pretty sure I can handle him if he tries to play alpha male." Something came into her eye then, a strength that made me realize John Buchannan might not be the toughest member of his family.

"I am. I'm used to dealing with Frederick." Though I was pretty out of practice. I'd barely seen him since Vicki had moved away from California shortly before I'd made my own move. It had been years now. As far as I knew, he'd grown twice as stubborn in the interim.

Still, I thought I could deal with him without causing too much trouble. He might insult me, might give me looks that would kill any lesser woman, but he wouldn't actually *hurt* me.

Unless he's the one who killed Cathy.

I squashed the thought before it could take root in my brain. The Pattersons were a lot of things, but they weren't killers.

"Thank you," Elsie said. "I'll call Ms. Patterson and let her know everything is under control."

Steeling myself for what was to come, I shook Elsie's hand once more, and then turned to face Vicki's father.

Frederick was no longer at the painting, but was now standing by a bookshelf at the back of the room, perusing the titles. He turned as I approached, already scowling. "I suppose you went against my wishes, and refused to consider a change," he said.

"Vicki wants to have the ceremony here," I said, refusing to let his condescending tone get to me. "There aren't many better places in town to hold a wedding, to be honest. While the church is old, there's a history here. She likes it, and I think she should get what she wants, don't you?"

He stared at me a long moment before saying, "I suppose there's little I can do about it, especially if what you say is true. I haven't seen enough of this town to know if anywhere else would be more suitable for what she deserves."

I blinked, surprised. I'd expected to argue with him for a good half an hour before I got him to concede, even a little. "Okay," I said, not quite sure where to go from there. "Good."

"It's just so damn frustrating," he said. "Gina and I are stressed, thanks to Cathy's demise. We want everything to be perfect for Vicki, yet it all seems to be going wrong." He glanced around the room. "When I walked in here, all I could see were the faults."

"Just because there are faults doesn't mean it's not good enough. She likes it here. The place has character." And yeah, there might be a few water spots on the ceiling, and maybe the stairs creak a bit too much, but that didn't detract from it in any way. In fact, I liked it all the better for it.

"I know." His shoulders sagged. "If you had children, you would understand, perhaps. When she was growing up, I imagined what her wedding would be like. There'd be thousands of guests, an outdoor ceremony with flowers blooming all around her." He spread his hands helplessly. "I feel as if I've failed her."

"She's happy," I said. "This is what she wants."

"I suppose it must be." He said it like he couldn't imagine anyone wanting to have a wedding here, let alone *live* here. "It's just not what I wanted for her."

"Sometimes, you've got to let your children make up their own minds about what it is they want."

He gave me a startled look, like he hadn't expected anything remotely philosophical coming from my mouth. Honestly, I hadn't either; it had just sort of popped out.

"You're right, of course." He grimaced as if the words tasted bad. "I'll let Gina know."

"Great." I probably should have left it at that, and walked away. My job here was done, and Vicki's wedding could go on as planned.

But the murder was still unsolved. If anyone would know more about the suspects, Frederick would. And I had him right here, alone, without anyone else around to influence what he says.

"So, who do you think did it?" I asked, leaning against the wall, crossing my arms. I was trying to act casual and relaxed, but I was all nerves inside.

Frederick's eyes narrowed, as if he was trying to decide if I was attempting to trick him into something. "Did what?"

"Killed Cathy," I said. "The police think it might have something to do with the fake necklace found in her possession."

"I don't know anything about that," Frederick said. "I'm sure it's some sort of mistake. That necklace was most definitely real." He paused, brow furrowed. "I suppose if someone tried to replace the real one with the counterfeit, she might have tried to stop them. Cathy was the kind of woman who cared about her friends." He said it like he didn't think I knew what that meant.

"Any idea who might have wanted Gina's necklace?" I asked, not wanting to mention Lyric's name up front. She believed it was hers, so she was the most likely suspect when it came to a theft, but murder? I wasn't so sure.

Frederick frowned, eyes darting from side to side as if looking for an escape. It was clear he didn't want to accuse one of his friends, but I could tell he had someone in mind.

"If you think you know something, it might be a good idea to tell someone now, before the police wonder why you withheld the information," I prodded.

"Tell who? You?" He chuckled. "What good could that possibly do?"

"It could take away any guilt you might feel about ratting on one of your friends," I said. "Tell me and if I think it's important to the investigation, I can tell the police in your stead. I'm good friends with a few people on the force." Or at least, I used to be. Paul still liked me, but I wasn't so sure about everyone else lately. "Tell me and I'll be the one turning them in, not you. It limits your culpability."

He gave me another surprised look. Apparently, he had assumed I didn't know many big words. "Lyric believes the necklace should belong to her," he said, slowly, as if it pained him to say it.

I nodded, and motioned for him to go on. I already knew that.

"She's had words with Gina about it on more than one occasion. I was surprised when she decided to come along for the wedding, to be honest."

I wasn't. I thought about telling him Lyric's real motive for coming, but decided that was for her to do, not me. "Do you think she could have tried to steal it?"

"I don't think she would do something like that on her own," he said. "Lyric likes to delegate." He smiled, somewhat fondly. "If she can get someone else to do something for her, she will. Usually, she has no problem finding some poor sap to run all her errands for her."

Theft and possible murder were a long way from an errand, but what did I know? She was a beautiful woman who someday might hit it big in acting. A lot of people would do anything for someone like that. "So, you think she might have hired someone to steal the necklace for her?"

He shrugged. "I don't know. She could have. But if I were to look at anyone specifically, I'd look at her suitor."

My mind immediately went back to when we'd gathered at Death by Coffee that first time, and the man who'd stared at her like he adored her. "Vince?" I wondered aloud. He'd stood right beside Lyric during the introductions, hadn't even noticed when attention turned his way. He'd looked at her like he would do anything for her. Did that mean he'd be willing to steal for her?

Frederick gave me an odd look. "No, not Vince. Jacques. He's called on her a few times in the past, and from what I've heard, he's been seen with her a few times here already."

"You think Jacques Kenway might have attempted to steal the necklace for Lyric?" I asked, before following it up with, "Isn't he related to you?"

Frederick chuckled, though it wasn't an amused sound. "Distantly related. At least, that's what he says. I'm not sure we've ever actually found a real connection between us. I think he wants to feel a part of something since he doesn't have a family of his own."

Could it be that easy? Lyric had wanted that necklace for years. Could she have gone to Jacques for help, and he'd then made up some story about being related to the Pattersons, just so he could get close to them so he could steal the necklace for her? It sounded a tad convoluted, but these were actors we were dealing with here. As far as I knew, he'd done the same sort of thing in a movie and decided to give it a try in real life.

"I should get back to Gina," Frederick said, cutting into my thoughts. "Tell Vicki the venue will suffice."

He turned and walked away without waiting for me to respond.

I wanted to ask him more questions about Jacques and Lyric, but I let him go. I now had two top suspects, and thankfully, they weren't Gina and Frederick Patterson. That was a win in my book, since I'd been starting to wonder about them.

The only question was, how could I get Lyric or Jacques to admit it?

Of course, I doubted they ever would, not without evidence they couldn't explain away.

Okay then, so where would I get that evidence?

If Lyric and Jacques had indeed stolen the necklace, and Cathy had been found with the replica they'd replaced it with, then that meant one of them would have the real one. If I found it on one of them, then that would be proof they'd had something to do with her death, right?

It wasn't perfect, but it was as close as I was going to get without having them break down and confess.

It looked like I was going to have to talk to Lyric again. And this time, I wasn't going to leave until I got some answers.

18

I made a quick stop at Death by Coffee to make sure Lena and Jeff were handling things okay, and I shot Vicki a quick couple of texts telling her about Robert's request and my thoughts on Beth before I made my way toward Ted and Bettfast. The smart thing to do would be to call Paul and tell him everything I'd learned, but I wasn't totally convinced Lyric and Jacques were the culprits. I figured if I asked Lyric directly—with someone else around, of course—I'd see something in her eye that would tell me whether or not she'd had anything to do with Cathy's death. I doubted she'd admit to it directly.

And, of course, if I could take a peek into her room, all the better.

Doubts ran through me as I pulled into the lot. What had made me think I'd be able to spot a lie in the first place? Lyric was an actress. She might not be a good one, or have ever been in any big movies, but that didn't mean she couldn't fool someone like me, especially when her freedom could be on the line.

But what else was I going to do? I couldn't simply drop it, not when I felt like I was getting closer to the truth.

I got out of my car and made my way into Ted and Bettfast, determined not to let anything get in my way.

A tall, scrawny kid I recognized was sweeping the floor when I entered. Well, at this point, I supposed I should call him a man since he was now past eighteen. His acne had cleared up and he was turning out to be a pretty good-looking guy, even if he still wore his hair long enough to cover much of his face.

"Hi, Justin," I said, approaching him.

He glanced at me, and actually met my eye. The Justin I knew had always been gloomy, and a little nervous, yet now it appeared as if his confidence had grown right along with his appearance.

"Hi, Ms. Hancock," he said, smiling. I wasn't sure if I'd ever seen him do that before.

"You seem to be in a good mood."

He shrugged and seemed to shrink in on himself a little. "I guess."

"How's your sister?" Justin used to steal from the guests of the bed-and-breakfast, which I couldn't completely condemn him for since it had helped me solve a case. He'd apparently been doing it to help provide for his little sister, selling what he stole for some extra cash. I didn't know what that said about his parents—if they were still alive, if they were too poor to help, or if they just didn't care. Either way, he had been doing it for a good cause, though I was glad he'd stopped.

"She's good." That smile returned. "Things have been looking up lately."

"That's good to hear."

His smile faltered, eyes darting toward the Bunfords' office door. "You probably shouldn't be here."

"Jo told me," I said, moving to stand behind a tall indoor potted plant so that if Ted or Bett did look out, they wouldn't see me. "I'm here to speak to Lyric Granderson. She's staying in one of the rooms."

Justin nodded. "She is," he said. "But she's not here right now. Left about an hour ago."

"Was she alone?"

"Yeah. But she was in a hurry. I think she was meeting someone."

"Any idea who?" I knew it was a longshot, but you never knew until you asked.

Justin shook his head. "No, but I assume it's the guy who's been coming around visiting her."

"Do you know this guy's name?"

"Sorry. Just some dude." He looked down at his Converse, as if embarrassed he couldn't be of more help. "Didn't even really look at him, so can't really tell you more than he's a guy and he's not from around here."

Typical Justin. I sometimes wondered if he actually *saw* anyone, or if he spent so much time with his eyes lowered, he only caught general impressions of them. He might be coming out of his depressed shell more and more, but he wasn't quite all the way there yet.

I looked past Justin, toward the stairs. Lyric's room was up there somewhere. She was gone now, but could be back at any moment. I doubted the Bunfords would let me sit around to wait for her, not that I wanted to. And if she didn't come back until late tonight, there was no way I could wait. I had too much to do.

An idea crept into my head then, one that had

been forming ever since I'd started suspecting Lyric of stealing the necklace. I tried to resist it, I really did, but I desperately wanted to get to the bottom of Cathy's murder before Vicki and Mason decided to postpone—or worse, cancel—their wedding.

"Do you think I could have a look around Lyric's room?" I asked, keeping my voice low, just in case someone was listening.

Justin's eyes widened. "I don't know about that, Ms. Hancock. I can't lose this job."

"Ted and Bett don't need to know," I said. "I could go up by myself, have a look around, and be out of there before anyone is the wiser. You could say you never saw me if someone does catch me. But they won't," I added when his eyes widened in alarm. "I'll be careful."

"Her door will be locked," Justin said. "She's pretty particular about that. She even warned us against cleaning her room. I guess she values her privacy more than she cares about clean sheets."

Either that, or she was hiding something. *Like a stolen necklace.* I wanted to have a look around even more now.

"Just a few minutes," I pressed. "I promise I won't get you into trouble."

Justin glanced toward the office door once more. He gnawed on his lower lip for a few seconds, before nodding. "Okay," he said. "What do you want me to do?"

I considered it. If I took his keys and was caught, Justin would get into trouble. They'd either think he'd helped me on purpose, or simply had been careless enough to leave his keys lying around where someone like me could snatch them up. Either way, it might get him fired, and I didn't want that to happen on account of my nosiness.

But if the door was unlocked when I went upstairs . . .

I told Justin what to do and then found a dark corner to wait in. He went upstairs, looking as nervous as a cat dropped into the middle of a dog kennel. He'd told me which room was Lyric's, and I was glad to note it wasn't one of the ones in which a murder victim had already stayed. That would have been a little too creepy, even for me.

I counted down the seconds, positive the Bunfords would come out and catch me at any moment, but after only twenty seconds or so, Justin returned. He flashed me a nod, and then went back to sweeping the floor, though now his back was stiff and he kept darting glances toward the stairs and the office.

If I don't hurry, he might accidentally give me away. The guy looked so guilty, he very well might confess without Ted or Bett asking him anything other than how he was doing.

I'd better make this quick, then.

I snuck up the stairs, taking them quickly, shoulders hunched, just in case. There were no sounds upstairs, which I took to mean there were currently no guests in house, though I supposed someone could have been reading or sleeping. I didn't want to wake them if that was the case, lest they call down and complain.

Lyric's room was at the end of the hall. I tried the doorknob and was happy to note Justin had done his job and unlocked it for me. I slipped inside, and closed the door carefully so that it made only the faintest of clicks. Then, I turned to take in the room.

The room was much like the others I'd been in at Ted and Bettfast. Simple. Wardrobe against the wall, a desk, a bed piled high with pillows. The TV here was small, attached to a wall that could use a new coat of paint. The smell of Lyric's perfume dominated the space, though I could still smell the faint hint of moisture, as if there was a leak somewhere in the room. If there was, I couldn't spot the source.

My gaze immediately moved to the dresser, where a jewelry box sat. Heart hammering, I hurried across the room. Could it really be this easy? If I opened it and the necklace was right there, then I'd have my killer, or at least, one of the co-conspirators. If it wasn't Lyric herself who'd done the deed, she would know who had, since they would have brought the necklace to her. I could hand the information off to the police and let them sort it out.

With trembling hands, I reached out and tested the box. It was the kind that looked like a mini wardrobe, complete with a lock, and I was afraid Lyric might have locked it before leaving, but the jewelry box opened when I tugged at it.

Diamonds, emeralds, even a few rubies glimmered from inside. Rings, and a few necklaces, were carefully hung from small hooks meant for that purpose. Many of the pieces had to be expensive.

But Gina's necklace wasn't there.

I closed the box and tried the desk drawers, but they were empty of all but blank stationery and a few pens. Moving to the bedside tables, I checked the drawers there and was likewise met with nothing but a ratty Bible and a balled-up tissue full of enough dust, I knew it had been there for the last couple of years.

Lyric's luggage wasn't immediately evident, so I

went to the wardrobe next. Inside, I found a few light dresses hung up on padded hangers, a couple pairs of shoes below. A carry-on bag lay next to the shoes. I opened it to find makeup, a couple of cheap, unopened toothbrushes, and other personal items. No necklace.

"Where would she put you?" I wondered aloud. The room had a closet that was too small to hang anything up without the shoulders rubbing the walls, hence the wardrobe. Inside, Lyric had stuffed her suitcases. There were three in total, and they were my last hope of finding the necklace before Lyric returned.

She could have it on her. I doubted she'd wear it in public, but that didn't mean she wouldn't keep it buried in her purse. It would probably be safer that way.

Doubt filled me as I pulled the first suitcase from the closet. I opened it to find more clothing, including four bathing suits, each skimpier than the last. I checked all the pockets, and felt around the edges, but there were no telltale lumps telling me she'd hid the necklace inside a hidden pocket or in the lining.

I zipped up the suitcase, and went through the final two suitcases, only to find more of the same. She'd packed as if she planned on staying for weeks. Odd, but it didn't get me any closer to learning whether or not she'd had anything to do with Cathy's death. Overpacking wasn't a crime.

I turned away from the closet and, for the first time, noticed something was lying on the bed, next to the pillow. In fact, I think I'd taken it for one of the white pillows when I'd first entered. The stack of pages was bound, and turned facedown, so I couldn't see the print. It looked to be a couple hundred pages.

I crossed the room and, curious, picked up the stack and turned it over to read what it said.

Return of the Pirate Thief.

I frowned at the title. Was this a movie script? The title sounded vaguely familiar—not that I'd heard it exactly, but it reminded me of something else I couldn't quite place. Lyric's name was scrawled on the title page, barely legible. Whoever had written it seriously needed to take a class on handwriting.

I was about to open to the first page when the door to the room flew open.

I spun around, denials already forming on my lips. When I saw it wasn't Lyric Granderson standing just inside the doorway, however, but a very angry Bett Bunford, the denials died, unuttered.

"What are you doing in here?" she asked, voice low, dangerous. She wasn't just angry; she was furious. I knew nothing I said was going to make her simply walk away and forget she'd seen me. Bett appeared far older than when I'd first met her, a product of everything that had happened around her property since people had started turning up dead in Pine Hills. Her hands, once strong, looked frail, but her voice was as firm as ever when she spoke.

"The door was unlocked," I said. "I was looking for Lyric and thought something might have happened to her." The lie felt weak on my lips.

Bett narrowed her eyes at me, and then shouted, "Ted! Call the police! We have an intruder."

I gasped and started forward, but she raised a hand toward me. I stopped, not wanting to agitate her any further. She was old and I probably could have shrugged her off if she tried to grab me, but that would only make things worse. She knew my name. If

I fled the scene now, who knew what kind of charges Buchannan would try to nail me with.

"There's no reason to call the cops," I said, hoping to reason with her. "I wasn't doing anything wrong. Like I said, the door was unlocked and I came in to make sure everything was okay. After what happened before, I was worried about Lyric." The last time I'd entered a room uninvited, I'd found a body, so I thought it was a believable lie.

Bett's mouth pressed into a fine line, nearly vanishing amid all the wrinkles. Obviously, she wasn't falling for it. "We'll let the police decide what your intentions might have been," she said. "Come on out of there. I'm not letting you out of my sight."

Knowing that this wasn't going to end well for me, I lowered my head, muttered, "Yes, ma'am," and followed Bett Bunford out of Lyric's room, and down the stairs, to await my doom.

19

"You know, you didn't need to put me in here," I said from my cell. I was sitting on an uncomfortably thin cot mattress, trying my best not to get angry. It would help no one.

Buchannan glanced at me and shook his head. He otherwise didn't respond.

"Fine, be that way," I muttered, propping my elbows on my knees so I could plant my face in my hands. I didn't want him to see my frustration.

Buchannan, of course, had been the cop to come get me from Ted and Bettfast. He had taken inordinate delight in hauling me away at Bett Bunford's behest. I'd tried to talk to him, to explain what I had been doing in Lyric's room, but how could I do that and *not* make myself look guilty. There was no way around it; I was snooping. And unless I wanted to get Justin into trouble, they could easily add breaking and entering to my list of petty crimes.

And what had I gotten out of it? I'd learned nothing. Lyric didn't have the necklace secreted away in her room, nor did she have some sort of damning piece of evidence lying around in open view. There was the script, I guess, but what did that tell me? That she was an actress? I already knew that.

I did wonder if it was the script to the movie Gina and Frederick were in. If so, how had she gotten it? Had one of them passed it on to her? The director? Or was it the script for another movie entirely?

And did it even matter?

I sighed dramatically, hoping Buchannan would take pity on me and at least let me sit somewhere that wasn't behind bars. At least he'd thrown me in one of the nice cells upstairs, rather than the disused basement ones. While the cot wasn't what I'd call comfortable, it was at least clean.

"I met your wife," I said, when he didn't react to my sigh. "She's nice. She told me you two have talked about me. From what I hear, you don't hate me as much as you pretend to."

He glanced up and strode over to my cell. "It appears I might have to reevaluate my opinion in that regard." He sounded mildly amused.

"Come on." I practically whined it. He was enjoying this *way* too much. "I didn't do anything. The door was unlocked! All I wanted to do was talk to Lyric."

"And go through her things?"

"There's no evidence of that," I said, face getting hot.

"Uh-huh. Mrs. Bunford said she caught you red-handed, with one of Ms. Granderson's belongings in hand. Are you calling her a liar?"

"Well, no." I rose and crossed over to the bars. "But I wasn't trying to cause any trouble. I shouldn't have gone in, but thought I should check on her, just in case the killer struck again. I saw the script, and was curious. There was no ill intent. It's just a big misunderstanding."

"Right." He drew out the word and rolled his eyes.

"Chief will be here any minute. You can tell her that and see where it gets you."

Great. Patricia Dalton was already disappointed with me. At the rate I was going, she was going to flat-out disown me. She'd always taken my side before, usually letting me off with a warning to keep my nose out of police business whenever I ended up on the wrong side of the law. I was pretty sure I was running out of warnings.

I returned to my cot and plopped down, dejected. It wasn't like I'd murdered anyone. The police were wasting their time dragging me in here, simply because I had been found in an unlocked room without the resident present. I hadn't stolen anything, so what could they really do to me?

Buchannan left the room, leaving me alone to contemplate where exactly I went wrong. Pine Hills wasn't normally a high-crime area, so the cells were usually empty, and other than me, they were now. In all the times I'd been locked up, I'd never seen another inmate. I thought I was the only repeat visitor, which said a lot about both me, and the town.

The minutes ticked by. I tapped my foot, before rising and pacing. After only a few minutes of that, I was seated again, wondering how I was going to talk my way out of this one. I *had* snuck into Lyric's room; there'd be no denying that. And since I'd found no incriminating evidence that proved she had been involved in Cathy's death, I wouldn't even be able to give the police a reason to look lightly upon my infraction.

"What am I going to do with you?" I looked up as Chief Dalton entered, shaking her head. She had her hat in hand, and was spinning it slowly, fingers running along the brim. "Every time I turn around, you're here."

"I'm sorry," I said, going for contrite. "I know I shouldn't have done it."

"You're right; you shouldn't have." She walked over to my cell and unlocked it. She opened the door and stepped aside. "After you."

I darted out of the cell, thankful I wasn't going to be spending the night there. I didn't want to have to explain *that* to my dad.

"We're going to interrogation one," she said, causing my heart to sink right back down to my stomach. Chief Dalton returned her hat to her head and leveled me with a stare. "We need to have a little chat."

"Sounds great."

She grunted an unamused laugh, and turned to lead the way.

Head down, I trudged my way through the station, to interrogation room one. Buchannan was standing at the front desk with a young female cop I didn't know. Behind him, Officer Becca Garrison looked on, frowning at me like I was a disobedient child.

Maybe I was. It seemed like I was finding myself in this position more and more lately. No matter how hard I tried, I couldn't seem to make anyone here like me—other than the Daltons. Each time I came close to winning someone over, I did something stupid and got caught where I shouldn't be.

Chief Dalton followed me into the interrogation room, closing the door behind us. She gestured toward the far end of the table, waited for me to take a seat in the hard plastic chair, and then sat down herself. She removed her hat, set it aside, and then folded her hands in front of her. She stared at them for a long couple of seconds before meeting my eye.

"Okay," she said. "Explain yourself."

"I was there to talk to Lyric Granderson," I said.

"About?"

I looked down at my own hands. "The necklace."

I could almost *feel* Chief Dalton's frown. "The one found on the victim?"

I nodded. "Lyric believes the necklace belongs to her." I gave the chief a brief rundown of what I knew in regard to the necklace, leaving out my own personal speculation about what I thought it meant when it came to Cathy's death. I'd leave that for her to decide.

Chief sat back in her seat and regarded me a long moment before speaking. "That doesn't explain why you were in Ms. Granderson's room without her present, nor without her permission."

"I went up to talk to her, found the door unlocked, and went inside." I tried not to flinch with the lie, and I think I mostly succeeded. I hated lying to Chief Dalton. If she knew the truth, that I'd talked an innocent man into helping me, she would lose whatever respect she had left for me. I didn't want that. While I might not be looking to date her son any longer, we *were* friends.

"Ms. Granderson believes she locked her door before she left."

Uh-oh. "You talked to her?"

"I did."

I scrambled for something to say, and only came up with, "What did she say?"

"Lucky for you, she doesn't want to press charges. Nor does Ted or Bett Bunford. You are not to go back to the bed-and-breakfast, however. If you do, you'll find yourself in a cell so fast, your head will spin."

I nodded, grateful. "I was only peeking," I said. "I thought that if maybe she stole the real necklace, then perhaps she'd have it in her room. When I saw the door was unlocked . . ." I trailed off at the shake of her head.

"You just happened to test the knob and found it unlocked? I find that hard to believe."

"I'm nosy."

I wasn't sure how to take it, but Chief Dalton seemed to accept that explanation. "Do you believe Ms. Granderson had anything to do with Ms. Carr's murder?"

My eyebrows shot skyward. Was she actually asking me my opinion? "I'm not sure," I said, carefully. This could also be some sort of trick to implicate myself in unlawful snooping. I had a feeling I wasn't completely off the hook quite yet.

Chief Dalton leaned forward again, forced me to look at her. "I'm not going to nail you for what you did. If Ms. Granderson and Mr. and Mrs. Bunford are comfortable with your banning, I am too." She held up a finger, much like my mother used to do when she was going to lecture me and wanted to cut off any objections I might have before I could start. "But if you know something and aren't telling me, I'm going to come after you. I know you. You couldn't leave a murder alone, even if you tried."

Compliment? I doubted it.

"I didn't find the necklace," I said.

"I didn't think you would. We found it on Ms. Carr."

"You found a fake one," I reminded her. "Gina insists the one she had was real."

"And you think whoever has the real necklace now could very well be our killer?"

"I do." Or at least, I hoped so. I supposed it was possible that whoever took it could have discarded it or, worse, planted it on someone else.

"And if this necklace has nothing to do with Ms. Carr's death?"

I shrugged. "Then I don't know what to tell you." And I was being honest. Other than rumor, I didn't really know anything. I was sure the police already knew about the various arguments between the actors and Cathy Carr. And if not, they'd find out on their own eventually. It wasn't like I had to force anyone to tell me about them, so the spats weren't any great secrets. If I did bring them up myself, it would only make Chief Dalton realize how much I'd been asking around, and I was pretty sure she wouldn't approve.

As much as I wanted the killer caught, I didn't want to spend the rest of the day explaining myself. Selfish? Maybe. But right then, I just wanted out of there.

Chief Dalton rubbed at her eyes and sighed. "Would you listen if I told you not to go near my suspects?"

"Of course, I'd listen." Obey? I wasn't so sure about that.

Chief seemed to realize the same. "You do realize you would be our top suspect if we didn't know you so well," she said. "You're the only person we can place at the house that night. You had the weapon in hand when the Pattersons returned home. If this was some other town, you'd likely already be sitting behind bars."

"Thanks?" It came out as a question.

"And I suppose I'd better tell you that we were at your place earlier. Got a couple of calls saying you might have evidence in your home."

Gina. Vicki had warned me her mom was pressing the police to look for her necklace at my place, but I didn't think they'd actually do it.

"And?" I asked, keeping my face neutral.

"Found nothing, as expected. Your father was friendly and cooperative, let us in without complaint. He did keep a close eye on us, though." She chuckled as if it amused her.

"I didn't kill Cathy. And I didn't steal anything," I said.

"I know." Chief Dalton gave me a weary smile. "Please, just tell me if you learn anything. I'd rather not have to investigate *your* murder because you got too close to the wrong person."

"I will," I promised. And I would; once I had some time outside the police station to reflect on what I actually *did* know. So far, it was all just speculation and rumor. You couldn't build a case on that.

"And stay away from Lyric Granderson. She has a solid alibi."

"She does?"

Chief Dalton frowned as if she hadn't meant to tell me that, and then stood. "Trust me. It wasn't her."

I tentatively rose from my seat. When she didn't tell me to sit back down, I followed her to the door.

"I'll have Officer Garrison drive you to your car. You won't make me regret letting you go, will you?"

"No, ma'am. I'll get right in and drive home as soon as she drops me off." My car was still at Ted and Bettfast. And while the temptation to go in and talk to Lyric, even to apologize, would be strong, I was determined to resist it.

For now.

"I guess I'll have to be satisfied with that."

Chief Dalton led me out of the interrogation room and to the front, where she handed me off to a grim Officer Garrison. She took me to her cruiser and opened the back door for me. I slid in, hating the fact I would look like a criminal to anyone looking. I guess, in some ways, I was.

But I was trying to solve a murder, just like the police were. So what if I didn't have the authority to do so? It was a free country. I should be allowed to talk to people, right?

I pouted all the way back to my car, which wasn't exactly adult of me, but darn it, I was frustrated. Garrison didn't say a word on the way there, nor as she opened the door to let me out.

"Thanks," I told her, hoping she'd at least speak to me. We'd just started to get to know—and like—one another better recently, and it looked like we were right back to square one.

She grunted, shook her head, and got back into her car. She drove away without a word, let alone a good-bye wave.

So much for our budding friendship.

I looked toward Ted and Bettfast. The Bunfords were inside, likely telling all their employees to keep a lookout for me and report to them the moment they saw me. It hadn't worked the first time, but I was betting no one would disobey them now. Upstairs, a curtain swished and I saw Lyric look out at me. I raised a hand and waved. Surprisingly, she returned the gesture before vanishing back into her room.

Maybe Chief Dalton was right and I was looking into the wrong person. Lyric might have wanted the necklace, but that didn't mean she would kill someone for it. I was even starting to believe she wouldn't even *ask* someone to do it for her.

But what exactly was her alibi? Did it exonerate someone else? Like, had she been with the mysterious man Justin had said she was going to meet today? If so, it would help me narrow down the suspects.

I got into my car and put any and all thoughts of talking to Lyric about her alibi—or the necklace—out of my mind. That path would only lead to trouble, and I'd had just about as much trouble as I could handle for one day.

20

Dad and Laura were watching a movie together when I got home, which seemed to be something they did quite often. I considered joining them, but honestly, I wasn't in the mood to sit and forget. And if I joined them, it would inevitably lead to conversation, and I didn't really want to talk about my day. I couldn't stand to see the disappointment on Dad's face when he learned I'd spent a part of my day behind bars.

So, like a coward, I headed straight for the kitchen and started up some coffee. Dad glanced back at me, as did Laura, but neither of them rose. I could tell they were both curious, but they remained seated, which I appreciated.

My coffee finished percolating. I doctored it up, and then sat down at the island counter to drink it and think. I refused to let my brush with the law deter me from finding out who had killed Cathy, and saving Vicki's wedding. I kind of felt like they were one in the same. I mean, how could Vicki get married knowing one of her guests might be a murderer?

"What's on your mind, Buttercup?"

I looked up from my coffee, startled. Dad was sitting across from me, giving me a worried look. I wasn't sure when he'd sat down, or if he'd been trying to talk to me for the last few minutes or what. Laura was no longer in the living room, and the TV was off. I had no idea that they'd moved, or how long ago.

"Nothing," I lied. "It's been a long day, is all."

"Has it? Want to talk about it?"

Did I? When I'd first arrived home, I sure hadn't. But now, I wasn't so sure. Dad had a way of comforting me when I was at my worst, and could often guide me in the right direction, even without realizing he was doing it.

"I'm just worried about the wedding," I said, which was the truth, if not the entire truth. "This whole thing has been stressful for everyone."

Dad smiled and took my hand. "We'll make it through it unscathed. You'll see."

"I hope so."

"The police were here earlier," he said, dropping his eyes. "They wanted to have a look around. I told them they could, since you have nothing to hide. I hope that was okay?"

"I heard," I said. "I think Gina sicced them on me."

"Would she really do that?"

I gave him a flat look.

"I guess she might," he said. "You aren't mad at me for letting them in, are you?"

"No," I said. "I'm annoyed that it came to this, but glad it's over with. Nothing was found, which means they have no reason to suspect me of anything. I'd count that as a win."

"I still don't like it. I should have called you and asked you what you wanted me to do."

"You did good."

My phone rang then, causing me to jump. I plucked it out of my purse and, noting Will's name on the screen, I hurriedly answered, rising from my seat at the counter as I did.

"Will! I'm glad you called."

"Krissy." He paused. "Would it be okay if I stopped by?"

I was barely able to contain my excitement. Dad was one sort of comfort; Will was another entirely. "Of course! I'll be here all night." And, oh, how I could use some Will-and-me time.

"Okay." Another pause. "I'll see you in thirty minutes."

"Great."

He hung up.

Dad was watching me with a knowing grin on his face. "Hot date?" he asked, causing my face to flame.

"No." Or at least I wasn't going to tell him if it was or not. "Will's coming over." I stated it casually, as if we'd simply sit around and play Scrabble. I was hoping for a lot more than that.

"Laura and I were thinking of heading out for a walk anyway," Dad said, rising. "I think we'll do that. It's a beautiful night."

I almost told him not to be silly and stay, but then realized I'd feel much more comfortable if they weren't here when Will arrived. It had been so long since I'd seen my boyfriend, I was practically giddy with excitement. I fully planned on planting a kiss on him the moment he stepped through the door, and that was something I didn't want my dad to see.

"He'll be here in thirty minutes," I said, hoping I didn't sound as eager as I felt.

"Then we'll stay out for a few hours." He winked, and then laughed when I blushed so hard, I felt faint. "Let me get Laura and we'll get out of your hair." He turned and headed for the bedroom.

Thoroughly embarrassed, I waited for Dad to step into the hall and around the corner before I pumped an excited fist. After all I'd been through over the last few days, I could seriously use the stress relief of a Will visit.

Then I looked around the house, and some of my excitement fled.

I hit the cleaning with determination, picking up a stray bowl that held only an empty grape stem, and running the sweeper to clear away Misfit's fur, which was coating the living room floor. Once that was done, I hurried into the bedroom to change—Dad and Laura had left while I was sweeping. I didn't have time for a shower, but I did take a moment to wash my face. I'd just finished fixing my hair when there was a knock at the door.

I gave myself a quick once-over, scratched Misfit behind the ears before shutting him in the bedroom— I didn't want him escaping out the door in case our hello lasted longer than was decent—and then rushed for the front door. I flung it open, and was about to fling myself into Will's arms when I saw the look on his face.

"May I come in?" he asked, brow pinched, eyes worried. He looked like he'd just received some bad news and wasn't looking forward to sharing it.

"Yeah, of course." I stepped aside, wondering if something had happened to someone in his family.

I hoped not; I liked every single one of them. Or at least, the ones I'd met.

Will entered and walked straight to the island counter. He didn't sit, but instead turned to face me. "Are you okay?" he asked. "I've heard about everything that's happened and, well, I'm concerned."

"I'm okay," I said. I refrained from adding, "Now that you're here," since it would not only be cheesy, but with the way he was looking at me, it didn't seem appropriate. I was becoming decidedly nervous, but was afraid to ask him about it outright.

"Good, good." He looked down at his feet and fell silent.

I studied him, his creamer-rich coffee skin, the dark eyes, and felt my heart do a double beat. He had all the looks a woman could want, the money—if you're into that sort of thing—and the charisma.

And yet, he was almost never there when I needed him anymore. Sure, he was here now, but I really could have used his shoulder to lean upon when I'd found Cathy. I'd talked to him on the phone, of course, but that wasn't the same as a face-to-face meeting where I could touch his hand, feel his warmth.

I couldn't hold back any longer. "Is everything okay?" I asked. As far as I knew, he had a disaster of his own that he'd been dealing with and *I'd* been the one who hadn't been around to make him feel better. With Vicki's wedding and getting Death by Coffee ready for the reception, I had been pretty lost in my own world as of late. And then, with the murder, it was a wonder I wasn't pulling my hair out.

"I'm good," he said, flashing me the briefest of smiles. "I had a strange day at work the other day. Some guy from out of town came in complaining of stomach pains. He wouldn't fill out any forms, just asked if someone could check him out. I think he was here for the wedding."

"What was his name?"

"Jack or something like that. I can't remember his last name. Carl looked him over and gave him something to calm his stomach. I didn't see him for much more than a few seconds."

"Could it be Jacques Kenway?"

"Yeah, I think that's it."

Hmm, interesting. "What was wrong with him?"

Will shrugged. "Ulcer, I think. I'd claim doctor–patient confidentiality, but he wasn't actually a patient. It was weird." He frowned down at his hands. "It was like he was trying to hide something. Either that, or he didn't want anyone to know he was sick. It made me wonder if he used other doctors like this for drugs. It didn't feel on the up-and-up, though honestly, he could just be on the odd side."

It wasn't surprising an actor had an ulcer, especially considering everything that had happened recently. Still, like Will, it made me wonder if there was more to it. Jacques's name had been coming up an awful lot lately, and not in a good way.

But I pushed all thoughts of that aside. There was something more Will wasn't telling me, and I could tell by the way he refused to look at me, I wasn't going to want to hear it.

"Coffee?" I asked, wanting to push that moment down the line as far as I could.

"Sure."

I entered the kitchen and put on a half pot. I motioned for Will to take a seat at the island counter and went about gathering the creamer and sugar.

I set them down, avoiding Will's eye, and then poured us each a cup before finally taking a seat across from him.

"Okay, lay it on me," I said.

Will looked pained, but didn't try to deny there was something more to say. He added sugar to his coffee, then a tiny touch of creamer, before speaking.

"I've been offered a job," he said, stirring his coffee. "A good job."

"That's great!" Yet, why didn't it feel great? It felt like someone had punched me in the stomach.

He nodded, smiled sadly. "It's in Arizona."

My heart hiccupped and then steadied. "Arizona?"

"Yeah." He shrugged one shoulder. "I applied for the position a year ago, thinking I'd never get it. They filled it briefly, but the guy they hired got sick and is going to retire. They called a few months back, telling me it was mine if I wanted it. I've had time to think about it since they were waiting to make sure the other guy didn't change his mind, but I'll have to let them know soon."

"Are you going to take it?" I asked, knowing the answer already.

"I want to," Will said, finally meeting my eye. There was a whole lot of concern there. And pain. "But, well . . ."

I got it. Me.

We looked at each other across the counter, and I realized I wasn't angry. Sad, yeah, of course, but not angry.

"You should take it," I said. "Especially if it's a promotion."

"It is," Will said. "I lose my own practice, but this is

a chance for me to move up, really make a difference."
He sounded excited, and I knew I couldn't take that
from him. "Carl and Darrin will stay behind with
Paige. They'll take over the office and take over my
patients. You won't have to look for another doctor or
anything."

"That's good," I said, though the thought hadn't
even crossed my mind.

"I'm sorry," Will said, entire body sagging. "I've
really made a mess of this."

"Don't be sorry," I said, and found I could smile,
despite the ache in my stomach. "This is a good
thing."

"It is," he said. "But you . . . I should have handled
it better." He fiddled with his coffee mug a moment
before going on. "I've been pulling away," he admitted. "Over the last few months, when I realized I was
going to be taking this job, I thought it better if we
eased off. I couldn't ask you to leave your life behind;
I'd never forgive myself if I did. So, I thought I'd
slowly break away, making it easier on the both of us
when I finally did have to go." He laughed a bitter
laugh. "Well, make it easier on me, I suppose."

I remained silent. I'd noticed how few and far between our dates had become. I'd feared it was because
he was breaking up with me or I'd done something to
offend him.

It appeared I was right on one count.

"I should have considered your feelings more," he
went on. "I mean, I did, but not in the right way. I
could see how my actions were affecting you, but I was
afraid that if I told you why I was staying away, I'd hurt
you more. I put myself in a position where no matter

what I did, I would hurt you, and that, in turn, made me miserable." Another brief, unhappy smile. "I really did mess up."

"It's okay," I said. "You didn't mess anything up."

"I should have told you up-front."

"You should have," I conceded. "But I'm not mad at you. I understand why you did it." I might not like it, but I understood it.

"And now, with everything else that's happened, I wasn't sure I should tell you. But I felt so guilty lately, I had to get it off my chest." He sighed. "I thought maybe we could try the long-distance thing, but that would never work, not with our jobs. We're both always so busy."

I rose and walked around the counter. Will watched me the entire way, as if he wasn't sure what I was going to do. There was a stiffness to his posture, like he was mere seconds from bolting.

I stopped before him, met his eye, and was forced to fight back tears. Good-byes sucked. I looked at him, and instead of loss, I felt relief that he'd finally found the strength to tell me. I smiled to show him I was happy for him, and then, I hugged him.

His reaction was immediate. His entire body sagged into me as he wrapped his arms around me. "I'm so sorry, Krissy." His voice was choked with tears.

"It's okay," I said again, struggling against crying myself. And it was. Now that I knew what was going on with him, it was a big weight that had been lifted from my shoulders. "We'll both be okay."

We parted, each of us having to pause to wipe away our tears.

"I can still go with you to the wedding," he said

once we both composed ourselves. "If you want me to. They wanted me to fly out in two days, but I can stay here."

"No, go," I said. "You don't want them thinking they can't count on you."

"Are you sure?" he asked. "I'd much rather stay with you. It might only be a couple of days, but . . ." He shrugged.

"I'm sure." I took his hand and squeezed to prove it. "Take the job. I'll be okay here." My face turned stern. "But you'd better write."

"I'll do better and call," he said.

"Good."

He rose and swallowed as if he was having trouble. If he cried again, I was going to completely lose it. I was barely holding on as it was.

"I should probably go," he said, sucking in a deep breath. "Thank you for understanding and not kicking my ass for dumping this on you with everything else that's happened."

"I'm glad you did." I paused, gave a little bark of a laugh that sounded as if I was near hysterics. "Well, I'm glad you told me. I'll miss you."

"I'll miss you too."

I walked Will to the door. He hugged me once more, kissed my cheek, and then stepped outside.

I watched him go, heart breaking just a little. I might be okay with him leaving, but it still sucked. It was a miracle that I'd landed him in the first place, and to have held on to him for this long was more than I could have asked for.

Will got into his car and started it. He honked his horn and waved. I returned the gesture, and then he backed out of my driveway—and in many ways, my life—for the last time. A moment later, he was gone.

I closed the door, made straight for the freezer, and removed a tub of rocky road ice cream. Eschewing a bowl, I grabbed a spoon and carried the entire container to the living room, flipped on the TV, and then dug in, determined to eat my troubles away.

21

I felt surprisingly good when I woke up the next morning. My stomach was a little on the icky side, thanks to all the ice cream, but otherwise, I thought I could face the day without breaking down over Will's imminent departure.

When I drifted out of the bedroom, I wasn't met with the smell of breakfast like I was accustomed to. I went out into the dining room, curious, to find both Dad and Laura sitting at the table, dressed as if they were planning on going out.

"Hey, Buttercup," Dad said, rising. He crossed the room to where I stood, and gave me a quick kiss on the cheek. "How are you doing?"

"Fine," I said, looking from one to the other. Laura had stood and was giving me a worried look. "What's going on?"

"Nothing," Dad said, glancing back at Laura. "Well, I mean, nothing bad."

"We just want to make sure you're okay," Laura said.

"I am."

"Are you sure?" Dad walked over to the trash and

picked up the empty tub of ice cream. "I know what this means."

"It's nothing." I looked at my feet, ashamed I'd given in and eaten the whole thing.

Dad started forward, but Laura beat him to me. She draped an arm over my shoulder and pulled me close so our heads rested against one another. "If you need to talk, I'm here," she said. "No need to include men." She shot a sly smile toward Dad.

Some of the sadness about Will's departure tried to sneak in then, but I swallowed it back. It's hard to admit when you're hurting. But while I was sad Will was leaving, I would get through it.

"Thank you," I said. "But really, I'm okay." I stepped back and smiled, showing the both of them how okay I really was.

"If you want, we can all go out and get some ice cream together," Dad said. "My treat."

My stomach did a little flip. "I think I'm all ice creamed out," I said. "But thanks."

"What about breakfast?" Laura asked. "We were thinking of going to the Banyon Tree."

Going out to eat with them sounded great, but I wasn't in the mood. "Perhaps later?" I asked. "You guys go ahead."

Dad and Laura shared a look, before Laura took my hand. "Okay. If you change your mind, you know where to find us."

"I do."

"Chin up, Buttercup," Dad said.

I raised my chin. "Yes, sir."

He laughed, and then both he and Laura gathered their things and were gone.

A part of me regretted turning them down, but if I

sat there with a happy couple, it might make me feel Will's absence that much more. And sitting around, thinking about him, would be just as bad, so I decided I needed to take care of a few things around town.

The first thing I did was pick up my phone and call Ted and Bettfast. Neither the Bunfords, nor Lyric, had pressed charges against me, for which I was thankful, but I didn't want to leave it there. I held my breath as the phone rang, worried Bett Bunford would answer. As much as I wanted to apologize to her for my actions, I thought it best to wait. There would be no forgiveness forthcoming from her, at least not for a while.

"Ted and Bettfast, this is Jo speaking."

I breathed a sigh of relief. "Hi, Jo. It's Krissy Hancock."

"Oh. You." She didn't sound happy.

There was a time Jo would have been happy to help me. Now, it was a wonder she hadn't hung up the moment I'd said my name. "I know Bett doesn't want me coming around anymore, but after yesterday, I feel like I need to apologize to your guest Lyric Granderson."

"I see," Jo said.

"I'd call her room directly, but I'm not sure how." I wasn't even sure the rooms had their own lines. It was more likely Lyric would be using her cell. Either way, I didn't have a number at which I could reach her. And sitting around town, waiting for her to wander by, would be a waste of time.

Jo was silent for a long moment. "I'm not sure I should get her," she said. "Bett was awfully clear about you."

"She doesn't need to come to the phone now," I said. "And you don't have to give me her number."

"I wouldn't do that anyway."

"But could you give her my cell number? She can call me if she wants to talk to me. It'll take the pressure off of you and let Lyric make up her own mind about whether or not she wants to talk to me. Bett can't get mad at you for doing that, can she?"

Another stretch of silence before, "Okay, fine. I can do that."

"Thanks." I rattled off my number. "Tell her she can call anytime." Though I hoped she'd call me back right away. I wasn't exactly known for my patience, and if forced to wait too long, I might do something I might later regret.

"I'll let her know."

"Good. Thank you, Jo."

"Uh-huh. Have a nice day." She hung up.

I settled back with a huff. Now what? I really wanted to talk to Jacques Kenway, but I had no way of contacting him. I supposed I could call up Gina or Frederick and ask them about him. They'd likely have his number, and might know where he was staying.

Then again, Gina had sent the cops after me. I'd find another way to contact Jacques.

Knowing I'd go crazy if I sat and waited for the phone to ring, I decided to watch a little TV to pass the time. Misfit had sauntered into the room sometime while I'd eaten, but hadn't bothered me like he usually would. In fact, he'd barely looked at me at all, choosing instead to sit in front of the front door.

"You like her more than me, don't you?" I asked, only a little jealous.

He looked over at me, and then stood up and walked away, tail swishing.

"Well, she'll be gone soon," I called after him. "You'll come crawling back to me then!"

He flipped his tail once, and then vanished back toward the bedroom.

I started for the living room, wondering if I should buy Misfit a new catnip toy to win back his affection, when the phone rang. I snatched it up and answered after only the first ring.

"Krissy, it's Lyric." She didn't sound thrilled. "I'm returning your call."

"I'm glad you did," I said. "I wanted to apologize for my behavior yesterday. I shouldn't have gone in your room, no matter the reason. I don't know what I was thinking."

"Thank you. Was there anything else?" She didn't sound as if she fully accepted my apology, which was okay. I hadn't expected her to.

"I was hoping we could talk," I said. "Do you have a few minutes?"

She sighed dramatically. "I was going to go out for a walk. I suppose you can join me if you'd like."

"Great! Where?"

"There's a nature trail not far from here. Do you know it?"

No, but I wasn't going to tell her that. "Sure."

"I'll be there." She hung up.

After a quick Google, I learned that Pine Hills did indeed have a nature trail called the Squirrel's Trail. It was only a couple of miles from Ted and Bettfast, tucked away past a golf course and a few large, private houses.

"I'll be back soon!" I called to Misfit as I gathered

my keys and purse. He didn't come running to see me off. I left the house, figuring that I would definitely need to get him something soon. I missed having him twined around my legs at every step.

I drove to the trail quickly, afraid Lyric would get started without me. If she did, there was no way I'd catch up to her, let alone find her, and I wasn't going to stand around the parking lot waiting for her to finish.

Thankfully, she was still stretching when I pulled into the lot. A big squirrel with the word "Trail" written stylishly along its tail made up the sign, which stood next to the entrance. There were quite a lot of cars here, most of them of the expensive variety. Apparently, the Squirrel's Trail was where the rich folk of Pine Hills went for their exercise.

The smell of pine and water hit me the moment I opened my car door. I sucked in a deep breath, which was a mistake. My nose started itching immediately, warning me there were quite a few flowers out here as well. I barely refrained from sneezing as I started across the lot.

Lyric was dressed in running shorts and a tight, stretchy shirt that left absolutely nothing to the imagination. I, on the other hand, was wearing a regular pair of shorts, the kind with actual pockets, and a T-shirt. Thankfully, I'd been smart enough to put on tennis shoes, rather than flip-flops, though it had been a near thing. I wasn't exactly on speaking terms with exercise.

She gave me a quick once-over, grimaced, and then started for the start of the trail. "We can talk while we walk," she said. "Do try to keep up."

I hurried after her, already worried this was going

to be a really bad idea. I normally didn't spend much time working out, and while walking wasn't as strenuous as running or lifting weights, I had a feeling I was going to struggle. Lyric walked with her arms pumping, in quick, determined strides that were just this side of a run. I sort of flopped my arms and dragged my feet as I moved.

I panted up next to her, only slightly disconcerted by the spongy feel of the track. What did they make these things out of? Old tires? "Thanks for taking the time to talk to me."

She nodded, but didn't speak.

I took that as an invitation to talk. "How well do you know Jacques Kenway?" I asked.

"Jacques?" she shrugged. "We're acquaintances."

"You aren't dating?"

She shot a glance at me. "No." She sounded offended. "Why would you think that?"

"The rumor mill," I said. "I heard someone was visiting you in your room at the bed-and-breakfast. A man. And since Jacques is good-looking . . ." It was my turn to shrug.

Lyric's nose wrinkled. "I don't think so. Jacques might be a pleasure to look at, but his personality leaves a lot to be desired."

"You have no interest in him?"

"None." She shuddered. "I don't even know why you'd think I'd have anything to do with him. He isn't my type."

We rounded a corner and passed two other power-walkers, who both nodded to Lyric and gave me a pitying look. I was panting, and seriously struggling to keep up with the much fitter woman.

"If it wasn't Jacques, who was visiting you?"

"First off, I don't know how that is any business of yours." Lyric stepped around a branch that had fallen into the trail, and pressed on. "And secondly, even if it was Jacques, that doesn't mean we are dating. Men and women can share the same space without being an item, you know?"

I frowned, and then grimaced as my legs started barking at me. "So, it *was* Jacques?"

Lyric, either frustrated by my questions or because she was taking pity on me, stopped. My hands immediately found my knees as I gasped for air. She'd said she was going for a walk, but what we had just done was a long way from a walk in my book.

"If you must know, we were discussing a movie," she said.

"The one you came here about?"

"No, another one. Jacques thinks he can get me a role in it. We were running lines so that when I get back, I can ace my audition. He knows what the director looks for in his actresses."

I thought back to when I'd seen her at Geraldo's. "Was he the one you were supposed to meet the other night, when you were with Trey and Sage?"

She nodded.

"He stood you up?"

"It wasn't a date," she said, biting off each word. "We were going to discuss the movie. Trey and Sage are having something of a dry spell too." She looked embarrassed to admit she was struggling to find work, but pressed on. "Since we were all in town together for this stupid wedding, I thought it might be a good idea if we all got together. Jacques, apparently, decided it wasn't as important as the rest of us believed."

"What about Vince Conner?"

"What about him?"

"Was he invited?"

Something came across Lyric's face then, something I couldn't pinpoint. Finally, she answered with a simple, "No."

We stepped aside as a group of joggers ran past. They were sweating, but didn't look anywhere close to slowing down. Lyric watched them go, and then looked at me, as if asking why I couldn't do the same.

"No one seems to have a lot to do with Vince," I said, refusing to give in to the challenge. If she was willing to stand here in the shade of the pine trees, I was all for it. It was going to be struggle enough to get back to my car without my legs falling off.

"He's . . . different," she said. "I like him, don't get me wrong, but he's a little awkward."

"He seemed pretty interested in you when we first met." Vince had been practically drooling, though Lyric hadn't seemed to notice.

Her eyes narrowed at me. "I don't like what you're implying. Just because I talk to a man doesn't mean we are sleeping together."

"I wasn't implying that," I said, though I was intrigued. I hadn't said she was sleeping with anyone, yet she'd quickly jumped straight to that conclusion. So, did that mean she *was* closer to Vince than she was letting on? Or was it Jacques she was concerned about? Something about her denials felt off, as if there was indeed something going on between her and one of the two men.

But which one?

Asking would be futile, I knew. Lyric was watching me, just waiting to put me in my place for pressing, so I moved on.

"Do you know anything about Jacques's stomach problems?" I asked. "Someone mentioned he went to the doctor to have it checked out."

"*Someone* does a lot of talking," Lyric said, casting a longing glance down the trail. She looked anxious to be running. "I don't know anything about that. You could always ask him yourself if you're curious."

"I wish I could," I said. "I don't know how to get ahold of him."

Lyric started stretching again, warning me she was about to resume her power walk. "That's not a problem." A sinister grin spread across her face. "I can give you his number."

"Great!" I waited.

Lyric rolled her eyes. "Not here. I'll text it to you when I'm done. I don't have it committed to memory, and my phone is in my car."

"Oh." I looked down the path. Just past the trees ahead, I could see the crystal-clear waters of a small lake. Birds were fluttering overhead in the breeze that was causing the branches of the trees to sway. It was beautiful, but I didn't think I could handle another leg of Lyric's walks.

"I think I'll head on back then," I said, shaking my legs as if I'd done a full set of squats. "You go on ahead."

Lyric gave me a cynical smile, and then started walking, arms pumping, entire body tensing and releasing with every step.

"Don't forget to text me his number!" I called after her.

She raised a hand and waved, though she didn't look back.

I turned back the other way, entire body slumping now that she wasn't watching me. We'd only gone a mile, yet I dreaded every step as I worked my slow way back to my car. My eyes were itching, and my nose running. I liked nature, but I'd prefer to watch it from afar.

I decided I wouldn't sit in the parking lot to await her return. There was no telling how long she'd be, and honestly, I wanted out of there. I desperately needed to find someplace where I could put my feet up and relax and that wouldn't trigger my allergies. And maybe have something cold to drink. And sit down. Yeah, I definitely needed to sit down.

And after? Hopefully, I'd get my chance to talk to Jacques. And then, once that was done, I could spend the rest of the day with Dad and Laura.

I just needed to make it back to my car alive.

22

My phone dinged as I was chugging my second bottle of water. Sweat was still dripping from my forehead where I stood in my kitchen, feeling as if I might die. The warm day had turned hot by the time I'd gotten back to my car, and to top it off, when I'd tried to turn on the air-conditioning, only hot air had blown out at me. My car, it seemed, was in its twilight years.

I finished my water and tossed the bottle into the trash with its companion, mind on my poor little Focus. It had served me well for many years now, but seriously struggled last winter, and had only gotten worse since. Once Vicki's wedding was over, it looked like I was going to have to make a trip to the local car dealership to find a replacement.

Feeling as if I might yet survive the day now that I had water in me—though, by now, my stomach was sloshing around and I was feeling decidedly seasick—I picked up the phone and checked the text. As promised, a phone number awaited me.

"Here goes nothing," I said to Misfit, who was perched on the island counter, watching me with a "When's she coming back?" look on his face. Laura and Dad were still out, though I found it hard to believe they were still eating breakfast at this point. Despite what the actors think, there's quite a lot to do in Pine Hills, if you don't mind spending your time in locally owned businesses instead of chain stores.

I scrawled the number down on a pad of paper and then dialed. It rang for so long, I was afraid Jacques was ignoring an unfamiliar number. Just as I was about to hang up, however, he answered with a jaunty "Yo?"

"Hi, Jacques, it's Krissy Hancock."

"Who?"

"Krissy. Vicki's friend. I met everyone at the airport and then again at Death by Coffee."

"Oh, yeah, Krissy." Pause. "How did you get this number?"

"Lyric gave it to me," I said, feeling only mildly guilty for ratting on her. Served her right for how she'd treated me at the trail.

"Really? Huh." Another pause, while he reflected on that. "What can I do for you, Krissy Hancock, Vicki's friend?"

"I was hoping we could talk." I thought about that, and added, "Face-to-face."

"Sure. What about?"

Not wanting to scare him off, I chose my words carefully. "I can't really discuss it over the phone right now. Can we meet somewhere? I promise not to take up too much of your time."

"Cute Cuticles."

"Excuse me?"

"I'm heading to Cute Cuticles now. Meet me there."

A niggling at the back of my mind. A pink, exaggerated sign. Fingernails the size of my head. "At a nail salon?" I asked, not quite sure I'd heard him right.

"I'm overdue," he said. "Come get a manicure with me and we can talk."

I wasn't so sure I wanted to discuss Cathy's murder in front of the manicurist, but this might be my only chance to talk to Jacques before the wedding. Time was quickly running out, and I was no closer to catching the killer.

"I'll meet you there."

Cute Cuticles was housed in a tiny building downtown. The big pink sign out front was just as I'd remembered: artfully drawn fingernails, and the name of the store, but little else. Large windows gave a good look inside, where I could see six chairs, two women dressed in pink, and Jacques Kenway. He was seated in one of the chairs, facing the windows, hands soaking in a bowl.

I entered, feeling about as out of place as I could get. I'd never gone to get my nails done before. No manicures, no hand baths or whatever people do these days. I could barely be bothered to use lotion unless my hands were so dry they were cracking. The only thing I ever did was clip my nails, and normally, that only happened after I broke one of them or sliced myself with a jagged edge, which happened more often than I cared to admit. I worked with my hands all the time at Death by Coffee, so it was inevitable I'd break a nail or two.

Jacques nodded to me as I approached. "I remember you now," he said. "I had a hard time placing you on the phone. They say the memory is the first thing to go." He chuckled. "And I have to admit, I wasn't my best after the flight into town and everything that's happened since."

I didn't know how to respond to that, so I took the seat next to him. One of the women in pink appeared and placed a bowl in front of me. She didn't so much as speak before turning and walking away.

"I went ahead and paid for you," Jacques said. "We can get the same treatment while we have our little conversation. It's supposed to be a good one—a house special. We'll see."

"Thanks," I said, dunking my hands into the water with a nervous frown. I wasn't sure what it contained, other than water. It smelled a little like lavender, actually. When the lukewarm water didn't cause my fingers to start burning or turn funny colors, I relaxed.

"So, what did you want to talk to me about?"

I took a moment to collect my thoughts. So far, Jacques had been the nicest person out of all the people the Pattersons had brought with them, but I didn't trust his smile, his friendly tone. His name had come up so much in conversation, I could be sitting with a killer, and I refused to be disarmed by his sparkling personality.

"How's your stomach?" I asked, just so I could gauge his reaction. I doubted his pains had anything to do with Cathy's death, but it *was* strange how he'd wanted to work around the paperwork at the clinic.

There was a flicker of something in his eye before he shrugged. "Better. When I get stressed, it acts up. Always has. I left my pills at home like a dope, so went in to pick some up. How did you know about it?"

I ignored the last question, not wanting to bring Will into this. "Are you stressed because of Cathy's murder?"

Another flicker in his eye, accompanied by a slight hesitation to his smile. "That's part of it, I suppose. Coming all the way here when I have so much to do back home adds to it. I have a movie coming up and I always get nervous the closer one comes to shooting, even after all these years." He laughed. "You'd think I'd be used to it by now."

I was going to ask him some more questions, but waited when the two women in pink removed our hands from the bowls. Jacques's manicurist was a pretty woman in her mid-twenties who couldn't seem to take her eyes off the good-looking actor. I had an older woman who appeared as if she was having the worst day of her life. She took my hands, looked down at them, scowling as if offended by my lack of care, and then started rubbing a lotion of some kind into them with all the force she could muster.

Jacques was getting a gentler application, and for a few moments, I was forgotten. He murmured something to his manicurist, who giggled and blushed like a schoolgirl before batting playfully at the hand she was holding. I noted how he squeezed her fingers every so often, and the way she would suck in a breath nearly every time it happened.

It was fascinating to watch, really. Did she know he was an actor? I had a feeling Jacques wasn't shy about telling all the pretty girls about what he did for a living, so it was possible.

This went on for a few minutes, and I was just starting to get used to the rubbing when the pain began.

Maybe it was because of my manicurist's bad mood, or maybe it was because of how bad my nails had become, but when she started pushing on the cuticles with this small, metal torture device, it was like she was jamming bamboo stalks up my fingers. I yelped and tried to pull away, but she held on with the fierceness of a tiger.

"Hold still," she barked, jamming at another cuticle.

"Never had a manicure before?" Jacques asked, grinning at my discomfort.

"No!" It came out at a near shout as she moved on to the next nail. "First time."

"I can tell."

Okay, I'm a wimp. I gritted my teeth and tried to find my center, in the hopes I'd somehow forget about the pain. It worked, kind of, and I decided it might be best to go ahead and continue with my questions. Maybe speaking would get my mind off of what this evil woman was doing to me.

"How well did you know Cathy?" I asked, sucking in a sharp breath as my manicurist dug at a particularly stubborn spot. She was biting her lower lip and glowering.

"Not too well, actually," Jacques said, seemingly unfazed by what was happening to his fingers. "I knew of her, of course. I've seen her around. People get married, divorced, married again, so there's always a never-ending supply of weddings to go to. I'm sure I've seen her at quite a few."

"I heard you went with her to Geraldo's here in town?" I asked.

"That's right," he said, not missing a beat despite the contradiction. "We did."

"You fought?"

He shrugged. "I suppose. It was nothing. We didn't actually go there together, if that's what you think. We happened to be hungry at the same time, and when I saw her there, I went over to say hi. Didn't take long before our personalities clashed, so, before things could get out of hand, I left."

"You didn't argue about anything specific?"

"Nah. She wouldn't shut up about the wedding, what she planned on doing with it, and so on. I got tired of it and asked her to stop. She didn't like that."

"It wasn't about any of the rumors?" I asked.

"What rumors?"

"That she liked to steal from her clients, for example."

Jacques shrugged. "If she did, I knew nothing about it." He smiled at his manicurist, who was taking far gentler care of his hands than the older woman was of mine. Of course, his fingernails were already near pristine, so there really wasn't much she needed to do. Maybe that was why he wasn't crying like I was very near doing.

"She was found with the necklace Gina was going to give to Vicki," I said. "Well, a fake one, actually. Do you think she might have stolen the real one and replaced it with the replica?"

Jacques laughed. "I don't think so."

I waited, but he didn't go on. "Why not?" I asked, and then, "Ow! That hurts."

The manicurist glared at me, and then jabbed all the harder.

"I suppose she might have been stealing it, but I doubt she was replacing a real necklace with a fake one."

"Why not?" I asked again.

"It was always fake," Jacques said, dunking his hands back into the water to soak. After a few seconds of that, he removed them again and turned them over so his manicurist could rub something into his fingers and palms.

"Why do you say that?" I asked. I found it hard to believe Gina would give Vicki a fake necklace.

"I've always thought so," Jacques said. "*The Nest of the Viper* was a low-budget flick that could barely afford to shoot in the studio, let alone use real props. Costume jewelry is pretty common in situations like that. I'll admit, it looks pretty real, but if you were to look closely, scratch away the shine, all you'd find is a common, pretty glass."

Could it be possible? Gina hadn't gotten the necklace appraised, so a professional hadn't had the chance to look it over to confirm its value. If the woman who'd given it to her said it was real, who was she to call her a liar?

"Does anyone else know?" I asked.

Jacques shrugged. At this point, his manicurist was wrapping his hands in warm towels. "I doubt it. Too many people see sparkly things and lose their minds." He winked at the young woman as she stood. She blushed and walked away with a giggle. "It's likely they all thought it was real enough, so if Cathy Carr *was* stealing it, she thought she was in for a big payday. Once she tried to pawn it, she would have been sorely disappointed."

If she hadn't been killed for it instead.

My manicurist stopped poking me and pushed my hands into the water, which had cooled. She held them down as if she thought I might pull them out, before tugging them toward her to rub a scented oil of some kind into my fingers and palms.

"Lyric says you two were discussing doing a movie together," I said.

He nodded. "I already have my spot—a cool-as-a-cucumber club owner accused of murder. She wants in on it. I figure I could grease some wheels for her." He looked at his nails briefly, as if appraising them.

"She knows how these things work and has already paid in full, if you know what I mean."

I thought I did, but really didn't want to know. "She said you two barely know each other."

He shrugged, dismissive. "You know how it is. What goes on behind closed doors and all that." He paused. "What's this all about anyway?"

"Nothing, really," I said. "I've been hearing a lot of things lately, and was curious what was true and what wasn't. I even heard one of you lost out on a role in a movie. Any idea who that might be?"

He didn't hesitate. "Vince. He shouldn't have tried to beat me out for the spot. There were better characters for his skill set, but he insisted on trying for the lead, the fool."

"*You* took it from him?"

"I wouldn't say I took it, but yeah, I beat him out for the part. I was surprised he'd agreed to come here at all, to be honest. The man has been a grouch ever since he realized he'd once again be relegated to doing stupid voices."

Grouchy and isolationist, actually. I'd barely seen Vince in town since he'd arrived. Was he keeping to himself because he was upset over the lost opportunity? Or was it because he had a murder on his mind?

"Do you know where I can find Vince?" I asked, thankful that the manicurist seemed to be done torturing me, and had wrapped my aching hands in warm towels.

"Try a bar." Jacques shook his head sadly. "The guy has some talent, but doesn't know how to handle rejection. His reputation has gotten around, so even if he did somehow manage to put on a better audition than me, his penchant for sulkiness and drink would work against him."

"Any idea which bar?" I asked. There weren't a lot of them in town, but I didn't want to go looking in every one on the off chance he'd be there.

"Try the one closest to where he's staying," Jacques said, standing. "It's some cheap hotel at the edge of town, if I remember right."

I thought I knew the place. "Okay, thanks."

"Anytime." He turned to the manicurist. "Hey, if you have time later, I might be free."

Her eyes lit up, and she grabbed a pen and wrote something down on the back of a business card. She handed it over to him with a, "I get off in a couple hours."

"Fantastic." Jacques kissed the card and shoved it into his pocket before turning to me. "Anything else?"

I started to say no, but one more thing came to me. "I heard Jacques isn't your real name. Is that true?"

Jacques's good humor slipped for an instant before his smile returned. "Stage names are common," he said. "Just ask *Toni*."

"Toni?" I didn't recall anyone by that name.

Jacques merely nodded and then, without another word, walked out of the salon.

23

Looking for a possible murderer in a bar while alone probably wasn't the best idea I'd ever had, but I didn't want to go home and see if Dad might back me up. I knew he would jump at the chance, and honestly, it would have been the smart thing to do, but I also didn't want to risk getting him hurt.

Besides, I didn't even know if Vince had anything to do with Cathy's death. He might just be a sad guy, bummed about his career tailspin. There was nothing dangerous in that, not unless he was an angry drunk. Even then, there'd be others at the bar who could step in if things got too heated.

Still, I made sure my purse was packed nice and tight, just in case he decided to come at me.

While Jacques hadn't known the name of the hotel where Vince was staying, I was pretty sure I knew where it was. Pine Hills was small, and as far as I knew, there was only the one hotel—outside of Ted and Bettfast, which didn't really count—so I made for the place simply called Hotel that sat at the edge of town. The place was as low budget as the last time I'd seen it. One of the windows was boarded up, and another door had old police tape strung across it. I wondered what had happened, but quickly decided it was none of my business. So instead, I drove past, looking for the nearest bar.

I didn't have to look far. The bar was within walking distance of the hotel, and as far as I could tell, had a similar naming style; the sign out front simply said BAR. The building was one of those old wooden structures that looked as if it should have been condemned years ago, yet was hopping with customers, despite the early hour. Picnic tables outside held a smattering of people, all eating fried foods and drinking. A half-dozen motorcycles sat outside, right next to a shiny silver Prius that looked completely out of place.

A ping at the back of my mind gave me pause. Hadn't I nearly been run off the road by a silver car near Ted and Bettfast? I couldn't remember if it was a Prius or not, especially since I was pretty sure Lyric's Audi was silver and I might be confusing them. Could Vince have been seeing Lyric, just like Jacques? If so, that meant she'd lied to me, more than once.

I parked beside the Prius, and got out of my car, drenched in sweat. My lack of air-conditioning was becoming a major problem, and with no end to the heat in sight, I wasn't so sure I was going to be able to continue driving it. Open windows didn't help when the air was hot and soupy.

A handful of bikers stood outside smoking. Their eyes swiveled my way as I moved to the doors to the bar. There were no flashing neon signs proclaiming what beers they served, just dirty windows with no curtains or blinds. The smell of fried fish and chicken was nearly overpowering as I pushed inside to a dimly lit room, buzzing with the murmur of voices. My gaze swept across the men and women, many with beards and long hair, until I spotted the one man who looked as if he didn't belong.

Jacques was right; Vince was already in his beer, looking dismally ahead at nothing. He looked worse than when I'd seen him at Death by Coffee, which was saying something. I headed straight for him, trying hard not to look at the floor, which was alternatively hard and squishy. Vince was seated at a table by himself, which served my purposes, though I did wonder why he'd come to a place like this. He might not be popular, but he *was* an actor. You'd think he'd have better taste.

"Mind if I take a seat?" I asked over the sound of country music being played. Thankfully, it was kept low enough to serve as background noise and wouldn't drown out our conversation.

Vince glanced up at me, forehead crinkling in confusion for a moment before recognition dawned. "Kris, right?"

"Krissy," I corrected. "Jacques told me where I could find you."

Vince scowled, but nodded toward the seat across from him. "What does he want? You'd figure he's beaten me down enough for one lifetime."

"He didn't send me," I said. "I was hoping to talk to you, but didn't know where you were staying, so I asked him. I hope that's okay?"

He looked curious, but shrugged. "Sure, I guess." He glanced around the room and, for the first time, looked embarrassed. "This kind of place isn't my usual scene," he said. "But it does have its own character. I don't have to worry about someone I'd rather avoid showing up and bothering me."

I followed his gaze around the room, and was surprised by what I saw, now that I was really looking. The bar felt more like some kind of lodge than the dive it appeared to be from the outside. Sure, the usual trappings were there: the long bar with bottles lined up behind it and a haggard man wiping down the counter. But then there were the mounted bear and deer heads, the unlit fireplace across the room. I wondered if it served as a clubhouse for bikers—or whatever they'd call it—when the place wasn't open for business.

"So, Krissy," Vince said, drawing my attention back to him. "What did you want to talk to me about?" He took a long drink from his bottle.

"I was curious to know how you're holding up?" I said, opting for concerned, rather than jumping straight for accusations. "It's been a rough couple of days."

Vince grunted and lifted the bottle, swishing around what little was left. "How do you think I'm doing? I shouldn't have come to this godforsaken town." He took another swig. "Honestly, I don't know what I was thinking."

"Why *did* you come?" I asked. "Do you know Vicki well?" I knew from my conversation with her the other day, he didn't, but was curious about what he'd say.

"No, I don't know her at all," he admitted. "I . . ." He scowled. "I was stupid. I thought I could, I don't know, talk my way into . . ." He met my eyes, shook his head. "You know, private stuff." He drained his bottle, and stood. "Excuse me a second." He headed for the bar, raising the bottle to let the bartender know he was finished and was ready for more.

While he got another beer, I thought about what I knew about him. Vince was obviously a private man, which was strange since he was an actor who, if he ever hit the big time, would have his entire life splashed all over the media. It was clear he also had a thing for Lyric. I'd seen the way he looked at her. And if that was indeed his Prius I saw at Ted and Bettfast, then I was betting he'd tried to tell her.

But had he made it to the door? It was just as likely he'd chickened out and left before going in to see her. He didn't seem the forceful, forward type, though how well did I really know him?

Vince returned and sat down with a pair of full beer bottles. He offered me one.

"No thank you," I said.

"Suit yourself." He took a drink and set the second bottle aside, apparently for later.

"You care for her, don't you?" I asked after a moment. "Lyric, I mean. I think I saw you leaving the bed-and-breakfast where she's staying."

"Yeah, well, I don't know why I bother," he said. "It's not like she's ever given me the time of day." He took a long drink this time, as if he thought he might drink himself into oblivion on that one bottle. "I figured this trip would be the perfect opportunity to get to know her. I mean, since we are all pretty much strangers here, we'd stick together. Or so I thought."

I wondered if Lyric even realized Vince had feelings for her. She'd told me she liked him a little, even if he was a bit awkward and weird. But that didn't mean she knew him well enough to know his true feelings for her. He was so detached from everyone, I wondered if anyone knew.

Vince was clearly a depressed man, infatuated with a woman whom he'd likely never get. That had to be hard on him.

And then there was the lost movie role.

Carefully, putting as much compassion in my voice as I could, I decided to bring it up. "Jacques was telling me you both were up for the same part in a movie."

Vince's face turned an ugly shade of red almost immediately. "He stole it from me," he said, leveling a finger my way. "It had nothing to do with talent. He used his influences to earn himself the part, a part *I* had already gotten."

"They told you you had it?"

"Well, no." Vince grimaced at his bottle. "But I *knew* it was mine. I met all the requirements. They didn't want a pretty boy to prance across the screen, but rather, they wanted someone with some actual talent. Jacques Kenway is a hack who sleeps or buys his way into his roles. I end up relegated to supporting actor, or worse, just some nameless extra who doesn't even get a line."

"That has to be hard."

"Tell me about it," he said. "The biggest roles I ever land are often voice, where no one actually sees my face. I get cartoons, or worse, end up just some invisible, disembodied voice. Not like Jacques Kenway." He changed his voice at the last so he sounded just like Jacques. I had to admit, I was impressed. If I hadn't been looking right at him when he'd said it, I might have thought Jacques himself was in the room.

He sucked in an angry breath and leaned back. He

looked a little better after his rant, if angry. At least he didn't look depressed anymore.

"Have you ever heard of someone named Toni?" I asked.

Vince's eyes narrowed. "Where did you hear that name?"

"From Jacques," I said. "He told me to ask Toni about stage names, but I'm not sure I know anyone by that name."

Vince snorted. "Jacques Kenway. As if he has any room to talk? Jason Kennedy more like."

"Jacques's real name is Jason?" He *did* look a lot more like a Jason than a Jacques in my opinion.

"Of course it is. There's nothing genuine about that man." Vince sat back and shook his head. "I'm done talking about him. The man doesn't deserve the breath spent on him. Same goes for Toni."

There was a lot more I'd like to know about this Toni character, and Jacques, like why he'd changed his name, but I decided to honor Vince's wishes. "What can you tell me about Cathy Carr?" I asked instead.

He looked startled by the question and took a drink from his bottle before answering with, "What about her?"

"Did you know her well?"

"No. It sucks she died, but I had nothing to do with it."

"I didn't say you did."

His eyes narrowed, as if he was trying to determine if I was trying to fool him in some way, before he shrugged and looked away. "I think the only people who liked her were Gina and Frederick. She had a tendency to rub people the wrong way. I think it was because of all that caffeine, made her too hyperactive for some people. She practically bounced from the walls wherever she went. I'm not even sure that woman ever slept."

"Do you have any idea why anyone would want to kill her?" I asked, lowering my voice so that no one else in the bar would hear.

"No. Why would I? I've been keeping to myself, if you haven't noticed." He frowned and gave me a meaningful look. "Well, I've been trying to anyway."

I ignored that. "She was found with Gina's necklace on her," I pressed. "I was told she stole from her clients, and I was wondering if you'd ever heard the same."

"Can't help you there."

"Did you know the necklace was fake? Or at least, the one she had on her was. Do you think she might have planned on stealing the real one and replacing it with the forgery?"

"Honestly, I don't know." He sounded frustrated by the questions. "I didn't know her well enough to form an opinion. If she was a thief, then yeah, I suppose it's possible." He leaned forward, locked eyes with me. "But I can tell you for a fact that necklace of Gina's was real. Someone must have taken it." His teeth clenched, eyes going hard, before he took yet another drink from his beer. It wasn't long past lunchtime and he looked as if he was already well on his way to drunk.

"How do you know for sure?" I asked. "Jacques said just the opposite."

"What would Jacques know? There's not a hint of intelligence in that man's head."

I couldn't say I totally disagreed.

Vince sighed. "Look, I don't know who killed her or why. I don't know why anyone would care enough to hurt her. I don't know why anything is happening. I just want to get this little trip over with so I can go back home and try to put my career back together before I'm too old."

"Did something else happen?" I asked. I had a hard time believing one lost role was enough to ruin an acting career. "To your job, I mean."

He shrugged. "With people like Jacques always taking the glory, even in our low-budget cheesefests, it's hard to make ends meet." He rose. "I'm going to go lie down. I'm not feeling too good."

I stood with him. "Thank you for talking to me," I said. "I hope you feel better soon."

He drained his beer, picked up the full bottle, considered it, and then set it aside. "Guess I best lay off, huh?" he asked, before barking a bitter laugh. "See you around, Krissy." He trudged off, head down, looking as depressed as any man I'd ever seen.

I followed him out the door. He didn't so much as look up as he got into his car and drove off. I briefly wondered how safe it was to have him driving after drinking, but noted he was heading for the hotel, so I guessed I didn't have to worry too much.

I got into my own car, but didn't start it right away, despite the heat. For a bunch of people who'd come together for a wedding, they didn't seem very festive. Or friendly toward one another, for that matter. Vince hated Jacques, who, in turn, didn't like Vince. Lyric wasn't Jacques's biggest fan, while she thought Vince to be an oddball, though she'd apparently spent the night with at least one of them, according to Jacques. Sage and Trey Herron were willing to sit and eat with

Lyric, but as far as I knew, didn't associate much with Vince or Jacques. And none of them had known, or liked, Cathy Carr all that much.

So, what did that mean when it came to her murder?

It appeared as if all the actors cared about were their careers. Cathy had nothing to do with that. The only people who well and truly disliked her were Sage and Trey. Could they have finally decided to take their revenge on her for her previous thefts?

I started my car and turned toward home. It looked like I was getting nowhere, and I doubted I'd talk my way into an answer. I hoped the police were having better luck piecing it all together, and considered calling Paul to check in and tell him what little I'd learned. But if I was being honest with myself, he wouldn't want me asking around. Talking to people wasn't a crime, but interfering in a police investigation was.

Fifteen minutes later, when I was nearly home, my phone rang. Thinking it might be Dad telling me he was finally back from breakfast, I answered without checking the screen.

"Krissy!" Vicki's voice was high-pitched and frantic. "Can you come to the police station?"

Adrenaline shot through me and my foot automatically pressed down hard on the pedal, ramping up my speed well past the legal limit. "I'm on my way. What's going on?" My mind was conjuring all sorts of terrible things, including the possibility the murderer hadn't been content with killing just Cathy, but had moved on to someone else, someone closer to me and my best friend.

"It's Mason," she said, causing my fears to double.

I could hear tears in her voice, as if she was fighting hard to hold them back.

If someone has hurt him . . . I didn't know what I would do, but it wouldn't be pleasant. "Is he okay?" I asked, heart in my throat. "Where is he?"

"He's okay," Vicki said, though she didn't sound convinced of the fact. "Physically at least."

"Okay, then," I said, somewhat relieved. At least he wasn't bleeding out or black and blue from a beating. "What happened?"

Vicki's voice broke when she spoke again. "The police have him," she said. "They've arrested him for Cathy's murder."

24

I screeched to a halt outside the Pine Hills police station, just barely missing a double-parked SUV. It earned me a hard look from a cop walking to his own car, but I paid him little mind as I rushed into the station, alternating between worried and hopping mad. There was no way Mason Lawyer would have killed anyone, let alone Cathy Carr. Sure, he wasn't happy she was interfering in his wedding, but I knew Mason; he wasn't a killer.

Vicki saw me the moment I was through the door. Her face was makeup-streaked, eyes red and swollen from crying. She came toward me, arms already outstretched, in dire need of a hug.

"I don't know what to do," she said, a panicked lilt to her voice. She squeezed me tightly and held on as if she was afraid I might abandon her.

"I'll take care of it," I said, voice coming out strained. "What happened?"

Vicki released me and stepped back. "Apparently, someone called in a tip." She wiped at her eyes, and took a deep, calming breath. "We were going over the rehearsal plans when the cops showed up out

of nowhere and took him away. I didn't know what
to do!"

"Which cops?" I asked, dreading the answer.

"Paul and John."

I closed my eyes and took a deep breath of my own.
Paul had to know Mason wouldn't do this. I'd expected it from Buchannan, but not Paul.

"Paul did his best to make me feel better," Vicki
said, correctly interpreting my reaction. "He said they
had to follow up on the tip, even if it's bunk. I can't
believe this is happening now."

"Did Paul tell you what kind of tip it was?"

Vicki shook her head. "All he told me was that
someone called in and claimed they saw Mason at my
house the night of Cathy's murder. But he wasn't
there until after it happened. You saw us come in together. We were home before that, and he never left
my sight, not once."

I had to believe that meant something, but with
how things were going lately, I wouldn't count on it.
"Did Paul say who called in the tip?"

"He never said. I think it was anonymous, but you'd
have to ask him to be sure."

I glanced around the room. Garrison was at a desk,
watching us. Another cop was sitting at the front
desk, typing away, seemingly oblivious to Vicki's near
meltdown. Otherwise, we had the immediate area to
ourselves. No Paul, no Buchannan, and definitely no
Mason.

"What time did all of this happen?"

"I called you the moment they took him away,"
Vicki said. She ran her fingers through her hair, and
I noted how her hand shook. She was doing a good

job not completely losing it, but she was far from okay. "I didn't know what else to do."

Was it just a coincidence that a call had come in, naming Mason, just after I'd talked to three of my top murder suspects? First Lyric, then Jacques, and finally Vince. All three would have had ample opportunity to call in the tip, especially if they thought I was getting too close to the truth. And if two of them were working together . . .

I took Vicki's hand and met her eye. "I'll get to the bottom of this. I promise. You *will* have your wedding."

A frightened smile flittered across her lips. "I know you will. I believe in you."

That made one of us.

Steeling myself for what was to come, I turned toward the hallway that led to interrogation room one. If Mason was anywhere, it would be there. The same went for both Paul and Buchannan, and quite possibly Chief Dalton, if she'd been called in.

Acting as if I had every right to do so, I marched straight for the interrogation room door. If Garrison or the other cop noticed, they didn't make a move to stop me. At this point, I was practically a regular, so maybe they just figured, "Why bother?"

I considered throwing open the door and demanding to be told what they thought they were doing. It would be dramatic, but it would also probably be counterproductive. Instead, I knocked, albeit angrily, and stood back, arms crossed over my chest, and waited.

The door opened after only a few seconds. Paul Dalton came to an abrupt halt when he saw me. A mixture of emotions flew across his face, before finally settling on resigned.

"Krissy," he said. "I suppose I should have expected you."

"What do you think you're doing?" I asked, looking past him. Buchannan was half-seated on the table, almost casually, looking my way with an annoyed frown. Mason sat across from him, chair pushed back, one leg atop the other. I noted he wasn't handcuffed, which I took for a good sign. He looked pretty relaxed for a man who'd just been dragged into the police station on suspicion of murder.

Paul stepped forward, invading my personal space until I took a step back. He pulled the door closed behind him. "We got a tip and had to follow up on it, Krissy."

"It's *Mason*," I said. "He didn't do it."

"The evidence is compelling enough, we had to at least look into it."

"Oh, really?" I tapped my foot. "And what evidence is that?"

Paul frowned. "You know I can't divulge that information."

"Who called in the tip?"

"I can't tell you that either."

I gave an exasperated huff. "What can you tell me, then? My best friend is terrified you're going to send her fiancé to jail right before their wedding, and you won't tell me why? That's not very nice of you, Paul Dalton."

He actually blushed. "I wish I could tell you," he said. "I really do."

"Then do it. Who's going to tell?" I glanced dramatically around. It was just us and the empty hallway.

Paul's frown deepened. He looked toward where Garrison and the other cop were, and then took my elbow. He led me farther down the hall, away from everyone else.

"The call was anonymous," Paul said, keeping his voice low. "I asked for her name, but she refused. I didn't recognize the voice. All I know for sure was the caller was female."

"What did she say exactly?"

"She claimed to have been out that night, walking alone, when she heard a scream. She said she was frightened, but went to investigate anyway, thinking someone might need her help. She claims she saw Mason Lawyer hurry away from the Patterson house, get into his car, and drive away at high speed."

"Did she tell you the make and model of the car?"

"No."

"The color?"

"No."

"So, she just said, he got into his car and sped off?" I gave him a meaningful look.

"I know," Paul said. "The call was light on details. I even asked about it, but she claimed it was too dark to see much else."

"But she could make out his face," I said. This was sounding more and more like a setup. "Mason was with Vicki at the time of Cathy's murder. She can vouch for him."

"She is also going to be his wife. We can't take her at her word, as much as we'd like to."

"Are you calling Vicki a liar?" Steam was practically pouring from my ears at this point. I couldn't believe Paul Dalton would even consider, for a second, Vicki would lie to him to protect Mason. She loved her

fiancé, sure, but if it turned out he was a cold-blooded
killer, she wouldn't hesitate to turn him in.

Paul stepped forward and put a hand on my shoulder. He squeezed. "I believe her," he said. "But we had
to follow up on this. You understand that, don't you?"

I sighed. "I suppose." But I sure didn't like it. "How
long are you going to hold him?"

"I don't think the chief is going to allow us to let
him go today. She's on her way in now. Buchannan
called her since it's a pretty big development. She'll
want a chance to talk to the suspect."

My anger peaked and I very nearly bit his arm off.
"Are you serious? Mason didn't do it! You said you
believed Vicki, and you're calling him a suspect?"

"I didn't mean it like that." He withdrew his hand,
and then looked down at them. "Mason has to go
through questioning, and once we verify his alibi, I'm
sure we will release him. There's little else I can do
now but promise we'll do our best to make sure no
one jumps to any unfortunate conclusions."

That wasn't enough. What happened if they didn't
find any other evidence? What if the real killer got
away with murder? What if the tip wasn't the only
thing this woman was willing to do to frame him? She
could very well be planting evidence now. If the police
found, let's say, Gina's necklace in Mason's underwear
drawer, they'd have no choice but to arrest him. Then
Mason would go down for a crime he hadn't committed and Vicki wouldn't get her dream wedding.

I would *not* let that happen.

"Take me instead."

"What?" Paul's brow furrowed.

"Arrest me." I held out my wrists for him. "Put the
cuffs on me right now and let Mason go."

"Krissy, I can't do that."

"No, Paul. You are not going to ruin Vicki's wedding. I won't let you. If I have to sit in a jail cell to make sure that doesn't happen, well then, I'll do it."

"Don't you think her wedding will be ruined if you aren't there for it?" he asked.

"Don't get all logical on me," I snapped. My eyes were brimming with suppressed tears. I knew I was overreacting, but at this point, I was having a hard time dealing. I mean, how could anyone, even for a second, think Mason could be guilty? And then, when you added in everything else that happened, I was seconds from a serious breakdown.

"What's going on?" Paul asked, face pinched in concern. "There's more to it than just this." He gestured vaguely back toward the interrogation room.

I sucked in a breath and held it. I was *this* close to telling him about Will and his new job, how it had caught me off guard even though a part of me had suspected. If I told him, he would hug me, would make me feel better, at least for a few minutes.

But it would do nothing to help Mason. *That* was the important thing right now, not my feelings.

I blew out my breath and forced myself to focus on what was most important. Mason was currently suspect number one, thanks to an anonymous tip that named him personally. Why would anyone want to do that? As far as I knew, he'd had no interactions with any of the people who'd come with Vicki's parents, other than that first meeting at Death by Coffee. I doubted any of them knew him much more than by name, let alone sight.

Did someone have a reason to stop the wedding? Raymond Lawyer and Regina Harper would rather he marry Regina's daughter, Heidi, but getting Mason jailed wouldn't accomplish that goal, so they were unlikely. And that's ignoring the fact Mason is Raymond's son. There was no love lost between the two of them, but I had serious doubts Raymond would call in a bogus tip implicating his son in murder, no matter his feelings on his upcoming nuptials.

Vicki was in love with Mason and would never turn on him like that. Gina and Frederick only wanted what's best for their daughter, even if they had a strange way of showing it sometimes. As far as I knew, they'd never once spoken ill against Mason, so I was pretty sure Gina hadn't made the call.

So, who did that leave other than a nosy neighbor or a prankster thinking it would be funny to call in a false tip?

It had to be one of the actors. It was the only thing that made sense. Whoever had killed Cathy was afraid I was getting too close to the truth, and had decided to try to throw off the police. No one else in Pine Hills had a reason to go after Cathy, which meant no one would have a reason to implicate Mason. Whoever it was had latched on to what they viewed as the likeliest suspect for the murder, a man angry with Cathy for ruining his wedding, and run with it.

"I talked to some people," I said, meeting Paul's eye. "Just before you got the call."

"What people?" he asked.

"Lyric Granderson, Jacques Kenway, and Vince Conner. They all came to Pine Hills with Cathy for the wedding."

"And you think one of them called in the tip?"

"I'd put money on it." Unless Sage Herron had done

it. Out of everyone, she was the one who disliked
Cathy the most.

But if she had, why wait until now to make the call?
She could have done it the moment I'd spoken to
her about Cathy's death. No, there was one other
woman who had more to gain, and I'd just recently
spoken to her.

"Do you really think Lyric Granderson is responsible for this?" Paul asked, following the same line of
reasoning.

"I think she very well might be."

"Why would she?" he asked. "She has a solid alibi
for the night of the murder, and it didn't include
taking a lonely walk out in the middle of nowhere.
And I'm pretty sure I would have recognized her voice
if it had been her."

"Are you sure about that?" I asked. "She *is* an actress."

"I'll give you that, but I still don't believe it."

I narrowed my eyes at him, wondering if he was
smitten with the pretty actress, but dismissed the
thought immediately. It was none of my business if
he was or not.

"What if she disguised her voice and made the call
for someone else?" I wondered aloud.

"Like who?"

"Vince Conner or Jacques Kenway. Do you know
them?"

"I've talked to them." Paul rubbed his thumb across
his lower lip in thought. "Well, we, as in the police,
have talked to them. I've only spoken to Mr. Conner
personally."

"They're rivals," I said. "Well, Vince sees it that way.
Jacques doesn't see much past himself."

"Okay, but how does that lead to Ms. Carr's murder and our tip?"

"I'm not sure," I admitted. "But maybe one of them was trying to get a leg up on the other somehow, and ended up killing her by accident."

"I don't see how," Paul said. "From what I've gathered, Ms. Carr had nothing to do with either of the two men. And if one of them was looking to frame the other, why not point the finger at the rival when they had someone make the call? Why target Mason?"

"I don't know." I made a frustrated sound. He was making too much sense, and it was causing all my theories to crumble. "But I'm sure it all connects somehow."

Chief Dalton's voice rang out from down the hall, causing Paul to tense. "I'd best get back in there," he said. "Go take care of Vicki, okay?"

"All right, I will. But don't you dare go accusing Mason of the murder or so help me, Paul Dalton, I'll never forgive you."

When he smiled, it was affectionate, which was surprising, considering the threat. "I'll do what I can."

We stood there awkwardly, facing one another, not quite sure if we should shake hands, or hug, or just walk away. Paul made the decision and clasped me on the arm briefly before turning and hurrying back to the interrogation room, just as Chief Dalton reached it. She glanced past him and gave me a disapproving glare before they entered the room together.

I took a moment to compose myself before leaving the hallway. Vicki didn't need to see me upset. I needed to be strong for her. I also needed to figure out who had killed Cathy Carr, and who had called in the bogus tip. And I needed to do it yesterday.

25

There wasn't much I could do for Vicki other than wait with her and provide as much support as I could muster. I did my best to let her know that it would be all right, that Paul was on her side, but it was of little comfort. Her husband-to-be *was* in jail. There was no remedy for that, not unless I produced the real killer.

"Go ahead and go home," she said after a while. "There's no sense in you sitting here with me." Garrison had brought over two chairs for us earlier, but had said nothing. I was thankful for the gesture, even if she'd done it grudgingly.

"Are you sure?" I asked. "I can stay for as long as you need me. There's no reason for you to be alone."

"I'm sure. There's nothing you can do now. But thank you for coming."

A big part of me wanted to sit right there, regardless. I know if it was someone I loved, I'd need all the support I could get.

But she was right; I couldn't do anything while sitting there. The real killer was out there, and I'd be of more use to Vicki and Mason if I found him or her.

If I could figure out who had called in the tip, I could very well end up uncovering the murderer.

Reluctantly, I said my good-byes and left Vicki to worry alone. It was still shining brightly outside, which was a stark contrast to the gloom inside the police station. I had to shield my eyes against the rays as I got into my car and started for home. Thankfully, I'd travel most of the way there with the sun at my back, lest I end up blind. I desperately needed to invest in a good pair of sunglasses.

I was halfway home when my phone rang. Thinking it might be Vicki with news, I snatched it up and answered with a worried, "Hello?"

"You won't believe what I've found out!"

"Rita?" Even though I recognized her voice, I pulled the phone from my ear to glance at the screen to be sure. She'd never called me out of the blue before.

"Who else, dear? I did as you asked and spent the last few days with my ear to the ground, listening for anything that might be useful for your investigation. The way people talk around here, you'd think nothing is private! It's almost obscene."

And Rita was the one who was often leading the charge on that front, but I didn't want to point that out. "What have you heard?"

"Well, the latest, it appears, is that the police have arrested Mason Lawyer for that woman's murder! Can you believe it? I sure can't." She tsked. "Someone must have made a mistake because the way I hear it, he couldn't have done it. Georgina's friend lives across the street from Mason and says he was in all night, and she would know. Nothing goes on in that neighborhood without her knowing!"

Creepy, but good to know. "Does she have proof that he never left?"

"She has her two good eyes, and that's enough for me. Of course, she does need reading glasses these days. It happens to the best of us as we get older, I suppose. But she said she saw Mason in the window just before the lights went out that night. And then a short time later, they came on again and both he and Vicki Patterson sped away, looking like someone died." She paused. "Well, I guess someone did."

It was great to know someone could vouch for Mason's whereabouts at the time of the murder, but I wasn't sure how that helped me when it came to finding out who had killed Cathy or, at least, had called in the tip. I already knew Mason was innocent, and I was pretty sure the police would do their due diligence and talk to Mason's neighbors. Knowing how Georgina was, I imagined her friend was much the same, and would be willing to talk their ears off if they let her. And if she was anything like my neighbor, Eleanor Winthrow, used to be, then she would have seen everything, right down to what Mason and Vicki had been wearing when they'd left.

Too bad Vicki didn't have a neighbor like that. It would have been nice if someone *had* been watching the house the night of the murder.

Then again, maybe someone had been. Could the tip be legit, but they'd made a mistake when they'd identified Mason? It had been dark and the tip was otherwise vague, so perhaps the caller had seen a man leaving the house that night and assumed it was Mason since he and Vicki were an item.

It made sense. Perhaps I would need to visit Vicki's neighbors and see if one of them had indeed made the call. With all the trees, they would have had to have been at the foot of the driveway to see anything. There was enough distance from the road to the front door, I could see someone mistaking a man like Jacques Kenway for Mason.

"Have you heard anything else?" I asked, my mind turning over the possibilities. Maybe I was going at this all wrong and it really was a case of mistaken identity. If the caller had gotten a good look at the car, but had forgotten when talking to the cops, all I'd have to do was jog their memory and we'd have our man.

"The usual tidbits here and there," Rita said. "Everyone has an opinion, and many of them are outright wrong." She huffed. "There are some that say Mason deserves this after what happened to his brother, the poor soul. Others are pointing to how these celebrities are treating us, saying it's justified! I can't say they're wrong, considering some of the things I've heard. Just this morning, Albie Bruce said he bumped into one of those actors and just about had his ear chewed off. I mean, Albie is well into his nineties. Who treats an old man like that?"

No one good, that's who.

"And do you know what else I heard?" Rita went on, after only a brief pause for breath.

"What's that?"

"There's something happening with all those actors as we speak!" She said it like it was the most shocking news she'd ever heard. "Apparently, everyone is gathering at Vicki Patterson's house at the request of her parents. I'm not sure what they're going to talk about, but I bet it has to do with the wedding. How can it go on now? It'll be canceled by morning, mark my words."

A cold chill washed through me. *They can't be talking about the wedding now.* Not without Vicki and Mason present.

Could they?

"Where did you hear this?" I asked, realizing that, yes, this was exactly the sort of thing Gina and Frederick would do.

I could hear the smug smile in her voice when Rita said, "I have to protect my sources, dear."

I could have pressed, but decided against it. Let her have her moment. "Do you know who all is going to this thing?" With Vicki at the police station, Mason behind bars, and me being, well, me, I had a bad feeling where this was going.

"Those out-of-towners, for sure," Rita said. "I also heard tell of Regina Harper and Raymond Lawyer heading that way too. It's why I'm sure it has something to do with the wedding. Why else would they be there when they have nothing else in common with those people?"

I was actually pretty impressed by her information, if it was accurate. Although, it did make me wonder how extensive Rita's network really was. Regina and Raymond wouldn't be happy to know people were watching them or, at least, reporting on where they were going. Heck, *I* wouldn't be happy either. But right now, I was thankful for the tip.

"Thanks, Rita," I said, pulling into my driveway. I had a feeling I wasn't going to be staying home for long, not if there was something going on that might affect Vicki's wedding. Things were already bad enough without Mason and Vicki's parents making it worse.

"No problem, dear. I'll let you know as soon as I learn something more."

We hung up and I got out of my car, noting the rental was back so Dad and Laura were home. Apparently, they were the only out-of-towners not invited to the little get-together at Vicki's house. I didn't know why that bothered me so much, but it did.

I entered to find Dad and Laura sitting on the couch, watching yet another movie. Either they really enjoyed relaxing together, or I seriously needed to reconsider my entertainment options around the house.

"Hey, Buttercup," Dad said, pulling his arm from around Laura's shoulder. "Missed you at breakfast."

"Sorry about that," I said. "Something came up." I briefly told him about Mason's arrest.

"That's terrible," Laura said. "Why would someone do that, especially right before his wedding?"

"I wish I knew." My phone rang. "One sec." I pulled my cell from my purse and noted Paul's number. My heart jumped. "Paul?" I asked, answering. "What's going on?"

"We're letting him go," he said, sounding as relieved as I felt. "He has multiple eyewitnesses vouching for him, and quite frankly, no one here believed he could have had anything to do with the murder. It just didn't fit."

"Thank goodness," I said, letting my entire body sag against the wall. My knees felt weak and I was decidedly light-headed. It was as if the tension were the only thing keeping me going.

"I have some free time." Paul sounded hesitant. "Would you mind if I stopped by for a few minutes? I promise I won't stay long."

"No, please do." As much as I wanted to get over to Vicki's and see what was going on, I wanted to see Paul outside the station. Maybe he could tell me something more about the caller, or perhaps some detail the police had picked up on that would connect with something I'd learned. It was time I spilled everything I knew before someone I cared about ended up behind bars.

"I'll be there in ten."

We hung up, but before I told Dad—who was watching me with a curious look on his face—what he'd said, I dialed and pressed the phone to my ear. "Vicki," I said when she answered. "I heard about Mason."

"He's shaken up, but doing good. We both are."

"I hate to be the bearer of bad news, but Rita told me Gina and Frederick called everyone over to your place to talk. Raymond and Regina are there too."

"That can't be good."

"That's what I was thinking."

"We'll head there as soon as Mason grabs something to eat. Thanks for letting me know. It's like the fates are trying to see how far they can push me before I snap."

"You'll make it," I said. "You're the strongest person I know."

We said our good-byes, and I finally turned to Dad and Laura and told them the good news.

"That's a relief," Laura said. "So, the wedding is still on?"

"It better be," I said, wondering if there was any way Vicki and Mason's parents could put a stop to it. Other than butting in and being disruptive, I didn't think so. Both Mason and Vicki were adults. Their parents could ruin the wedding, and make the both of them miserable, but I didn't think they could actually put a stop to the thing.

Then again, how long before enough was enough? Unwanted guests, a murder, and now an arrest? There had to be a point where they'd throw in the towel. I desperately needed to step in before it came to that.

"Do you think the real killer tried to frame Mason?" Dad asked.

"It's likely." Someone screamed on the TV, briefly drawing my attention, but I was too distracted to actually take the time to watch. "Paul said it was a woman who called in the tip."

"So, if it was the killer who called, it was either one of the women who came with the Pattersons, or they're helping one of the men." Dad rubbed at his chin, brow furrowing in thought. "Or it could be someone else entirely, a disgruntled neighbor, perhaps."

"Which doesn't really help us," I grumbled. Not unless that neighbor actually had seen something and I could get it out of them. No idea how, but darn it, I was willing to try anything, just as long as it led to Cathy's murderer.

"I know I didn't get to know them all that well," Laura said, "but I can't see any of the women killing anyone. They're rude, but not hateful, or even violent."

"I got that impression too," Dad said.

I had to agree. As much as Lyric rubbed me the wrong way, she didn't seem the type to commit murder. The same went for Sage. I *could* see Lyric covering for someone if she thought it would help her in some way, however.

A car door slammed outside and I opened my front door to wait for Paul. He looked haggard, and tired.

"Krissy," he said, stepping inside. He removed his hat when he saw Dad. "Mr. Hancock. Ms. Dresden."

"Officer Dalton," Dad said. "Is there anything we can do to help?"

"I'm afraid not," Paul said. "At this point, we're chasing our tails. No one saw anything, and without evidence, all we have is speculation." He looked at me. "I'm assuming you haven't come up with anything concrete either?"

I blushed. Of course, he knew I'd been snooping around, asking questions. "Nothing," I admitted.

He sighed, eyes drifting toward the television, which was still on in the other room. He frowned as a high-pitched, nasally voice begged a man in a pair of tight leather pants to save the children.

"That's it," he said, taking a step toward the living room.

"What's it?" I asked. I had no idea what was playing on my TV, other than the fact it was terrible. The brief snatches of dialogue I'd caught were stiff and stilted, the camera shots shaky. We're talking B-movie material, if not worse.

"That woman's voice. That's the one who called in the tip."

I spun to Dad, heart doing a little hiccup. "What are you watching?"

"Your friend Jules brought over a movie called *The Pirate Heist*," he said. "Apparently, you two talked about it and he thought you might find it amusing to watch."

"One of the actors who came with us is in it," Laura added. "Jacques Kenway. He's not very good."

Even as she said it, Jacques came into the picture. He smiled directly at the camera before delivering a wooden line about doing what was right and saving not just the children, but the world.

"That's not it," Paul said. "It was the woman's voice, the beggar."

I hurried over to the couch and picked up the remote. I rewound until I was back at the begging of the scene. The woman's face was obscured, but her voice was clear as day. I, however, didn't recognize it in the slightest.

Paul did.

"That's the one," he said, pointing. "Who is that?"

I rewound again and watched intently as the woman whined. She was shrouded from head to foot, so her body was completely covered, all but her face, which was turned away from the camera. All that could be seen was the vaguest of features; nothing we could go on to identify who it was.

Still, I found something familiar about her, something I couldn't put my finger on. I could tell it wasn't Gina; I'd recognize her anywhere. And while it might be Lyric Granderson, I doubted it. This woman held herself differently, almost awkwardly, like she was too embarrassed to be seen.

If I was in this movie, I'd be embarrassed too, I thought as I pressed fast-forward. Lyric was self-centered and wouldn't want anyone to see her looking like a common beggar woman.

I supposed it could be Sage Herron. If so, she'd masked her voice, but as I said, this wasn't a good movie. She probably wouldn't want any of her friends to know she was in it.

I zipped through the rest of the film, not stopping until the end credits rolled. I then set it to play at half speed.

No one spoke as we watched the names roll by. It was ponderously slow, but I was afraid to go any faster, just in case it wasn't immediately obvious who we were looking for. The woman had a line, so I was guessing she'd be listed in the end credits, but from what I saw, it was unlikely she was playing anything more than a bit part, meaning there was no specific character name to look for.

"There," Paul said. "Pious woman."

We read the name next to it together.

"Who's that?" Dad asked with a frown.

"I don't recognize it either."

I looked back at the others, eyes wide, as pieces started to fall into place. Then, without even bothering to stop the movie, I hurried for the door. I turned when no one moved. "Come on," I said. "I think I know who killed Cathy Carr."

26

I was first to arrive at Vicki's place, my mind jumping from conclusion to conclusion. I had no real proof of who'd killed Cathy, but that one name had triggered something, a memory of scripts and actors, that I hoped would all connect once I confronted them about it. While I'd said I thought I knew who had done it, that wasn't entirely the case. I had my suspicions, though, and that was good enough for me.

Mason's car was parked just ahead of mine, telling me he and Vicki had already arrived. Beyond that, I saw Raymond's vehicle, and then various rentals, almost all of them silver.

Paul pulled in beside my car, leaving just enough room for Dad to pull his rental in behind him. Dad and Laura could have stayed behind, but I was glad he was going to be here to back me up. This was already going to be challenging enough on my own, so his support meant a lot.

"Are you going to tell me what this is all about?" Paul asked, getting out of his car.

"I will once we're inside and I can see their faces."

Paul crossed his arms and gave me a stern frown.

"Are you holding back on me, Krissy? If you know something, you should tell me. I don't want this getting out of hand."

"Trust me," I said, resting a hand on his arm. If I told him what I had was mere conjecture, he might turn and walk away. I couldn't do this without him. In fact, I *wouldn't* do it without him. There was no telling how the killer might react if and when I got them to confess.

"Krissy," Paul warned, but I was already moving toward the door.

It probably would have been better to simply tell Paul my theory, but then again, we were dealing with actors here. They'd enjoy the drama. Well, the innocent ones would, anyway. The killer, not so much.

Admittedly, I did have ulterior motives for wanting to do this in dramatic fashion. A lifetime of the Pattersons looking down on me, of chiding Vicki for spending her time with someone as lowly as myself, was grating on me. I thought that if I were to show them I wasn't a total loser, that I could discover who'd killed their friend all on my own, then maybe they'd treat me with a tiny bit more respect. I didn't think anything would ever make them actually *like* me, but if it stopped the looks and the constant put-downs, I'd take it.

So, yeah, this time, it was going to be all about me.

I didn't bother knocking. I pushed open the door and strode inside, hoping Paul, Dad, and Laura would follow without comment.

They did.

"No!" Vicki shouted from the dining room. "You have no right to do any of this."

"We're only doing what's best for you, Victoria," Gina said.

"It's all for the best," Regina added, sounding as if nothing could sway her and that her opinion was the only one that mattered.

"It's our decision," Mason said. "Not yours. I don't care who you are, none of you have any right to step in like this."

"Mason, sit down," Raymond barked.

"No!"

I rushed into the room before the argument could completely blow up. Mason and Vicki were standing at the head of the table, Vicki's army of porcelain dolls looking on behind them. Mason's face was bright red and a vein was pulsing in his temple. Right then, he looked a lot like his dad, which was kind of frightening. Raymond Lawyer wasn't someone you messed with, and if Mason had some of his dad in him, that meant he could be a serious force to be reckoned with when he wanted to be. I only hoped he never turned that stubborn forcefulness onto Vicki, or else we'd have some words.

The others were sitting around the large dining room table, looking on as if amused and, in some cases, confused by the display. Raymond and Regina were nearest me, backs my way. Lyric sat to their right, followed by Jacques and Vince. Gina and Frederick were across from them, with a horrified-looking Heidi between Frederick and Regina. Trey and Sage sat across from one another, on either side of Mason and Vicki. If the table was any smaller, they all wouldn't have fit.

"She's a perfectly nice girl," Raymond said. "And you're insulting her by your refusal to see reason."

"*I'm* insulting her? She doesn't even want to be here!"

By the look on Heidi's face, I'd agree.

Knowing things weren't going to get any better if I waited them out, I cleared my throat, drawing every eye in the room. Vicki and Mason looked relieved to see me. Everyone else, not so much.

"Oh. You." Gina frowned as she looked past me and to Paul. "Who called the police?" Her accusatory gaze swept to Vicki.

"I did," I said.

"Why would you do that?" Frederick asked. "There's nothing wrong with having an adult conversation." He glanced at Vicki when he said "adult" as if he thought her refusal to do as they said made her little more than a child.

"No, there's nothing illegal about that," I said. Though I'd argue that there *was* something wrong with trying to force your children to marry someone else, just because you liked one match over the other. This wasn't *Game of Thrones*. "But murder is."

A look of confusion swept around the table. I watched each face, hoping to catch a sign of guilt, but got nothing. Based on the quality of the actors here, I was actually surprised.

"Are you going to tell us what this is about?" Paul asked, clearly impatient with my method. I didn't blame him, but I wasn't going to hurry for his benefit. As sure as I was about the killer's identity, I could be wrong. I needed to do this right.

"First off, Vicki and Mason are getting married."

I held up a hand to silence Gina when she opened her mouth to speak. "There's nothing you can do about it." I took in the Pattersons and Regina and Raymond as I made that statement. "They love each other, and while you might not approve, it's what they want. If you think their marriage is a mistake, and if it turns out you're right, then they'll figure it out eventually. They should be allowed to make up their own minds on how they want to live, and who they want to live it with."

"Hear, hear," Laura said from behind me.

I shot her an appreciative smile. "We all make mistakes," I went on. "Some of us more so than others." I walked slowly around the table. All eyes followed me, some with continued confusion, others with annoyance. "Which brings us to the reason I'm here tonight: Cathy's murder."

There was no startled gasp, no shout of outrage—only the stares.

"At first, I couldn't figure out why anyone here would want to kill her. She was annoying, sure, and many of you fought with her, but was that reason enough to kill her? Why here? Why not in California, where there were a whole lot more people to blame it on?"

"No one here would have harmed her," Gina said.

"Really? What about Sage and Trey? They believe she stole from them, ruined their wedding even. Wouldn't that be cause to be outraged?"

"I never harmed a hair on her head," Trey said, his tone of voice telling me he was offended. Sage nodded, but did look decidedly nervous, like she wasn't entirely sure about that.

"I believe you," I said, which caused Sage to suck in a relieved breath. "While you disliked her, and thought she stole from you, it did happen a long time ago. You argued with her before boarding your flight, but at this point, it's just a sore point between you. Killing her wouldn't get you your jewelry back."

Trey put an arm around his wife and pulled her close, eyes hard while he watched me. Just because I'd declared him innocent, that didn't mean he liked me bringing up his grievance with the deceased in front of everyone else. I had a feeling I wouldn't be getting a Christmas card from him any time soon.

"Cathy was found with a fake necklace on her," I went on. "A forgery. Some believe the real one is still out there somewhere. Others believe the necklace was always a fake. Who's correct?" I paused a heartbeat, before. "Honestly? It doesn't matter, because if someone *was* trying to steal it, then all they needed to do was *think* it was real."

"It was," Gina said, crossing her arms over her chest and glaring at me.

Jacques snorted from across the table, causing her to swivel her glare his way.

"What if Cathy tried to steal it, like she supposedly stole from the Herrons?" I asked. "What if someone caught her in the act?" I looked right at Frederick.

His eyes widened. "She wouldn't have done such a thing. *I* wouldn't have done such a thing!"

"We were out getting dinner," Gina added. "There's no way either of us could have done it."

"They were," Paul said from behind me. "We finally got confirmation of that earlier today. A camera from across the street picked them up heading into the restaurant at the time of the murder."

A part of me breathed a sigh of relief. For as confident as I was feeling about who I thought had killed Cathy, there was that niggling concern in the back of my mind that the Pattersons had had something to do with it.

"I never thought you did," I said, not wanting to voice my concern, lest they hate me forever. "Out of everyone here, you two were the only ones who actually liked Cathy. Even if you did catch her stealing from you, you probably wouldn't have done much more than scold her for it."

Gina looked offended by that, but said nothing.

"Vicki and Mason are clearly innocent," I said, hoping to move on from them quickly, but it wasn't to be.

"Why do you say that?" Jacques asked. "Wasn't Mason detained earlier? Hard to believe the police wouldn't have a reason for that."

"He was," I admitted. "And he was cleared of any wrongdoing. Whoever called in the tip made a mistake. Mason has a nosy neighbor who could place him at his house when the murder took place. The neighbor was also able to confirm what time Mason and Vicki left to come here. That means they both have solid alibis. That's more than I can say for some of you." My eyes scoured the table, hoping someone would show some kind of reaction, something I could latch on to.

But other than Gina's glare, and a few confused looks, I still got nothing from them.

Raymond heaved a heavy sigh. "Can we hurry this along? I don't want to spend my entire night sitting around, speculating on something that can't be proven one way or the other."

"Ah, Raymond and Regina," I said, turning on them. "What about the two of you? You want Mason to marry Heidi." I put a hand on Heidi's shoulder and squeezed. She was tense, but leaned into the gesture.

The poor girl had gone through so much in her life already; she didn't need this. "How could he do that if he was marrying Vicki?"

"If you are accusing me of killing that woman, I'm going to sue you so hard, your grandchildren will be paying for it," Regina said.

"I'm not," I said. "You could have used Cathy's death to try to break Vicki and Mason up, but I don't think either of you would go as far as killing someone to accomplish your goals. And I'm sure you both have solid alibis." I glanced at Paul, who nodded. "Instead of killing anyone, you decided to use this unfortunate situation to your advantage. You should both be ashamed."

Much to my amazement, both Raymond and Regina lowered their eyes. Had I actually hit a nerve?

My gaze then moved on to the three people sitting together across the table. Lyric was frowning down at the table, looking as guilty as anyone could. Jacques was sitting back, arm flung casually across the back of Lyric's chair, calm as could be. Vince was much the same as when I'd last seen him. He looked haggard, and in serious need of a drink.

"Lyric Granderson is at the center of our murder," I said, causing her head to jerk up.

"I had nothing to do with her death, if that is what you are implying," she said. "In fact, I won't sit here for it." She started to rise.

"Please take a seat, Ms. Granderson," Paul said, stepping forward. "Let's hear her out." He turned to me. "She wasn't the one who called in the tip. That wasn't her voice."

"No, she wasn't," I admitted. "But she did think the necklace Gina was giving to Vicki belonged to her by right. Everyone here knew it."

"It was given to me," Gina said, stabbing the table with her index finger hard enough it had to hurt. "I don't care what she believes."

"Get over yourself, you hag," Lyric spat, then turned her anger on me. "I don't know what you're trying to pull here, but I killed no one. I was in my room at the time of her death. Ask anyone."

I glanced at Paul, who nodded to confirm her story, as expected.

I moved on. "While you are, in some ways, responsible for Cathy's death, I don't think you were the one who actually did it." I turned my attention to the two men sitting beside her. "But one of you did."

"This is absurd," Frederick said, standing.

"Sit down, Mr. Patterson," Paul said, voice harsher than when he'd told Lyric to do the same. I needed to hurry this along. "No one is leaving until we get this sorted out."

Frederick dropped as if he'd been shot.

"Jacques, you are interested in Lyric, are you not?" I asked.

He glanced at her, and shrugged nonchalantly. "She's not bad."

"Oh, please," Lyric said. "You come panting after me like a dog in heat every time we're in the same zip code together."

Jacques snorted. "You wish. I could have my choice of any woman I wanted. She knows." He grinned at me. "Right, Kris?"

"I don't think so," I said, truly seeing him for the slime he was. The man had no scruples, cared about no one but himself. He might be interested in Lyric, but I doubted he cared about much more than how she would look on his arm, personality be damned. The guy was a pig.

I turned my attention away from him, both in disgust, and because of the man next to him.

"And you, Vince, you are just as infatuated with her as Jacques."

He gave me a strained smile, but unlike the better-looking man beside him, he didn't try to deny it.

"You both knew what Lyric wanted. She might have come to Pine Hills in the hopes of landing a movie role, but that's not truly what she desired. Gina's necklace—that's what she wanted, and both of you knew that."

"What are you saying?" Gina asked.

"I'm saying that both men want her. Both have tried, in their own way, to gain her affections. Vince stalked her, showed up where she was staying, all in an attempt to find the right time to approach her."

He winced when Lyric looked at him, eyes wide and accusatory.

"And Jacques convinced her to sleep with him, claiming it might help earn her a role in the movie he was going to be in, isn't that right?"

Lyric's face turned an alarming shade of red, while Jacques simply shrugged off the comment with, "It happens."

"I don't see how any of this leads to Cathy's murder," Frederick said.

"It's ridiculous, that's what it is," Gina added.

"I think I know where you're going with this, Buttercup," Dad said. I was thankful for his support because, quite frankly, I was worried I was wrong.

"Both of you wanted to win her over," I said. "Both of you failed." I paused dramatically, meeting every-one's eyes before saying, "So, you came after the necklace."

Gina's hand crept to her mouth as she stared

wide-eyed at the two men whom she thought of as her friends. They might have been, but not so much that one of them wouldn't have stolen from her without batting an eye. For the first time, I thought, she was realizing how shallow many of her relationships really were.

"I couldn't figure out which one of you did it for the longest time. You both care about her, you both had opportunity. Unfortunately, Cathy had the necklace on her and she ended up dead, which put a serious crimp in your plan. You might have gotten away with the murder because, quite frankly, the police had nothing to go on."

Paul cleared his throat and gave me a disapproving look when I glanced back at him. I held up a finger, telling him to wait and hear me out.

"You could have gone home, put it all behind you, and lived out your life without worry that you'd be caught," I went on. "But then, instead of just letting things play out as they would, you made a mistake." Another dramatic pause. "You called in a tip."

"I thought it was a woman who called it in?" Vicki said.

"It *sounded* like a woman," I said. "And if Jules hadn't brought over a movie for me to watch, I might have continued to believe it was a woman. But it wasn't, was it?"

No one had anything to say to that.

"It was in the credits," I said. "A name not many people here would recognize. Not all of you use your real name, or at least, not in all your roles, right, Jason?"

Jacques's eyes widened. "I . . ." He glanced around the table. "I didn't do anything wrong."

"I wondered why you didn't want to give me your real name when we talked about it before. It seemed strange, but I guess Jason Kennedy isn't nearly as famous as Jacques Kenway." Not that Jacques was winning any awards with his acting.

"You're grasping," he said. "I don't do voices."

"No, you don't." My eyes slid sideways. "But you do, right, Toni?"

There was a moment of silence as all eyes turned toward Vince.

When he didn't speak, I went on. "It was a short little clip, maybe five seconds long, but it was more than enough for me to figure out it was you."

"His name . . ." Dad said.

"He changed it," I said. "Or at least, he used a different name back then. Was it because of the voices? Didn't you want anyone to realize the woman's voice was really that of a man? Toni could be either, couldn't it?"

He looked as if he might deny it before his shoulders slumped. "Okay, fine," he said. "I called in the tip. I wanted to go home and thought if the police arrested Mason, the rest of us could leave." He looked up, met my eye. "But I did not kill Cathy Carr."

"Didn't you?" I asked. "I might have believed you, if it wasn't for the fact I kept seeing your car everywhere. I even saw it that night, before I found the body. I didn't put it together until now, but when I got here, I saw a silver Prius in the driveway. I thought it was Cathy's car, but she didn't have one, did she?"

"She rode with us," Frederick said, eyes never leaving Vince. "How could you?"

Vince rose, backed away from the table. "You have no proof of anything, just speculation."

"Don't I?" I asked. "Do you think you managed to go unnoticed in this town?" At this point, I was winging it. I had no idea if anyone had actually *seen* Vince around town, or even on the night of the murder, but he didn't know that. "If I saw your car that night, don't you think someone else might have? All it takes is one person."

"I'd take Krissy's word," Paul said, stepping forward, hand going to the butt of his gun.

Vince took another step back. So often, when I accused a killer, they made a run for it. And since Vince was an actor, I figured he'd be all for the dramatic escape.

He looked to Lyric then, eyes pleading with her. "I did it for you," he said at a whisper. "I didn't mean to hurt her—she just . . ." He swallowed with some difficulty. "She got in the way."

"Vince Conner, you have the right to remain silent," Paul said, advancing.

I braced for the inevitable escape attempt, but Vince simply raised his hands. "I'm sorry," he said.

And then, he broke down into tears.

Paul walked across the room, took him into custody, and then led him from the room while everyone else looked on in shock.

And just like that, the drama was over.

27

"Maybe we should wait, do it another time."

Vicki was standing in front of a mirror, looking at herself. She looked gorgeous in her wedding dress, which was to be expected. Trouble sat next to her in a box on the floor, put there for him, glaring as much as a cat could glare. He had a pillow on the back of his neck, held in place by a white ribbon. On top were the wedding rings. It had been a nightmare getting him to sit still long enough to get it attached, but I'd managed, though I had the scratches to show for it. Now, all we had to do was convince him to walk down the aisle using treats. It had worked in rehearsal, but I doubted it would be so easy with guests looking on.

"It's going to be okay," I said.

"But after everything that's happened, don't you think it's insensitive to get married?"

"Do you love Mason?" I asked.

"I do."

"Do you want to marry him?"

"I do."

"Then do it!"

She smiled. "You're right." She sucked in a breath

and let it out in a huff. "I'm just so nervous. What if something else happens? I don't think I could handle it."

"I won't let anything get in the way of your wedding," I promised her.

Vicki turned away from the mirror and wrapped me in a hug. "Thank you. For everything."

"Of course."

We parted. "Help me with this." She picked up the necklace Gina had given her. Apparently, sometime after Vince had been taken away, Vicki had given in and agreed to wear it. Paul had brought it to her personally, amusingly wrapped in Christmas wrapping paper.

Vicki turned so I could clasp the necklace around her neck. When she turned back to me, she looked nervous again. "Do you think it'll be okay?"

"Who cares that it's not real?" I said. "It looks real enough. And it's the thought that counts, right?"

There'd never been a "real" necklace, just the fake. All the fuss had been over a piece of well-made costume jewelry. Gina had just about died of embarrassment, but that was nothing compared to how Vince must have felt. If just one person would have had the thing appraised, or even asked someone who would know, then maybe this entire mess could have been avoided.

"I'd better check on everyone," I said, stepping back. My eyes kept wanting to tear up, I was so happy, and standing in Vicki's presence only made it worse.

"See you soon," she said.

"Count on it."

I left Vicki to finish getting ready, and decided to poke my head into the church to see who all had made it. Most everyone was there, including the uninvited guests. Lyric and Jacques were sitting in the same pew as the Herrons. Sage and Trey were between them. It didn't look as if the drama had drawn them together, but at least they were sticking close to one another. I had a feeling that once they were back in California, none of them would be calling on the others any time soon.

There were other faces I knew around the room as well. Rita was here with Andi and Georgina. Lena and Jeff sat next to one another, and were laughing at some shared joke. Regina and Raymond actually looked happy as they sat up front, Heidi next to them, smiling herself. I supposed they couldn't be angry and gloomy all the time. Even Robert and Trisha had scored invites, much to my amazement.

My gaze continued around the room, noting Jules and Lance, a few actors I knew from the currently closed community theater.

But of Paul Dalton, I saw not a hair.

"You okay, Buttercup?"

I turned to find Dad standing with his arm around Laura. He looked a little stiff, like he was still afraid I'd disapprove, but at least this time he didn't pull his arm away. I definitely approved of that.

"Nervous," I said. "I don't like the idea of standing up there." I nodded toward the front of the church.

"You'll be fine," Dad said. "All eyes will be on Vicki. You won't be the center of attention this time."

"I hope so," I said, causing them both to laugh.

A door opened behind them somewhere, then closed, causing Dad to glance back.

"We'd better take our seats," he said, an odd smile on his face.

"You'll do fine," Laura added, touching my arm briefly before allowing herself to be led away.

"Thanks," I muttered. I really hoped so, but was starting to doubt it.

They headed down the aisle together, and I wondered what it would be like seeing that in the future. There was no doubt in my mind that was where Dad and Laura were heading. They were perfect together. And sure, sometimes things came up—little differences, or a need to stay single—that broke up relationships. But looking at the two of them, I doubted they'd be unmarried for long, and that was a good thing in my book.

Of course, thinking of marriage made me think of Will. While I hadn't really thought that far ahead, it did make me miss him terribly. I regretted telling him to go to Arizona before the wedding. One last day together would have made me feel a whole lot better.

"Krissy."

I sucked in a breath and turned to find not Will Foster, but Paul Dalton standing there, dressed to kill in a dark blue suit and tie.

"Paul," I squeaked, feeling suddenly self-conscious in my dress. I immediately started to smooth out the fabric, though it really didn't need it.

"You look beautiful," he said.

"Thanks." I couldn't meet his eye. "Vicki decided not to embarrass me with an ugly bridesmaid's dress."

He laughed. "I bet you're happy about that."

"I am." I felt the need to hide my feet, but had nowhere to put them. I should have worn heels, but was afraid I'd end up flat on my face, so I'd worn white sandals instead. Suddenly, they didn't feel appropriate anymore. "Did you come alone?" My gaze traveled past him, but no one was back there.

"I did," he said. "Things, uh, didn't work out between Shannon and me."

"I'm so sorry," I said. "I didn't know."

"That's okay. It happens." It sounded like there was more to his meaning than just his failed relationship with Shannon.

"Did Vince confess?" I asked, changing the subject before both of us became too embarrassed to speak.

"He did," Paul said. "He maintains it was an accident, that he was only going to knock her out. Apparently, he went after the necklace, but found the jewelry box empty. He remembered what the Herrons said about Ms. Carr stealing from her clients, and went after her. He surprised her, hit her, and she choked. He panicked and ran before thinking to search her for the necklace."

"That's horrible."

"It is." He shook his head sadly. "He didn't try to deny anything. I think he believed we had more on him than we really did, thanks to you. Without the confession, I'm not sure we would have gotten a conviction."

"That's good," I said. "I should have realized he was the guy all along." The car. The way he kept himself separate. It was all right there, but I'd missed it.

"You know, you could have told me your suspicions before we got there." There was only a little reprimand in his voice. "I could have helped."

"I wasn't totally sure I had it right," I said. "I wanted to see his reaction as I went around the room, see if he'd give anything away."

"Did he?"

"No, not really."

Paul laughed. "Well, we got him."

"We did."

Our eyes met. He looked away first.

"You should forget about Vince Conner and this whole murder business," Paul said, straightening his tie. "You have a wedding to worry about."

"I do."

A look of melancholy must have passed over my face then, because Paul put a hand on my arm. "You okay?"

"I am."

"I heard about Will."

I flashed him a smile. "Yeah? I'll be fine."

He studied me a long moment before removing his hand and nodding. "I know you will."

Music started playing and my nervousness ratcheted up a good dozen clicks.

"I'd better find a place to sit," Paul said. "See you at the reception?"

"Of course."

He reached up as if to touch the brim of his missing police hat. And then, with a bow, he turned and headed down the aisle to take his seat.

I watched him go, knowing that as long as he was there to keep me from doing something too incredibly stupid, that I'd definitely be okay. We didn't need to be dating for that.

"Ready?"

I looked up to see Mason's best man, Charlie Yow, waiting for me, elbow extended.

"I am," I said, taking his arm.

I took a deep breath, steeled myself, and then, together, we started down the aisle.